A HARMLESS LIE

A HARMLESS LIE

A NOVEL

SARA BLAEDEL

Translated by Mark Kline

DUTTON

DUTTON

An imprint of Penguin Random House LLC

penguinrandomhouse.com

LIBRARY OF CONGRESS CATALOGING-IN-PUBLICATION DATA

Names: Blædel, Sara, author. | Kline, Mark, 1952– translator.
Title: A harmless lie: a novel / Sara Blaedel; translated by Mark Kline.
Other titles: Pigen under træet. English
Description: New York: Dutton, 2022.
Identifiers: LCCN 2021017340 (print) | LCCN 2021017341 (ebook) |
ISBN 9780593330944 (trade paperback) | ISBN 9780593330951 (ebook)
Subjects: GSAFD: Mystery fiction.
Classification: LCC PT8177.12.L33 P5413 2022 (print) | LCC PT8177.12.L33 (ebook) |
DDC 839.813/8—dc23
LC record available at https://lccn.loc.gov/2021017340
LC ebook record available at https://lccn.loc.gov/2021017341

Printed in the United States of America
1st Printing

BOOK DESIGN BY TIFFANY ESTREICHER

For Gitte—
my wonderful lifelong friend, my class field trip sidekick.
You are my rock.

A HARMLESS LIE

PROLOGUE

BORNHOLM, 1995

She spotted the cave, barely visible in the pale moonlight filtering through the dense treetops. She began stumbling up the slope toward it, fighting through the fog in her brain. Hearing voices on the path below, she began to rush. But this only made her slip, though she managed to save herself at the last second by grabbing onto a spindly bush and using it to find a foothold. Seconds later, she was pulling herself up to the entrance to the cave. Shelter, at last. The rain had started falling again, the drops slapping her face and rattling the leaves in the branches above.

The voices vanished into the darkness that surrounded her now. But she still needed to hide, and she frantically groped the rocks, searching for an opening into the cave she'd glimpsed from below. Her heart hammered against her ribs, and she was gasping for breath.

The blow had knocked her out; she knew that, though she had no idea for how long. When she'd come back to herself, she had seen them watching her. But she'd managed to crawl away—slowly at first, then somehow making it to her feet and forcing herself to run. She'd managed not to fall in the dark, though she felt dizzy. Now the pain in her head was intense, the dim world spinning and careening in front of her.

Touching her temples, she felt wet hair and a stickiness—blood. She would never speak to them again; all she wanted was to be left alone.

The rocks scraped against the soft skin of her bare arms as she wriggled through the narrow mouth of the cave. Once inside, she hugged her knees, shivering, and focused on breathing slowly and evenly to calm herself. For a long time, she listened intently, straining to hear through the howling wind and rustling treetops, until at last she was certain they'd given up looking for her.

Pain arced from her head down through her body, nausea ebbing and flowing. The cold rain began coming down harder and splashing her through the narrow opening. The wind whipped and tugged at her, and outside, the creaking of the enormous trees split the air.

She felt dizzier and dizzier. She tried closing her eyes to make it go away but jerked them open again as a huge tree branch crashed to the ground only feet away from her. The storm and the groaning branches were terrifying. She closed her eyes again and pictured Skipper, hoping it might help her feel calmer. Next she pictured her brother, whispered to him about how scared she was.

Her queasiness was unbearable now. Feeling a sudden need to vomit, she leaned out into the rain, accidentally ramming her shoulder hard into an outcropping in the process. Woozy and trembling now from the frigid air, she cried as she wiped her mouth and crept inside the cave as far as she could, looking for a dry place to lie down. Her head felt like it was about to crack open. She lay on her side and curled up to keep warm. When she closed her eyes once more, the earth beneath her swirled. Then all was quiet. Suddenly she jerked awake at the sound of an explosion outside, and the blackness thickened.

Darkness. The space inside the cave shrank even smaller.

ONE

"Louise Rick, Louise Rick!"

He pronounced her name "Lois Wreck."

The evening sun cast a deep golden glow over the ocean that stretched out before her, deep blue as far as the eye could see. She'd been sitting on the beach all day—and it had been an insanely hot one—and was still sitting there, unable to muster the enthusiasm to move.

She ignored him. She felt heavy, slow, and sluggish from the emptiness inside her.

"Emergency!" he yelled. "It's about your family. Please come to the phone!"

He approached where she was sitting at the water's edge, leaving a trail of footprints behind him in the wet sand. He was wheezing, out of breath. As his words finally sank in, she turned and stared at him in alarm. "What is it? What's going on?"

He held his hand out to help her up off the small towel she'd brought along from the hotel room.

"Please come," he repeated, his voice shrill now. He turned and began running back across the street to the hotel, darting past the food stands that had been set up between the parked cars. The scooters that zipped down the street in front of the hotel day and night were making their usual racket, but Louise didn't hear them as she followed the man through a small opening in the palm trees.

Thailand hadn't been her choice, but the family had made a deal when she'd taken six months' leave from the police department. Louise was between jobs; she'd just left the Missing Persons Department to take on a new role as the head of the Homicide Department. But before beginning her new job, she'd wanted to spend some time traveling, and the family had come to an agreement that each of the four members would be allowed to pick out one place they wanted to see. They'd started in Mexico, which her foster son, Jonas, had chosen. After exploring Mayan ruins, they had journeyed on to South America, Africa, and India. They'd been on the road for four months so far. A small double family: Louise and Jonas, her partner, Eik, and his daughter, Stephanie. All that was in the past, though. Now she was still in Thailand, but alone.

In the reception area, the man led Louise to a desk behind the counter, where the telephone was waiting for her. Her own phone was in her room. Shut off.

"International call," he said, pointing at the receiver.

Louise froze. Lately, she'd been doing everything she could to shut out reality and now this call was about to confront her with it.

She sank down on the chair by the table, and the man put the receiver into her hand. She raised it to her ear and spoke in a hush.

"Hello."

"It's Mikkel." She barely recognized her father's voice. "He tried to commit suicide. He's in the hospital in Roskilde; we're here with him."

He paused for a moment and took a deep, trembling breath. "They don't know if he'll survive. I think you should come home."

. . .

Mikkel. Her brother was two and a half years younger than her. They were close, though not as close as they would have been if Louise had stayed in Mid Sealand instead of running off to Copenhagen after her boyfriend Klaus had died. But Louise had been desperate to get away at the time—Klaus's death had traumatized her so much that she hadn't even been able to attend his funeral. Still, she and Mikkel kept in close touch, and she was godmother to both of his children. "The Terrorists," as her mother had called her grandchildren when they were toddlers. Now they were four and six, and not quite as wild. At least Kirstine wasn't. Malte was still a handful, but Louise had a soft spot for her nephew, even though a houseful of screaming kids wasn't exactly her cup of tea.

"I'll come."

She had trouble letting go of the receiver once they'd said goodbye. Her Mikkel, who had gone to Klaus's funeral and placed a red rose on his coffin for her. The brother whose world had collapsed when his wife left him with two small children and a house in Osted, with bills he couldn't pay. He'd taken on extra work as a deliveryman and had driven all over the country, in the little time he had left over from his job selling spare parts for Volvo in Roskilde.

That had gone on for almost a year, until Trine had finally come back to him. And since then he'd seemed genuinely happy. Louise had often thought that Trine's year away might actually have been good for them because they now seemed closer than ever. There was an air of peace about them, a new sense of comfortableness in their relationship. Louise hadn't cared much for her sister-in-law while she had been away from her family. But that was ancient history now; as long as her brother was happy, so was Louise.

She'd always thought she would do anything for her little brother. Climb any mountain, walk any desert, though he would have been irritated to hear her say that. He was a head taller than her and didn't look at all like someone who needed his big sister to take care of him. Still, she'd vowed that she'd always be there for him, no matter what.

Louise slept for most of the flight home. After Eik, Jonas, and Stephanie had left, a local Thai pharmacist had begun supplying her with sleeping pills. Normally they required a prescription, but she had smooth-talked her way out of needing to see a doctor. The pills had gotten her through the nights alone.

Because it was an emergency, she was allowed to leave the small, sleazy tourist hotel without paying for the entire week, which they could have insisted on. There wasn't much good to say about the room, and nothing good at all to say about the bed or the tiny shower stall, which specialized in icy water at a trickle. On the other hand, she had nothing but praise for the man at the reception desk, who turned out to be the owner—he told her so on the way to the airport. He had offered her a lift, and he'd also been the one who'd figured out the fastest way for her to get back to Denmark.

Which turned out to be three connecting flights, though with short layovers between them. She spent the trip in a fog of sleep, anxiety, sorrow, and a sense of unreality. Like a bad dream that had somehow invaded real life, making her head spin and her joints feel stiff. On top of that was the fact that she hadn't managed to eat since her father's call, and she hadn't drunk much, either. In fact, she hadn't taken in much at all during the past few weeks after saying goodbye to the others. Her body had come to a standstill; it felt like torture when she tried to force something down. She was off her feed, as her father would have put it, though he was usually referring to birds.

Her suitcase was one of the first ones to pop out, thanks to the red tag the hotel owner had convinced the woman at the airport to fasten onto the handle in order to expedite its voyage through the airports. Louise had lost all sense of time. She glanced at her phone and saw that it was nearly seven-thirty in the evening.

She spotted her father immediately after she passed through customs. He was standing off to the left in the arrivals hall. The second he saw her, he engulfed her in a huge hug, which roadblocked the other passengers trying to drag their suitcases through the gate.

He held her so tightly that Louise couldn't breathe enough to even ask about her brother. Or maybe she just didn't dare. More than a day had gone by since his call. The first twenty-four hours were crucial; she knew that from experience. They were the hours that separated life from death. When her father finally let go of her, she took a step back and quickly studied his face.

"They say he'll survive," he whispered with relief, though his voice was husky. "The doctors don't think he suffered any permanent damage, but it was close. If your mother hadn't gone over to visit when she did, Mikkel would be dead. He was unconscious when she found him."

The anxiety drained out of her body, leaving her giddy and light, almost as if she were floating. "Can we drive over to the hospital now?"

He shook his head. "They told us he needs to rest this evening. He's not well, he's not himself, but you can visit him tomorrow."

Her father grabbed her suitcase and led her to the exit. Still in a daze, she barely registered the hum of voices and the low sun on her face as they walked out. The specter of an impending disaster had overwhelmed her, put her body on high alert. And now it was slowly loosening its grip. At last she could breathe. They stashed her suitcase in the trunk, and he backed the car out of the parking space.

When they reached the freeway, he asked about the others. Specifically about Jonas. Louise answered vaguely. She told him everything was fine, that they all said hello. She assured him that Eik and the kids understood she had no choice. She'd needed to come home.

"You can fly back and join up with them again," he said, as if apologizing for interrupting her vacation now that her brother wasn't about to die after all.

The freeway signs flew by. Though she'd been gone a long time, the way home was still familiar to her and she didn't pay much attention. She thought about Mikkel. How could her brother have even considered committing suicide? He knew how devastated she had felt during all the years she'd believed, falsely, that her boyfriend Klaus had killed himself. She was the one who had found him hanging above the stairway in the house they'd just moved into.

After several minutes of silence, she asked, "What happened? How did he do it?"

Her father stared straight ahead at the cars in front of them as the silence lengthened. After what felt like forever, he said, "Car exhaust. Mikkel closed the garage door and started the car. We were taking care of the kids; they'd stayed the night. But your mother wanted to pick something up at the house the next morning before taking them back, and she heard the car idling out there."

"Car exhaust!" Louise knew that nowadays people seldom did it that way. Only the very poor or the very rich, the pathologists liked to say. It didn't really work with new cars that were equipped with catalytic converters. So it was usually someone with either an older car or an antique one.

She felt her father's eyes on her. "He must've been out there a long time." Her throat clogged up; if the garage was sealed tight enough, in time he would have easily died of carbon monoxide poisoning. "What about Trine? Didn't she hear him go out?"

"Your brother was alone."

Her father's voice was still raspy. Louise studied him, but then she let it go. She was too tired, couldn't handle it right now. She turned on the radio, leaned her head back, and listened to the news.

"Police have identified the remains of a body found last week on Bornholm. Susan Dahlgaard, a fourteen-year-old girl who disappeared more than two decades ago during a field trip with her class from Osted School in Mid Sealand, was found in a cave in Echo Valley, a popular site for visitors on the island. Identification was made difficult by the condition of the body, and at this moment, the cause of death is undetermined."

Louise straightened up in her seat. This was one of the cases the Missing Persons Department had been involved in back when she was working there. Her former colleague Olle had a picture of Susan Dahlgaard on the wall behind his desk, along with photos of several other people from cold cases the media often returned to, keeping their memories alive. Back when the young schoolgirl had disappeared, there had been an exhaustive search. Bornholm police had requested the assistance of the Mobile Crime Unit, and the best canine trackers in the country had been called in to aid the local dog patrols. Thirty men with highly trained dogs had combed the entire area around the Svaneke Hostel, where the girl's class had been staying. The next week, a new team had been sent over to relieve them, and the search had gone on this way for several weeks before being abandoned. With no evidence having been turned up by the dog teams, the police theorized that she'd been abducted and taken off the island. The girl's photo had been shown on newscasts and posters around the country. The department called a search like this "the whole package," and it included reviewing all pertinent international records.

The three friends Susan had shared a room with had last seen her at the harbor in Svaneke, where they'd split up. The four girls had left the hostel while they were supposed to be asleep in their rooms, sharing two bikes between them. During questioning, the girls stated that they had biked down to the harbor, where Susan had agreed to meet up with some Bornholm boys they'd met earlier. The other girls left her in front of the convenience store at the harbor and never saw her again. The boys confirmed meeting the girls there, but they claimed Susan hadn't been with them later in the evening. There'd been no further traces of the fourteen-year-old.

Louise had been in high school in Roskilde when Susan disappeared. That had been several years before she applied for police school, but even back then the case had intrigued her because Osted was close to Hvalsø, where she had gone to elementary school. Her class had also taken the traditional weeklong field trip to Bornholm, and her memories of it had been fresh. The day before they left, she had broken her collarbone playing soccer. She still went on the trip even though her shoulder and left arm had been bandaged tightly, and her friends had to help dress her and tie her shoes. At the same time, it had been a great excuse to duck out of the long bike tours of the island, which suited her just fine.

Now Louise closed her eyes and recalled the trip. How hard the Bornholm ferry had rocked, causing many of her classmates to throw up. How they had bought a smoked herring packed in newspaper at the smokehouse. And a gigantic ice cream cone at the Gudhjem harbor . . .

I must have dozed off, Louise told herself when she opened her eyes and looked up at her brother's red house. Her father had pulled in and parked, and her mother stood in the doorway, waiting for her to step out. She looked old. As if the four months Louise had been gone had aged her. Or maybe because these days she seldom saw her mother without her smock. At their farmhouse in the country, her mother was always marching back and forth between the living quarters and her small ceramics workshop at the far end of the wing, and her clay-stained work clothes were so much a part of her that normal clothing looked strange on her.

On the way to the front door, Louise realized it wasn't age treating her mother's face harshly. Worry showed in every line, as if she hadn't yet understood that her son was going to survive. The worst had blown over. But then it hit Louise: The worst had *not* blown over.

Her brother had wanted to die, and that hadn't changed just because his suicide attempt had failed. He'd been so unhappy that he was ready to sign off on life despite having two small children and a wife he loved.

Louise spread her arms and embraced her mother; let herself be surrounded by her familiar fragrance.

"I can't tell you how glad I am that you're back home," her mother whispered into Louise's long hair. Louise didn't know exactly how she looked; she hadn't checked in a mirror, but she was sure it wasn't pretty. She'd left the hotel in Phuket so suddenly that she was still wearing shorts and the hooded sweatshirt she'd thrown on during the plane ride. Her mother led her inside while her father unloaded her suitcase.

"Where are the kids?" Louise looked around. "And Trine?"

"The kids are asleep." Her mother pushed open the kitchen door. She'd set the table for three. Louise smelled curry on the stove, which made her stomach lurch, but she smiled and plopped down on a chair at the table. Her mother handed her a wineglass.

"How was he doing when you were at the hospital? Did he seem relieved?"

Louise had often seen that reaction from people who had tried to kill themselves. It wasn't uncommon for the police to get a call from someone who regretted swallowing the pills.

"More often than not, it's a cry for help," she added.

Her father came in and sat down. Her parents exchanged a quick glance and then her mother looked gravely at Louise.

"It wasn't any cry for attention," her father confirmed. "He meant to kill himself."

"But why?" Louise said. "Why now? If he wanted to, why wouldn't he have done it when Trine left him? For a while back then I was even afraid he might do something stupid. But why now, when everything is going so well?"

Silence. Once more her parents glanced at each other.

"Trine has deserted him again," her mother said.

Louise put down her wineglass. "Deserted him . . . What do you mean, deserted?"

Her father took over. "She's gone. She didn't give him a reason or any sign that she was about to leave. He came home from work Wednesday and she was gone. He checked her closet and saw that she had taken her overnight bag and a few clothes."

"And she emptied the jar with the no-smoking money." Her mother nodded over at the cupboard where a brown clay jar stood on the top shelf. Louise could never understand why her brother and Trine kept calling the cash they put aside "cigarette money" several years after they'd stopped smoking. They could have just called it vacation money. But every week for years, the money they saved by not buying cigarettes was stuck into the jar and spent on weekend trips.

"He hasn't heard from her, so he doesn't know where she is. Or if she's with another man," her mother added sharply.

"It could be," Louise's father mumbled. "I mean, it's almost like she was trying to show Mikkel that she wanted to start a brand-new life. Otherwise, she would have taken more of her things with her."

Her mother began speaking softly. "He never should have taken her back. She left him once; she could do it again. That's what I've always thought. And he was so broken up."

"Had they been fighting?" Louise was trying to make sense of it all, but her parents shrugged.

"Not that we know of," her mother said. "And I didn't have the feeling anything was wrong."

"Mikkel and Trine and the kids came over not long ago for dinner," her father said. "They seemed happy enough that evening; they'd just rented a vacation house for the first part of July. We saw no sign they'd been arguing or had any tension between them. It seemed completely out of the blue, her leaving like this."

Her mother stared down at her hands, as if she could hold back her anger at her daughter-in-law if she concentrated hard enough. "But she could have been putting on an act until she was ready to leave."

"So both of you think that's why he did it?"

Her mother nodded and looked up. "Yes, I think so. I imagine your brother couldn't bear the thought of going through it all over again."

"But we haven't had the chance to talk to him all that much," her father said.

Her mother handed her a plate of curried meatballs. Louise looked at it and asked for a smaller portion, but her mother had other ideas.

"It'll do you good to get some decent food after that long trip." Her mother firmly set the plate in front of her.

The kitchen in her brother's house reminded Louise of a cave. He'd renovated it himself. All the drawers and cupboard doors were painted dark green; a man at work who painted cars had helped him. The rest was built from used lumber and looked like something out of a home decor magazine.

During the year of Trine's absence, Mikkel had restored most of the house. When he hadn't been working one of his two jobs, he'd been hammering away inside. He'd claimed it saved him a lot of money on psychologists. Looking around now, Louise thought there might not be anything left to do that could help him. No more projects to occupy his time, keep his mind off things.

She didn't touch her food. "I ate on the plane." She set her glass down. "How are the kids taking it?"

"They don't know yet. We told them their father's in the hospital, but he's coming home soon. Yesterday we feared the worst, so we couldn't tell them anything. We had to wait to hear more about his condition. It wasn't until we spoke with him today that we learned about Trine leaving. Mikkel hadn't told us anything."

"How much money did they have in the jar?" Louise asked. All the animosity she'd felt the first time her sister-in-law had left Mikkel flared up again. If she had to squeeze that money out of Trine with her bare hands, she'd do it, and enjoy every second of it.

Her mother poured more wine into their glasses. "Mikkel thinks there was around seven thousand crowns."

"She won't get far on that, if she's on a little love trip," her father said.

"We don't know that's it," her mother snapped. "At any rate, we can't fill Mikkel's head with notions like that. It might be that she just needs to be alone for a while."

Her father wouldn't let it go. "She's gone, and what's more, she left the kids behind. Mikkel must be sure she's left him, otherwise he wouldn't have let himself hit rock bottom."

Louise stopped listening to their bickering. She was tired. And heartsick. She was certain that no matter what, Trine would have a lot to think about when she came home and found out what she'd caused. Suddenly it hit her how much worse it could have been: for some men, the extreme desperation Mikkel had experienced drove them to kill their wives and children, too, before committing suicide. What the media liked to euphemistically call a "family tragedy," but in reality was more like a liquidation. Thankfully, her brother hadn't tried to take his children to the grave with him. It hadn't been about punishing Trine that way. He'd put only himself in danger. Thinking of all the cases she'd worked on during her years in Homicide that had ended up much worse, Louise felt relieved. No one had died. Fortunately.

Louise nearly jumped when her mother stood up.

"I've made up a bed for you in the rear bedroom." She grabbed Louise's suitcase and pulled it down the hall. "We'll sleep here tonight so we can get the kids off to school tomorrow. But if they want to keep Mikkel at the hospital, I think you and the kids should come out to the farm. At least until they release him. It might do him good to have some peace and quiet here when he gets back, too. We can talk about that tomorrow."

Louise had no intention of staying with her parents, that much she knew, but she was too tired to get into it at the moment. Her mother had laid out towels for her in the guest room, and added that if Louise needed anything, she could use whatever was in Trine's closet.

"I just need a shower, is all," Louise said. "And it's going to be nice to lie down after all those hours sitting in airplane seats."

Her mother walked over and cupped her hands around Louise's cheeks. She stood for a moment before letting her hands fall. "Should I wake you up when we leave?"

"No. If I can get a decent night's sleep, maybe I can avoid jet lag."

She was already searching for the small, transparent plastic pouch in her bag. Her sleeping pills.

TWO

For a long time, she lay completely still, staring into the darkness without really seeing. Her body ached and felt heavy, as if it belonged to someone else. Her nose stung from the rancid smell of moisture and musty earth, and the quiet around her felt claustrophobic.

She listened intently for the slightest sound but heard only silence. She panicked, tried to sit up, but her body refused to move. When she attempted to scream, no sound came out of her mouth. It was as if the air around her stood still, as if fresh air were far, far away.

The searing pain in her nose reached all the way up into her sinuses; she squeezed her eyes and felt the tears running into her ears. She couldn't roll onto her side, but she managed to tilt her head a bit when a violent spasm racked her stomach, causing her to throw up. The thin slime ran down her face; she wanted to wipe it off, but her hands weren't her own. Seconds, maybe even minutes went by before she slowly came to fully understand her inability to move. Desperately, she sent signals to her feet; she tried to raise her toes, but nothing happened.

THREE

Coffee sloshed over the edge of the cup and burned Camilla Lind's fingers as she hurried down the hallway toward Terkel Høyer's office. The editorial meeting had just begun. She had gathered up all the clippings she'd had time to print out, and felt armed and ready to fight for her story.

When she opened the door, the chief editor was going through the story ideas that had already been presented.

"Glad you could stop by," he said, looking at her in annoyance as she closed the door.

Høyer had been her boss the entire time she'd been covering crime at *Morgenavisen*. He'd been the one who put her back on the crime desk now that she'd returned after a long, self-imposed hiatus. She had witnessed a brutal murder in Sweden's underground crime world, and she'd needed to spend some time in a psychiatric ward to deal with the trauma. Some of her colleagues had feared that Camilla wouldn't recover from the experience, that she didn't have the strength. They'd been wrong.

While she had been away, life had thrown her some curveballs that had distracted her from thinking about work at all. But finally, she'd come to the realization that she wanted to return to the paper. And having a full-time job again suited her well now that her husband, Frederik, was in the States, working for a film company on a TV series.

"Bornholm," Camilla said, after Høyer finished and glanced over at the stack of papers she'd laid on the table. "I spoke to the police in Rønne; they still can't say if Susan Dahlgaard's death was a homicide. But I did learn that the body is decomposed, and it was hidden behind some rocks under a fallen tree. They said it's almost certain she's been there since her disappearance, and when the tree trunk rotted away enough, there she was. Someone walking through Echo Valley reported it to the police."

She picked up her notes. "The rocks and the tree had her penned in so tight that no animals could get to her body."

"That's already on the website," Jakob said. The young reporter had interned on the crime desk, and despite the fact that the paper had been making budget cuts, he'd managed to get himself hired in Camilla's absence.

She pulled out a chair and sat down. "I went to grade school in Osted; I was a few years ahead of Susan," she said, ignoring Jakob. "I didn't know her, but I know the teacher who was on the class field trip. And I checked the students in that class; I recognize a few of the names."

"And do you have access to any of them?" Høyer asked.

"One of them had an older brother I went out with. And there's another woman who was in the class who I run into now and then. She lives close to the school. I'm sure she can steer me to the others who were on the class trip."

Høyer broke in. "Let's hold up on this. We don't even know yet if there's a crime involved."

"So you're saying we should just twiddle our thumbs and wait while the other papers lock up the people who can tell us what happened?"

She kept her eyes glued to him. Almost nothing irritated her boss more than when the competition beat them to the sources, sometimes even going so far as to prevent them from speaking to others in the media.

"I went to the same school. I even visited Bornholm myself. The same place. We stayed at the same hostel in Svaneke. I might have even slept in the same bunk bed as Susan Dahlgaard. I can do a feature. Describe what happened before she disappeared."

"But isn't it an old case?" Jakob looked over at Ole Kvist, the reporter who had been with the paper the longest.

Camilla's older colleague nodded. In recent years he rarely showed even a hint of interest in any of the story ideas floated at the editorial meetings.

Camilla felt like biting Jakob's head off. "This is the type of case people are always fascinated with, because no one ever found out why she disappeared. It's like an unsolved murder—we want to know what happened. Susan had just turned fourteen when she disappeared in 1995. We've all been on a school trip; people will identify with this."

"I've never been to Bornholm," Jakob answered.

Camilla glared at him; he'd barely been born back then, she thought. She noticed that Ole looked as if he was about to say something but then decided to hold back.

"There was a shooting last night on Tagensvej," Høyer said, glancing at Camilla.

She leaned back in her chair and folded her arms. "If I get one more gang-related assignment, I'm quitting!"

Ole laughed. "You just got back." He seemed to be enjoying the show.

"I'm covering the class trip. I can get access to the people who were there, I'll find out what they remember, where they are now. They can tell us what Susan was like, and they might have some ideas about what happened back then."

"But somebody must have already written about that," Jakob said. "Surely reporters talked to them back when it happened."

"*I* didn't write about it," Camilla snapped. "*I* didn't talk to them."

It looked like she'd successfully persuaded Høyer. He nodded. "Jakob, you take Tagensvej; Camilla, you get busy with the girl's classmates. If it turns out there's no crime, you'll have to go with how they feel about the case being reopened. Old wounds ripped up."

Camilla nodded with satisfaction. It would take her forty minutes to get to Osted, and she knew exactly where to begin.

The summer rain pelted Camilla's windshield as she turned off the freeway and drove past Glim and Øm on the highway to Osted. She thought about her husband, Frederik, who was staying in his house in Hawaii. His father was there, too, visiting him. Camilla had been there, but not since they'd been married. Several times Frederik had asked her to join them, but her son, Markus, would soon be home from boarding school for the summer. She didn't want to travel without Markus, and he wanted to stay at home through the summer to be with his girlfriend, Julia.

Crazy, Camilla thought. She looked across the fields toward a farmhouse where one of her friends from high school in Roskilde had lived. She had no idea how her son had turned into someone who didn't jump at the chance to go to Hawaii. But really, though, was she so different? After all, she'd rather be here with him than in Hawaii. Even in the middle of the Danish summer.

Markus and Julia had started going out at the beginning of the school year, and Camilla was surprised it had lasted this long. Now

Markus didn't want to do anything without Julia. And she was a sweet girl, to be sure. But Camilla was disappointed that she never had her son to herself anymore.

Her thoughts drifted back to Frederik. Moments later, her phone rang. It was him, as if her thoughts had summoned him. There was a twelve-hour time difference between them, but he sounded as if he were sitting right beside her.

"I'm on my way to Osted," she explained when he asked what she was doing.

"To the used-car dealer, huh?" He laughed. Camilla's father had sold used cars from a lot on Hovedvejen, the highway that passed by Osted. Camilla pictured the rows and rows of cars with price stickers inside the front windshields.

Frederik had never met him; her relationship with her father had been difficult until recently.

"Hardly. It's been twenty-five years since he closed up shop, remember? But I did have lunch with him yesterday, as a matter of fact. He was in town and wanted to see me."

Frederik's family had had a falling-out after his mother died, which Camilla believed was why it meant so much to him that she kept her own family together. But her dad was an asshole. Or at least he had been.

"He still won't talk about their divorce," she said. "Every time I bring the subject up, he just says it wasn't easy after my brother died. It wasn't very goddamn easy for any of us. It's never easy when a sixteen-year-old boy dies."

Camilla had been fourteen when her older brother, Lasse, was killed while riding his moped. The accident had happened less than two hundred meters from Hestehaven, where they lived. He'd pulled out on Hovedvejen just as a car sped by.

"Grief is hard to handle; we all react differently," Frederik said.

He'd said it many times, but it didn't help, not really. Her father had been a big shot in Osted; a firebrand with a broad network of friends and business connections. Shortly after Lasse's death, he'd left. Less than a month after the divorce, he was already living with a younger woman who Camilla hated from the moment she first laid eyes on her.

"But obviously you know that's not all," she said. She slowed down and kept her eyes on the houses on the other side of the street. "He's never been there for Markus. He's never volunteered to help or done anything, never offered to watch him, or even pick him up for that matter. He's never been someone we could count on. But . . ." She signaled to turn. "We had a good time together at lunch. It was nice seeing him. Maybe now that he's older, he's got a little more room in his life for people other than himself. We're getting together again sometime this week. I haven't been to Præstø in a long time."

Her father had taken over his parents' farm. He'd also sold used cars in that part of Southern Sealand for several years, but now he was retired. His young girlfriend had moved on a long time ago, and Camilla had the feeling that sometimes the days were awfully long for him to get through by himself.

"That's nice," Frederik said. She could tell that he was trying not to sound too enthusiastic about her reconciliation with her father. "And how's my mother-in-law doing?"

"Fine. She's teaching dream interpretation and Pilates; it keeps her busy. It seems like her social life has exploded over there in Skanderborg. Especially since she can't spend all her time on her grandson anymore now that he's too old for that."

Frederik laughed. "I Skyped with him earlier today. He asked if he could take the boat out this weekend."

Typical Markus! Going through Frederik because he knew the

combination of a seventeen-year-old, a motorboat, a summer evening, and a lot of friends on board would worry her way too much.

"And you gave him permission, I suppose."

Camilla had had a hard time getting used to having a boat. Having money. Things that Frederik had brought into their marriage. She was worried that it might not be good for Markus. He enjoyed it; that was obvious. Much more than she did.

"I did, yes. But on one condition."

"Which is . . ."

"That he convinces you to take a summer vacation and fly over to us."

"Not without him," Camilla shot back. They'd talked about this before; Frederik knew very well how she felt.

"Two weeks. He'll come over with you for two weeks. But only after the Roskilde Festival."

"Really?" She tried to remember if anyone else on the crime desk would be on vacation in early July. Happy butterflies were churning in her stomach and suddenly she felt an overwhelming longing for her husband. But she stopped herself; before she got too excited, she needed to find out if she could get away from work.

"Whoops, there's her house; I'd better go," she said. Vacation plans would have to wait for later. "I'll talk to you tomorrow. Say hi to your dad, and thanks for handling everything with Markus."

Camilla sent a few quick kisses through the phone and tossed it down on the seat, then pulled up in front of the house.

Trine had been in her class at school, but she didn't remember much about her, though in the past several years she'd run into her several times at birthday parties for Louise. Her friend's sister-in-law had also been at Jonas's confirmation. Every time they met, they talked about Osted School and their old elementary-school teachers.

And the school parties, and how they and their friends had often played hooky by heading down to the grocery store or hanging out on the soccer field instead of going to class.

It was just small talk between her and Trine. Once Camilla had remarked to Louise that her brother's wife was a bore, but her friend had only frowned and retorted that her brother was happy with her. And that had been the end of that.

But Trine Madsen *was* boring. Madsen—when she'd been married to Mikkel, her last name had been Rick, but after Mikkel took her back following their brief divorce, they hadn't remarried.

No other cars were parked in front of the house, which was a good sign, Camilla thought as she opened her door and got out. Trine was a podiatrist with her own clinic in the addition in back, and it looked like she might not have any clients at the moment.

The doorbell echoed all the way through the house, an incessant monotone that slowly pulled Louise out of a deep sleep. The bedroom was dark, and at first she had no idea where she was. Then it came back to her in small, painful drips. The trip home from Thailand, Mikkel's suicide attempt. And then everything with Eik and Jonas. She rolled over to face the wall and pulled the duvet over her head. The doorbell rang again. Suddenly fear gripped her, and she tumbled out of bed. What if someone had been trying to reach her and she'd slept through it? What if it was bad news about Mikkel and someone was here to tell her in person, something that couldn't be told over the phone?

She ran to the front door. The doorbell rang one more time before she flung it open and then stepped back in surprise.

Her voice was hoarse as she stammered out, "Hi!"

A deluge of questions rained down on her.

"What are you doing here?" Camilla's voice thundered.

The effects of the sleeping pill hadn't fully left Louise's body, and she felt like she was in a surreal daze. All she could do was stare speechlessly at her best friend, who kept yelling at her.

"Why didn't you call? When did you get home? How long have you been here? Why the hell didn't anyone tell me you were back in Denmark?"

Instead of answering, Louise stepped forward with widespread arms as she felt tears rising up through her exhaustion.

"Mikkel tried to kill himself," she whispered against her friend's shoulder.

"Oh no!" Camilla hugged Louise tightly.

"I got in yesterday evening."

They stood for a few moments in each other's arms, then Louise showed her friend to the kitchen and went back to the guest room to look for some clean clothes to put on. Her hair had dried on the pillow after her shower the evening before, and it lay strangely flat on one side of her head.

The house was quiet. Louise hadn't heard her parents and the kids get up, and only now did she see it was a quarter past twelve. She'd slept through it all. Several messages had come in from her mother.

"Visiting M this evening at six. Conversational therapy now, waiting for doctor."

Her mother had never been one for long text messages. And though Louise was anxious to see her brother, it was also a relief to know the effects from the pill would have time to wear off before she went to the hospital. She wouldn't be much use to him the way she felt now; she wasn't even much use to herself.

She sent an "Okay" back to her mother and asked if they had seen him, and how he was doing.

"Yes. Very depressed," she answered. "Afraid he'll do it again."

Louise closed her eyes and pictured her brother. They had the same dark, curly hair. His was short and lay tight on his scalp. They also both had a slightly pointed nose and blue eyes.

She rolled up her curls into a bun and fastened it with an elastic. Then she joined Camilla out in the kitchen and brought down a teapot from a shelf, filled it with water, and put it on to boil. Her friend asked her how it had happened.

"Car exhaust." She heard the professional tone in her voice. The one she used as Detective Louise Rick when she informed a family about a death. Empathetic, but professional. "He let the car idle out in the garage. Mom found him."

"I'm so sorry to hear this. When did it happen?"

"Day before yesterday. I came home as soon as I heard, but it took me a day to get here."

"Have you seen him?"

"Not yet, but I'm going in around six. He's supposed to talk to a doctor this afternoon, so I have to wait."

"But he's okay?"

Louise shrugged; she couldn't imagine that he was. She knew her friend had asked out of concern, but really, no one who wanted to end their life was okay.

"Was it Mom who called and told you I came home?" Louise found a tin of tea in the cupboard.

Camilla looked confused. "No one told me you were here; I had no idea. That's why I almost had a heart attack outside; you were the last person I expected to see."

Louise turned to her friend in surprise. "Then why in the world are you here?"

The teakettle shot a thick cloud of steam up onto the kitchen window as Camilla pulled out a chair and sat down at the table. "I drove over to talk to Trine. It's better that I'm the one who writes the story; I'll make sure it gets told the way she wants it to be."

"What do you mean? You know where she is!" With one quick step Louise was leaning eagerly over the table. "Have you heard from her? What story are you talking about, that it's better you write?"

They stared at each other for a moment, then Camilla, puzzled, shook her head. "I don't know where she is; I just assumed she was here."

Louise backed away from the table. "Trine's gone," she said, calmer now. "She left."

Camilla lifted her eyebrows. "Left?"

"That's why Mikkel hit rock bottom. What's the story you're writing? Did she do something?"

"Not that I know of. I'm here to talk to her about what happened on Bornholm, back when they were on the class field trip."

"Bornholm?"

"Your sister-in-law was in the same class as that girl Susan who disappeared over there in 1995. They've just identified a body found last week; it's her."

Louise nodded and said she'd heard about it.

"On the way here," Camilla continued, "I heard on the radio that the police believe Susan could have been in this little cave when a tree fell and blocked the entrance."

"So no one walking in the woods there could have seen her?"

Camilla nodded. "I want to talk to Trine about the trip. Just to hear what she remembers so I can piece together what happened leading up to the night Susan disappeared."

"Looks like you're out of luck with Trine."

Louise poured the tea. She'd had no idea her sister-in-law had been in that class, and at the moment, she couldn't care less. She saw that her mother had left some bread in a bag on the kitchen counter, and suddenly she was starving; she absolutely had to stuff something soft and filling into the emptiness inside her.

Louise handed Camilla a cup of tea.

"What's this about her being gone?" Camilla said.

"She's left him. Again." Louise brought out butter and cheese from the refrigerator. "We don't know where she is. No one's heard from her, so like I said, it doesn't look good for your story."

"But did she move out?" Camilla glanced around the kitchen, as if it could somehow show her where Trine had gone. "When did it happen?"

Louise sat down and buttered a slice of bread. "A week ago. The kids don't know anything yet. It's so terrible of her to do this. She knows how hard it was on all of them the last time she left."

Louise managed only a single bite before her stomach cramped up.

"Markus is going to be happy to hear Jonas is home. They've been writing each other and Skyping, but I know he misses him."

The two boys had gone to school together since they were young. Louise knew that Jonas missed his friend, too, even though he was having a great time on vacation.

"You look like hell," Camilla said as Louise pushed her plate away. "How was the trip? Are the others in town?"

Louise sat for a moment and stared at the table before shaking her head.

They'd left South America for Africa, which had been Louise's dream to visit. Botswana, Zambia, Tanzania, and then on to Madagascar. Then Eik took over. He'd traveled extensively in India many times, and he wanted them to see the country, too.

Eik's daughter, Stephanie, had seen photos of Phuket from some of her school friends who had been there on vacation, and it had been her dream to go there. Thailand was supposed to be only their first stop in Asia. Stephanie . . . Louise's stepdaughter. Louise had been getting used to the idea that they were a family traveling together. She no longer thought of Jonas as a foster child; he'd become a real son to her. She'd even been getting comfortable with the fact that within six months Eik had gone from being her new boyfriend to the man she would marry, and Stephanie—Steph, as she insisted on being called—fit so incredibly well in the little family, even though Eik was only just beginning to get to know his daughter. Her mother had hidden her existence from Eik for many years, and it was only recently that Stephanie and Eik had been able to meet each other.

"They're still in Asia." She couldn't stop the stream of tears, couldn't control her sobbing. She hid her face in her hands and slowly rocked back and forth, trying to get ahold of herself and seal away the despair inside her.

"My God." Camilla's voice seemed to come from another world. "Easy now, easy. What in the world happened?"

Her friend gently helped her up from the chair, and soon she was sitting on her brother's sofa, wrapped in a blanket with her legs curled up.

She was still crying, though more softly now.

"Easy, easy." Camilla nudged Louise's feet for room to sit down. "I can't believe they didn't come back, too. Eik ought to be here with you. That's how it should be when you're getting married—you're there for each other. And Mikkel will be his brother-in-law, so clearly he should be here."

Her friend kept on talking, comforting her, but Louise wasn't listening. Finally, to put a stop to the flow of words, she said, "He's ended it."

Camilla straightened up and set her teacup down. "What do you mean?"

"We're not getting married. We're not together; we're not a couple anymore."

Neither of them spoke. In the pin-drop silence, Camilla appeared to be processing this information.

"But he was the one who proposed," she said, as if there must be some mistake. A misunderstanding.

Louise nodded. "And he's the one who ended it. Took back his proposal. Broke up with me." It felt as if she suddenly had to do his explaining for him.

She sank back, exhausted now. Her tears had stopped, but she'd pricked open the wound inside her, the one that had been there since the evening she and Eik had sat out on the balcony after saying good night to Jonas and Steph.

He had simply said he wasn't ready to get married after all. That he couldn't share his life with her, the way he felt right now.

Louise had been shocked. At first, she thought he was joking, but no. She couldn't remember how she made it through that night. She hadn't told anyone, hadn't spoken it out loud until now, and even though the words made the breakup feel more real, they were also a release.

"What the hell happened? Did you have a big argument or what?"

Louise shook her head, but before she could answer, Camilla went on.

"Because it sounded to me like everything was going great. Like you two were so happy together. All four of you. And you looked so much in love in the pictures you sent."

"It's true, we *were* happy. Jonas and Steph get along so well, but I think Eik feels guilty about not being there for her while she was growing up. He feels like he failed her, like they missed out on so much together."

"But he didn't even know he had a daughter, for chrissake! You can't not be there for someone when you don't know that someone even exists! And it's so new for Steph, finding out about her biological father."

"Eik feels that he needs to focus on his daughter, catch up on everything they missed out on. He's also afraid that Steph's going to have an emotional breakdown at some point, from seeing her mother killed. And I understand that, of course I do. Jonas went through the same thing. It was so hard for him, for so long."

Camilla nodded thoughtfully. She'd been there herself, up in Sweden, when Jonas's father, the pastor Henrik Holm, was murdered right in front of them. She'd known Jonas and his father because Markus and Jonas had played together when they both lived in Frederiksberg.

"All right, but if there's anyone who can help Steph deal with what she's going through now, it damn well should be us," Camilla said, as if they were all one big family.

Louise nodded. "I think Steph talks about it to Jonas once in a while." Her son had told her that Steph often had nightmares that woke her up, which he could relate to; the same thing had happened to him. "But when I ask him about it, he clams up. He won't let me in on what the two of them talk about. It's like it would be a breach of confidentiality. I can respect that. The important thing is that she has someone to talk to."

"Okay, but it's just completely insane of Eik to push all of you away."

"He's not pushing all of us away. Just me." Her voice clogged up again; she had to clear her throat. "I think in a way he still wants to be with me, he just doesn't want to get married and have a life together. Right now, the only commitment he wants to make is to Steph."

"So okay then, do it that way! You said yourself it was strange, him all of a sudden wanting to get married. Keep on with what you had before."

Louise shook her head. "It's not about getting married. What matters is that apparently he feels I'm not worth making a commitment to."

It took a lot for her to say that last sentence. And as she said it, she stared down at her hands to avoid Camilla's eyes. But her friend understood; Louise sensed it in the silence that fell between them.

They'd known each other way back when Louise had been under the impression that her boyfriend Klaus had committed suicide. And although she had later found out that Klaus's death had been much more complicated than it had seemed, the idea that he would rather die than be with her had still left her with the lingering feeling, throughout most of her adult life, that she wasn't worth loving.

"You can't compare this with what happened back then," Camilla said, her voice firm. "And Klaus didn't take his own life; it had nothing to do with you."

Louise shook her head; of course she was aware of that. Now. But for almost twenty years, she'd lived with a lack of self-esteem. And it took so very little for that feeling to return.

"But I understand how Eik feels," Louise said. "I just can't go through the same thing again. The insecurity."

She thought about Mikkel. Maybe it was a family thing, the fact that both of them couldn't deal with being abandoned. For a moment she'd even thought it could have been her lying there in the hospital. But only for a moment. She wasn't the kind of person who got depressed; she was the kind who closed up their feelings and got angry. The anger just hadn't come yet.

Camilla brought the teapot in from the kitchen and poured them both another cup. "So it's actually you who broke up with Eik, then."

Louise could hardly believe her ears. She frowned and shook her head.

"Oh yes, you did. He says he's not ready to get married yet, but he still wants to be with you, and then you end it."

Louise opened her mouth to argue, but Camilla beat her to it.

"And you didn't even want to get married in the first place. You thought it was absolutely ridiculous when he got down on one knee. You said so yourself."

"Okay, but I don't want a boyfriend I can't count on," Louise snapped.

"And what about Jonas?"

"He stayed. At first he wanted to come home with me, but then Eik said he was welcome to stay on with him and Steph if he wanted to."

Camilla was indignant. "You're saying that Eik just accepted you not going along with them?"

Louise considered that for a moment before nodding. "He did, actually. After I said I was stopping, that was the end of the discussion."

It looked like Camilla was about to say something, but she held back. A few moments later, she said, "It must have been a difficult situation for Jonas."

"I'm glad he stayed with them. Traveling is an incredible experience, and all three of them get along so well. But I think seeing me so miserable affected him. He's not used to that. He writes almost every day to check in and see if I'm okay." Louise smiled, and for a moment, the warmth from that thought held back her gloom.

"He's a wonderful boy, really," Camilla said. She told Louise about how Markus had been spending most of his time with Julia's parents in Vanløse, where the two of them had a room in the basement. "I mean, we have this enormous apartment, a big roof terrace, it's in the middle of Frederiksberg, he has two rooms and his own bathroom, for chrissake, luxury, but do you think he wants to be there?"

Camilla was trying to be funny, but the words came out with a hint of bitterness. Clearly, she was hurt.

"Frederik and I are talking about a last-minute addition. To the family."

Louise's eyes widened.

"I always wanted one more, and Frederik doesn't have any kids."

"You're over forty!"

"Yeah, and in Hollywood, they're over fifty, so I've got lots of time." Camilla laughed.

"Honestly! Have you thought this through? Is Frederik coming home then, or are you planning on moving over there?"

"The plan is that I handle the pregnancy by myself. Most women do anyway, even when the men think they're so involved in it all. And Frederik will be back as often as he can when the baby comes. And I might take my maternity leave over there with him. It depends on what I feel like doing at that point."

Louise shook her head; though she'd never been pregnant herself, she thought the plan sounded irresponsible. In theory it might sound like it could work, but when reality hit, her friend would regret it. She kept that thought to herself, though.

She heard a text message arrive, and went to get her phone from the kitchen.

"We're picking the kids up and bringing them home with us. Write after you've seen Mikkel; he might open up more for you. Love, Dad."

Her father was a chattier texter than her mother.

"They don't think I can take care of the kids," Louise said as Camilla joined her in the kitchen. "They don't even dare let me pick them up."

She shook her head at her overprotective parents. Jonas had been eleven when he came into her life, so she'd never had much experience with younger kids. No experience, actually, at least in her own life, though she'd taken care of her niece and nephew a few times and it had gone just fine.

"I guess I'd better try to track down some of the others from Susan Dahlgaard's class, so I don't go back to the paper empty-handed. Or do you need a lift to the hospital?"

Louise shook her head. "I'll take Mikkel's car; it's right outside."

Right outside, where her brother had tried to end his life. But Louise cut off that thought.

"Call when you've seen him," Camilla said as Louise followed her out.

They hugged. Louise watched her back out and then drive away.

FOUR

Louise was just starting to clean up the kitchen when the doorbell rang again. She glanced around to see if Camilla had forgotten something, then walked over and opened the door.

Two uniformed police officers were standing on the front stoop. One of them asked if she was Louise Rick.

She hesitated a moment before saying yes. The officer asked if they could come in, and she stepped aside to let them pass through the door. They introduced themselves and explained that they were with the Roskilde Police. They added that they'd been trying to get in touch with her at her home address in Frederiksberg.

"We understand you've just returned from a long trip abroad," the officer said. "We'd like to speak with you for a few minutes."

Louise nodded as the part of her brain currently in working order tried to figure out what this was about. Their manner would have been different if something had happened to Jonas. Or Melvin, their downstairs neighbor. During the past few years, he'd become one of her closest friends, and he'd survived a heart attack a while back. At that time, she and Jonas had been registered as his nearest family. But Melvin had a girlfriend now, Grete Milling, and she would have called if he'd suffered a relapse. And if they'd come to deliver tragic news about Trine, they would have stood outside a bit longer before asking to come in. This was a more aggressive arrival. They were alert, observant.

She showed them into the kitchen. "What's this all about?"

"We're here to talk to you about your brother," said the female officer. She was a bit taller than Louise, with short blond hair. Louise didn't recognize either of them from the times she'd worked with the Roskilde Police, but they might not have been in the crime division.

"My brother?"

"Mikkel Rick."

Louise nodded and waited.

The male officer pointed at the table and asked if they could sit down. Louise wasn't eager for them to settle in, but she pulled out a chair for the sake of politeness.

"Trine Madsen," he continued. "Disappeared last Wednesday. She's been missing for eight days."

Louise nodded again.

"Four days ago, her mother, Liselotte Madsen, reported her daughter missing."

"Her mother!" Louise was surprised. Her brother's mother-in-law had been a high school teacher in Dåstrup, but for the past several years she'd spent most of her time in Málaga, where she'd bought a small apartment with an ocean view. She usually came home for Christmas, but the rest of the time she preferred her active retirement life in sunny southern Europe.

"Trine hasn't disappeared," she continued. "She left my brother, and it's not the first time; her mother knows that."

She felt her cheeks redden. It was ridiculous to let these two officers get under her skin; she knew that, but if they had come barging in here unprepared, she wasn't going to make it easy for them.

"The last time she left him and the kids, he was stuck with the house, the bills, and the sole responsibility for their two kids. And back then, her mother was busy with her retired friends down in Costa del Sol; she didn't have time to come back and help my brother with her grandkids. The ones her daughter had abandoned."

The officer ignored her. "It's been four days since Trine Madsen was reported missing. In all the time she's been gone, there's been no indication that she's alive. No digital traces, no physical sightings. Which means we've opened an investigation into her disappearance."

"I'm aware of what that means." Louise was even more annoyed at their lack of preparation; they didn't seem to know she worked in the Missing Persons Department. Or at least she had. "Did you know my brother just attempted suicide? Do you know how serious this is? How close he came to succeeding? And where is Trine's mother, by the way?"

She looked around the kitchen. "Obviously she's not here helping him pick up the pieces."

"Liselotte Madsen is at the station right now. She's with one of our colleagues, trying to put together a timeline of her daughter's whereabouts up to the time of her disappearance."

"Trine was *here* up to the time of her disappearance. What is there to put—"

Suddenly Louise understood what was going on. She folded her arms.

"We want to talk to you about your brother," the female officer said, clearly trying to get things back on track. "When was the last time you spoke with him?"

Louise took the time to think before answering; she wanted to stay one step ahead of them. "I've only spoken with him once since I've been gone. We left in February, and I called him on April 10, his birthday. We've texted each other, though, and written on Messenger. And I talked to my niece and nephew on FaceTime, and I usually said hi to him, too. But the only time we really talked was on his birthday."

"So you don't know how he's been doing? His mental and emotional state, I mean. If he was feeling unhappy, depressed."

She shook her head.

The male officer looked grave. "Do you have any reason to believe that your sister-in-law was suicidal? Tired of living?"

Tired of living! Louise rolled her eyes. "If she was depressed, I haven't heard about it."

"Did she have emotional problems?"

"Not that I know of."

"Do you know if she packed a suitcase before she disappeared?" the male officer asked.

Louise nodded. "An overnight bag. She took a few clothes with her. And money."

The officers glanced at each other.

"And no," Louise continued, "I don't know if she's having an affair. I don't know if she took any money out of their joint account before she left. And I haven't checked to see if my sister-in-law has been on any social media over the past week. I got home last night, and the only person who concerns me right now is my brother."

The female officer didn't bat an eye. "She hasn't. Hasn't taken any money out or been on any social media."

Louise looked back and forth between the two of them. "If it's been four days since my sister-in-law was reported missing, I assume you've checked her phone, traced her debit card, and questioned their neighbors and friends."

She could hear herself sneering at them. But the search must have started the day before her brother's attempted suicide, when his mother-in-law had reported Trine missing, and she could imagine how they had gone at Mikkel when they'd questioned him.

The two officers glanced at each other before the male officer leaned over the table. "We suspect your brother of being involved in the disappearance of his wife."

Louise stared coldly at them before shaking her head. "And what precisely is your suspicion based on?"

Neither of them answered. "Trine hasn't really disappeared," she continued. "Seven thousand crowns from their vacation savings is also gone, but my brother's mother-in-law doesn't know that, because she didn't respond when my parents left messages on her answering service. They called several times to ask if she knew where Trine was. If she'd heard from her. But instead of talking to the family, apparently she'd rather talk to you."

Louise was boiling mad.

"We're aware that your brother has attempted suicide, and this is looking very much like it could be a 'family tragedy,'" the female officer continued, using the media's favorite term for a murder-suicide. "And we intend to find out what happened to your sister-in-law."

Louise jumped out of her chair and leaned over the table, glaring at them. "My brother didn't kill Trine," she spat. She was about to add that Mikkel couldn't kill anyone, he wasn't the type, but after all her years in the Homicide Department, she knew it was an idiotic thing to say. With some people you just never knew.

"He's absolutely devastated about her being gone. He loves her, she's the love of his life, otherwise he'd never have taken her back after the first time she left him."

"We have to be rational about this," the male officer said. "Let's try to keep our emotions out of it and concentrate on the facts. At the moment it appears your brother is the last person to have been in contact with Trine Madsen, after she picked up their two children, one at school and one at day care."

"What do you know?" Louise's voice was trembling.

"Trine Madsen didn't show up for a dentist appointment the day after she disappeared. She didn't cancel her appointments with clients at her clinic. Your brother was the one who called and canceled. She didn't call her mother in Spain on her birthday last week. None of her friends have heard from her."

Louise stopped listening. She got it—they'd contacted her, and probably her parents, only after speaking to everyone else. Everyone knew Mikkel but wasn't necessarily on his side. They had opened an investigation based on suspicion of murder. And her brother was their prime suspect.

"Is anyone staying here while your brother's in the hospital?" the female officer asked. Louise hadn't bothered to remember her name.

"I am. And his children, and my parents are in and out. My apartment is sublet until August; I'm on leave from my job." As head of Homicide, she was about to add, but of course she hadn't officially begun yet. And right now she wasn't sure she even wanted to take the job anymore.

The female officer nodded. "Yes, we know."

Louise understood they *had* done their homework; they'd done a background check on her. In fact, they'd checked everything before contacting her. *So much for staying a step ahead of them*, she thought.

"Have you spoken to my brother?"

"He said the same as you. That she just disappeared. She picked up the kids that day, and he did the shopping on the way home, so he didn't get home until five-thirty. The door wasn't locked, and the kids were in the living room watching TV. Trine was gone. Neither of the kids noticed their mother leaving. They didn't hear anything, didn't see her walk out. They weren't aware she was gone until your brother came in and asked about her."

"So my brother wasn't the last person to talk to her after all," Louise quickly pointed out.

"The last adult," the female officer replied, just as quickly.

"But Trine had time to pack and take the money out of the jar," Louise said, mostly to herself. She wanted to defend Mikkel, say that he would never hurt Trine, but instead she said that she wanted to visit her brother at the hospital now, if they had no objections.

They considered that for a moment, but then the male officer shook his head and said that as long as Mikkel wasn't charged with a crime, she had the right to speak to him.

"Does he know you suspect him of harming her?" Louise asked. The words sounded all wrong coming out of her mouth.

"He's not officially under suspicion yet," the woman said. "But he knows we're investigating the case."

And he thinks you're on his side, Louise thought bitterly.

FIVE

Mikkel was lying with his back to the door when Louise walked in.
He'd pulled his duvet so far up that the only thing visible was his hair
on the pillow. He was alone in the room; the patient occupying the
bed by the window had flung the duvet carelessly aside and piled
magazines and plastic cups on the bedside table.

"Hi." Louise spoke softly as she approached him, thinking he was
probably asleep. She circled around the foot of the bed to check.

But he was awake, staring straight ahead as if he hadn't heard her.
His dark hair was uncombed, and his forehead glistened with sweat.
He might be too hot under the duvet, she thought.

"Hi," she repeated. She bent down to his eye level, then reached
out and gently touched his shoulder. He didn't move. She shook him
lightly and whispered his name until at last he blinked. Slowly and
carefully he turned his eyes to her. For a moment, they simply looked
at each other. Several thoughts flew through Louise's head. He might
be sedated; they might have given him something. Or maybe he'd
just woken up and wasn't himself yet. Meals were being served on

the ward and the smell of food filled the hallway outside. The clatter of silverware and plates rang out from the other rooms, but time had come to a halt in here, as if his room was separate from the rest.

"Mikkel," she said, lightly squeezing his arm.

"What are you doing here?" His voice sounded hoarse, and Louise smiled at him.

"I'm here to make sure you behave yourself." She tried to look impish, but it fell flat.

He shook his head weakly and didn't reply.

Louise pulled the chair over to the bed. "Would you like to sit up a bit?"

He didn't react. Nor did he move or speak when she began raising the head of his bed.

She pressed her hand to his cheek, the way she had when he was a little boy. While driving to the hospital, she'd thought about what to say to him and resolved not to say anything critical, nothing about how he had terrified them all, made them worry about him.

She noticed two drawings on his bed table. On the first, "Dad" was written in crooked letters over a red heart that filled most of the sheet of paper. The other was more abstract. Maybe a rocket, she thought. It was also for "Dad," which was written in a corner. Suddenly it was difficult to find something to say. Mikkel sat stiffly under the duvet, apathetic, his eyes averted.

"I got home yesterday," she said, thinking that her parents must have told him she was coming. "And I'm staying in your guest room. I hope you don't mind."

He shook his head weakly and reached for a plastic cup on the table. Louise reached to help him with it but then stopped herself.

She watched him empty the cup. "How long are they going to keep you here?"

"Christ, that's bad," he said when he put the cup down. His voice sounded more like it usually did. "What do the kids say, how are they taking it?"

"I haven't talked to them, actually. I was still asleep when Mom and Dad left this morning, and they were planning to pick them up. It might be because they don't dare leave the kids with me."

He smiled faintly. "Yeah, I'll bet that's so. Did you have a good trip?"

Louise leaned back and nodded, said it had been exciting.

After a few moments, the silence became awkward. She wanted to shake him, yell at him, but instead she just looked at him, unable to find the right words.

He was the one who spoke first, his voice low as he shook his head. "I just couldn't."

Louise nodded. She assumed he meant that he couldn't go through being left by Trine again.

In a monotone, he explained that first he'd decided to hang himself but had lost his nerve after putting the rope up. He hadn't dared.

The moment of silence that followed was deafening at first, until Louise exploded angrily.

"What the hell were you thinking? Hanging yourself? Who the hell did you expect to walk in and find you? Your kids? Trine? Were you trying to punish her? Did you fantasize about how horrible she'd feel when she found you? How fucking dare you! And Mom, how do you think she felt, finding her son half dead in the garage?"

The blood roared through her veins; she was furious at Mikkel but also at Eik, at everything. She gripped the duvet with both hands to keep from punching him.

"I'm sorry," he whispered.

"Shut up!" she shouted, just as the door opened and a middle-aged man in a robe and slippers shuffled in. He stared at her in fright before turning around and leaving again.

"Goddammit, Mikkel!"

Louise felt the tears running down her cheeks. She leaned over and pulled him to her. Hugged him, hard, rocking back and forth until the heat from the duvet was too much.

"I was so scared," she whispered as she sank down into her chair. "Scared you would die before I got home. I said my goodbyes to you so many times up there in the air; the whole time I was afraid it was too late. I'm sorry, I shouldn't have screamed at you. I didn't mean it. I've just been so, so scared."

"I'm sorry," he said again. "This time Trine isn't coming back."

Louise sat up and studied him carefully. His eyes were focused on his hands, which were folded on top of the duvet. He was pale, and small drops of sweat still glistened on his forehead.

"What makes you say that?"

He hesitated a moment. "It's just what I think."

There was something nearly childish about the way he said that. Louise tried to get him to look at her, but he kept averting his eyes.

Another silence arose between them. This time, though, she had plenty of questions to ask. She forced herself not to bombard him with them, though it was difficult to hold back.

She took a deep breath. "The police stopped by to talk to me before I came here."

She'd planned not to say anything about it, but that wasn't in his best interests, she realized that now.

He nodded and said they had been by to talk to him, too. "She's been reported missing," he continued. "I told them where you work, that you'd pull all the strings you could to find her."

"Where I *used* to work," she said.

"It wouldn't have helped, anyway; the police over here are the ones looking for her. Even though I tried to get them to send the case to Missing Persons, where the real experts are."

"The Roskilde Police know what they're doing," she said.

He nodded hesitantly. "What's important is that they're looking for her. Mostly for the sake of the kids. She can't just turn her back on them like she did the last time."

Back then, over a month had gone by before Trine had felt ready to see her children again. She'd needed to clear her head. Alone time, as she'd put it.

"Mikkel. The police think you had something to do with her disappearance. They think something has happened to her. They don't have any proof yet, but you need to be prepared. They're investigating her disappearance as unintentional, as a crime. And I wouldn't be surprised if they show up at your door with a search warrant."

He stared at her in astonishment, suddenly alert and wide awake. "Me! What could I have done? I wasn't even home when she disappeared."

She spoke quietly, holding his eyes. "That's what we have to prove."

He looked back at her and again there was something a bit childish about his reaction. Or maybe he didn't completely understand what she had just told him. She reached out and took his hand.

"We'll get through this. I just need to understand what happened the day she disappeared."

She'd said those words before. Under different circumstances, in another life. A life in which she'd been the officer looking for answers, needing to either prove or disprove a suspicion. But now she was on the other side, and it didn't feel any easier.

"Are you up to talking about it?" she asked.

Her brother nodded and sat up straighter. Just then the door opened and the man in the robe peeked in.

"Come on in," Louise said, waving him in. She turned back to her brother and leaned closer. "Tell me about what happened leading up to the day Trine disappeared."

He bit his lower lip and thought for a moment, then shook his head. "I've gone over everything so many times, trying to figure it out. Why did this happen now? But I can't think of one reason why. We were doing so great, no big arguments, no big ups and downs, nothing that made me feel like maybe she was tired of me. On the contrary."

He glanced up at Louise. "The sex was good. We laughed a lot; we'd just rented a vacation house and we were really looking forward to it."

Louise suddenly realized she was stroking his hand. She let go.

"That morning, Trine said she'd pick the kids up, which she usually does, but sometimes she likes to go out running or work out after finishing at the clinic. But that day she was picking them up, and I said I'd stop for Mexican food on my way home. And if the kids weren't too tired after dinner, we were going to drive out to Malerklemmen for doughnut holes. I talked to her before I left the shop; she was on the way to get them."

Louise let all that information sink in.

"I got home a little before five-thirty. The kids were on the sofa watching TV. I asked them where their mother was; they said she was out in the kitchen. But she wasn't. She wasn't anywhere in the house or over in the clinic. Her running shoes were out in the back hall. Although she would have let me know if she'd changed her mind and decided to go out for a run. The kids would have been okay alone, she knew I was on the way. But she would've left a note."

"But she packed a bag."

He nodded. "I found that out later. I was sure she'd be back. There'd been some small emergency maybe, over at the neighbor's or somewhere close by. We all know one another out here. Her bike was still there, so I figured she wasn't too far away. I took the food out and set the table and everything, but still no Trine. So, after we ate, I called a few of her friends, asked them if they knew where she was. Nobody'd heard from her. I tucked the kids into bed and told them Mom just had to leave for a while. But I'm pretty sure they knew something was up. After they fell asleep, I started going through her stuff."

"Did you find anything?" Louise asked.

He shook his head. "That's when I realized she'd left me. I knew it even before I saw her bag was missing and that she'd taken the money in the kitchen. And it was so much worse than the last time, because I had no idea it was coming. The first time she left, things were really bad between us. We'd drifted apart, we were terrible at making the marriage work. Lots of couples have trouble when their kids are young, and I guess we were one of them. Back then she'd threatened to leave. Several times. But this time, like I said, things had been going great for us."

"Do you know what she took with her?"

Her brother shook his head. "The overnight bag she keeps in the hall closet, it's gone now. And I guess she took some clothes; I can't see what's missing. I can't remember what she had on that day."

"Could her overnight bag have been missing before then? Before she disappeared?"

"What do you mean? Why would it be?"

"I don't mean anything, I'm just asking. The thing is, we can't be sure she packed the bag that day before she left."

After chewing on that a few moments, he shrugged. "I didn't notice it was gone before, anyway."

"And the money, are you sure she took it that day?"

"I don't understand! What are you getting at?"

"I'm not getting at anything, I'm just trying to get a clear picture of what could have happened."

A second later, he whispered softly, "Do the police think I killed her?"

She bit her cheek and nodded. "I get the impression they suspect you did."

He turned away, and she gave him a few moments before asking if he'd spoken to Trine's mother.

He looked back at her and nodded. "I called her two days later. I don't think I had a lot of nice things to say."

Louise could imagine. "She's back here in Denmark. She reported Trine's disappearance to the police."

Mikkel shook his head. "She's never been there for us. Not for Trine, either, not even when Trine was really hurting. Once she wanted to stay a while at her mother's apartment in Málaga, but her mother wouldn't even loan it to her. She told Trine she might want to go down there herself. That was in July, when she was always up here. And later on, whenever Trine asked, the woman kept coming up with some lame excuse. I'm surprised she makes herself out to be so worried all of a sudden; she's never really taken an interest in her daughter. Or her grandchildren, far as that goes."

Louise nodded; this fit her impression of her brother's mother-in-law.

A few moments later, he said, "You even have to wonder if she'd have helped Trine, if Trine had been the one left alone with two small kids."

Again, Louise had the feeling his suicide attempt had been more of an infantile wish to punish Trine than a true desire to die.

"Mikkel," she said, ignoring his last remark, "it doesn't look great that you didn't report Trine missing. And that it's her mother who has come home from Spain and set off an investigation. Why didn't you contact the police?"

Her brother looked pissed. "Come on, honestly. She left me. You think the police want all these husbands coming in every time a couple breaks up?"

Louise nodded; he had a point. "So you don't think anything happened to her?" This was her roundabout way of feeling out whether he could have been involved in Trine's disappearance, as unthinkable as that would have been.

"Why should anything have happened to her?"

"Because she's disappeared without a trace!" Louise was annoyed, but then she remembered why they were there in the hospital. It wasn't the right time to push him.

Another silence fell. This time when she spoke, he didn't react; he seemed apathetic again.

She squeezed his hand. "Mikkel, are you okay?"

Slowly he faced her and shrugged. "I don't want to be here any longer," he said, so weakly that the words barely made it out of his mouth.

"Here? At the hospital?"

He shook his head. "Here in life. I don't think I have it in me to deal with things."

"Stop it. You have to be here, otherwise your kids won't have anyone."

"She'll take care of them."

"You want her to hear about what happened. Is that what's going on here?"

Her anger rose into her throat once more.

He looked startled. "No." He glanced over at the man by the window; Louise had almost forgotten him. "I just can't bear to lose her."

"But don't you think about what your kids will lose if you kill yourself?"

"Well, excuse me," he said angrily, "but maybe not everybody is as strong as you are."

"As me!" Though it was totally inappropriate, she couldn't help but smile. If only he knew! "Mikkel, the way you're feeling right now, it can only get better."

"Better!"

She nodded. "I just can't imagine it getting worse."

He shrugged vaguely; he supposed she was right.

She lowered her voice to make sure the other patient couldn't hear. "There are some things I need to know and you have to be honest with me. And when I say honest, I mean *honest*."

He leaned forward, and she asked in a whisper if he was responsible for Trine's disappearance.

His face betrayed no emotion as he shook his head.

"Is there anything in your house you don't want the police to find?"

Again, he shook his head.

"Nothing at all?"

"I don't have any secrets," he said. "There's nothing to hide. They can turn the whole place upside down; I just hope they come up with some answers."

"Is there anything that might reveal where she is or what happened?"

"If they can find something I missed, that's great." Now they were back to where they'd started, with Mikkel completely convinced that Trine had left him. In a way, it eased her mind. She was certain she'd know if he tried to hide something from her.

"We'll find her," she said. "We will."

"But she'll never be mine anymore. She left me with no explanation, which means I'm just not what she wants anymore. She knows well and good that I won't take her back this time, and yet she

decided to leave anyway. I have to accept that. Right now, I'm thinking mostly about the kids, how it's going to be for them."

"If you're thinking of them, then you have to promise to forget
about taking your own life. Is that a deal?"

There, she'd said it. And she'd tried to keep it light. But she meant
every word. She hoped it sank in.

SIX

When Louise got back from the hospital in Roskilde, she found a paper bag on the front steps. Inside was a plastic container with chili con carne, a carton of sour cream, and a note from her mother, explaining that the sour cream was to be poured over the chili.

She carried the bag into the kitchen. She was exhausted and felt like heading straight for bed, but if she was ever going to get her brain cells back up to speed, food was necessary. While she searched for a pot, a text from Jonas came in. He'd sent several photos she hadn't had time to look at, and now he was asking what she thought.

She dumped the chili into the pot, then reached for a bottle of wine from the rack and found a corkscrew. After pouring herself a generous glass and making sure the sophisticated induction burner was on, she began opening the photos he'd sent.

He'd shorn off his hair. The long front bangs were completely gone. She stared at the photos of her son for several moments; he looked older. Some were close-ups, others had been taken from a distance. She noticed two thin strings around his wrist. Exactly like what Eik had been wearing when they'd met. All he needed was a shark's-tooth necklace and Jonas would practically be an Eik clone.

The photos made her feel melancholy; she felt a pang in her stomach as she filled a bowl with chili and added a large spoonful of cold sour cream. Then she carried the bowl and her phone and the glass of wine into the living room.

"Cool," she wrote, adding a sunglasses smiley. She should have written that it looked good on him. No doubt he'd had to work up the courage to do it. Several more photos were attached, one of them with Eik in the background. He had the same short haircut, the same style. They'd gone to the same barber.

Louise laid her phone aside and finished eating while watching some boring TV program. She missed both of them. But just then she missed Jonas the most, which was actually a relief. She missed laughing with him. And lounging with him on the sofa, watching *Game of Thrones*. He'd had to guide her through it, explain to her who was in the Stark family and who was a Lannister. And then there was the girl with the dragons. She loved it. But it would be almost two more months before he came home and they could watch it together again.

Louise got up and started to clean the dishes. She was wide awake now, which annoyed her. Stupid jet lag! She corked the bottle of wine and started the dishwasher, then began wandering around the house. First into the kids' bedrooms, one on each side of their parents' room. They were quite neat; clearly her mother had been busy. Then she walked into Mikkel and Trine's room. The bed was made with a dark green quilt. Louise was sure this was also her mother's work. A door led to a large bathroom with a tub and a double sink. The shelf under the mirror on one side was filled with jars of cream and small bottles. Perfumes and facial serum. Red nail polish. A cup with a pink toothbrush, toothpaste, and a small pale yellow blister pack of birth control pills. A month's worth, each pill nestled into a plastic bubble. The pack was half full.

Louise picked it up. The last pill had been taken on Wednesday. The day Trine disappeared. The pack slipped back down into the cup when she let go of it, and she returned to the bedroom. The built-in closet had space on both sides of the hallway door. Her sister-in-law's side had two sections with rods for clothes hangers and two broad drawers below. Shelves took up the third section, the middle one, and were filled with underwear, socks, and tops in separate baskets.

She couldn't reach the top shelf, so she fetched a stepladder from the kitchen. Then she systematically went through Trine's closet. On the top shelf, she found heavy blouses and sweaters and stacks of winter clothing stowed away. She laid it all out on the bed and separated every piece to see if there was anything hidden in between.

More blouses and sweaters lay on the next shelf. The cardigans were buttoned and neatly stacked. Again, she carefully went through each article of clothing before laying it all back into place on the shelves. The T-shirts looked ironed. One large stack of them was the white T-shirts she knew Trine wore in the clinic. There were others in various shades of blue, which she knew was the color her sister-in-law preferred to wear. Everything was so neat and orderly that she was certain she was wasting her time, yet in her work as a police investigator there had certainly been times when she'd felt that way and yet still a clue had turned up.

Her brother was right; it was hard to see if anything was missing. The stacks of clothes filled most of the closet. And while nothing you'd find in a normal closet seemed to be lacking, it was impossible to say whether or not a few things might have been removed.

Louise was going through the next-lowest shelf when her fingers caught on a sharp corner.

Pulling on it eagerly, she slid a folded sheet of paper out from between some workout clothes. She opened it and realized it was a class picture. It was of Trine's seventh-grade class, 7C, from the Osted elementary school. She sat on the bed. Three faces had been circled with a fat red permanent marker. Immediately she recognized one of them: Trine, with long pigtails, sitting in the front row. She drew a blank on the two other marked girls, but Susan Dahlgaard, the girl who had disappeared on Bornholm, was standing in the back row next to the teacher. Her hair was golden brown, and her smile was dazzling. The photo used in connection with the search had been her individual class portrait, and it must have been taken that same day because she was dressed identically in both photos.

In the photo, Trine looked like her daughter did now, though Kirstine's smile seemed happier. Louise grabbed her phone so she could send the class picture to Camilla. She also tapped out a short message to her friend, asking if she knew who the other girls were.

Camilla answered a few moments later. "The girl to the left is Pia Bagger; I dated her big brother. I know where her parents live. Will try to find her tomorrow. Thanks. Hugs."

Louise studied the class picture for a moment longer, then laid it on the night table so she could finish going through the closet. But there was nothing more. Not even an embarrassing sex toy. She checked the shoes and the clothes on hangers. Then she leafed through the four-ring binders in Trine and Mikkel's office. One of them was filled with personal papers. Birth, baptism, and marriage certificates; divorce papers. A plastic folder held car information and garage bills. Another was filled with the kids' documents and vaccination records. Everything someone would need if they were planning on moving was still there, seemingly untouched.

Suddenly, Louise spotted a wallet on the floor, halfway under the bed. A Louis Vuitton Mikkel had given Trine at Christmas. Louise had been there when she opened the present—they had spent the holiday in Lerbjerg with her parents. Trine had nearly cried with joy.

Her medical card, driver's license, and debit card were still inside, but there was no cash. She tossed it down and opened the drawer in the bedside table. A sleeping mask and hand cream.

She took the class picture with her and went to find one of the sleeping pills from Thailand.

SEVEN

BORNHOLM, 1995

It stunk horribly on the lower deck where they were supposed to sleep. The stench of gasoline combined with the clammy funk of adolescent sweat and stinky socks. Trine's stomach felt queasy. She was still dizzy from riding all the roller coasters in Tivoli, before the class had boarded the Bornholm ferry. The enormous cotton candy she'd eaten wasn't helping, either.

Susan had stashed some Bacardi rum in her backpack. It was hidden in a half-liter cola bottle with a screw-on lid. They called it half-and-half, and it was more than lukewarm when they boarded the ferry.

Trine kicked her tennis shoes off as soon as she was assigned a bunk—her feet were sore from hours of running around between the rides at Tivoli.

"Move those," Mona said, on her way to the top bunk. Without looking at her, Trine pushed her shoes out of the way.

They'd met at the school at two. The bus had almost left without Carsten, who was late as usual, but their teacher had talked the driver into waiting. They'd teased Carsten about it all the way to Copenhagen. *That idiot,* Trine thought.

She leaned out to see where Mads was sleeping. They'd done the bumper cars together. She hated ramming into the other cars, but they'd gone four rounds because Mads liked it. And she liked being close to him.

There was a shout, and then the ferry roared and shook as the engine started. Trine grabbed a sweater from her bag and sniffed the arm, but fortunately Pia had missed it when she threw up. They'd gone to the women's bathroom together; Trine had known Pia was drunk, but not *that* drunk. Several of the boys had also smuggled alcohol onto the bus, and Pia had hung around them. Mostly because of Aksel. Trine had no idea what her friend saw in him, with his stringy hair that stuck straight up. But Pia wasn't picky. You could learn a thing or two from her, Nina had told Trine, more than once. Nina, always so sensible. Susan, on the other hand, could afford to be picky. Ever since she and her long hair and white Kawasaki sneakers had joined the class in fifth grade, she'd had the boys in the palm of her hand. Even though Trine, Nina, and Pia had been friends since grade school, they'd accepted Susan into their clique. Nina had been against it, but Trine and Pia convinced her that hanging out with Susan would give them plenty of advantages.

The ferry was sailing now.

Someone yelled a line from the old song "In a Little Rocking Boat." Someone else yelled at him to shut up. Trine was tired. It was noisy, with all the classes from all the schools in the area in one room, but she tried to close her eyes and shut it all out. She wanted to sleep, even though Susan and the others had headed for the top deck after the teachers said good night.

She'd drunk too much, and the ferry was rocking. More than she wanted it to. She lay on her back, staring up at the bottom of the top bunk. Up where Mona was stretched out. The mattress wasn't moving, there was no sign she was awake, but Trine had the feeling that she was staring straight up, too. There was something strange about Mona. Pia was the one who had brought it up. First there had been the scene at school; she'd been the only one who hadn't wanted to go on the class trip. Every time they talked about it, it was like Mona spaced out. She hadn't helped plan it or anything. She even went to the teacher and tried to get her to cancel the trip, because she said she had a feeling something terrible was going to happen. Several of the boys teased her about it, said it was because she was afraid to be away from her mommy and daddy. Or afraid the cave people or Curly-Burly, the stupid, naughty little Bornholm troll, would capture her.

It was easy to tease Mona because she never said anything. She just stared straight back at the bullies, like she was hoping a trapdoor would open under their feet.

Truth or consequences, somebody yelled, right before Trine fell asleep. Their voices seemed to blend together with all the sounds of the ferry. The rumble of the engine sent small shivers through her body. She didn't feel Pia and Nina shaking her. She slept through all the singing and everyone yelling at one another. She slept through some of them sneaking away and kissing, and through some of them pretending to be asleep, because they had other plans.

"When we ring the bell, it's breakfast time," explained Kirsten, the manager of the hostel. She glanced around at the class. "And the same goes for dinner. You make and take your own lunches."

Lena and Steffen had already explained all that while they were on the bus. But several of them had slept on the way from Rønne to Svaneke. Trine sat with Pia, who told her that she'd kissed Aksel up on deck. That's why they'd tried to wake her up. And apparently Susan had ducked into the bathroom with a boy from a school in Helsinge.

"They were in there a long time," Pia whispered. Susan was the oldest of the girls; she'd turned fourteen in January. Pia was also fourteen now, and only Nina and Trine were still thirteen.

"The showers are over here, and the bathrooms are down the hall," Kirsten explained. Nobody was really listening. Their new teacher, Steffen, cleared his throat. He taught math and biology. None of them had been very happy to hear he was coming on the trip. He was a lot more uptight than Lena, who had been their teacher since third grade.

"Where's the TV?" Carsten yelled.

Kirsten, whom they were already calling "the maid," shook her head at him and pointed out the window. "Right there. It's called nature. Try it out for a change."

Some of them laughed. Trine whispered back and forth with Nina about Pia and Aksel. If Nina thought they were going together now. Nina didn't think so.

"And it's lights-out at ten o'clock." Kirsten glared at all of them. As did Lena and Steffen. They all nodded in a show of agreement, though of course they really had no intention of respecting the curfew.

Kirsten continued anyway. "I know all about the hormones cooking in seventh graders like you." She had their attention now. "But don't sneak out at night, and don't hang out with the local boys and girls. Not because they're not nice, because Bornholmers are. Nice."

"Second-team Swedes," one of the boys whispered.

"I won't have any running around at night, and you will be sent home if we catch you. Consider yourselves warned."

Lena and Steffen nodded in agreement, then looked meaningfully at each of them, to emphasize what Kirsten had already said.

"*Beverly Hills 90210* is on later," one of the girls said, after raising her hand. "Can we watch it?"

Kirsten repeated that there was no television at the hostel. "But

Jeppesen has a TV store down in the square, with a TV in the window. Maybe he'll let you choose the channel."

They had heard about Jeppesen's TV back home. Some students from the upper classes had been on the school trip when the national soccer team had been playing, and most of the class had stood on the sidewalk watching the match. Until a local came up with the idea of charging admission—five crowns to watch the rest of the match in his living room.

"Where can we buy candy?" Carsten asked. Kirsten referred them to the convenience store at the harbor. What Carsten really wanted to know was where he could buy cigarettes, but only the other students knew that.

Rooms had been assigned before the trip. It had been a battle. Trine and her friends had threatened to stay home if they didn't get to share a room together, and Pia's mother had called the teacher to plead their case. She'd reluctantly agreed, but only if the four of them promised not to make any trouble.

Suddenly, Anja piped up. "I forgot to bring bedding and a towel." She was known as the teacher's pet, and Trine couldn't help but laugh; it was the kind of stunt Carsten would pull. Kirsten shushed them and said they could rent bedding and towels.

"Does anyone else need anything?" She glanced around, but they all shook their heads. Lena had pounded it into their heads: remember to bring bedding, raincoats, and pants, as well as warm sweaters, even though it was early June.

"We've set up an orientation activity for you," Lena said when Kirsten had finished. "It starts after we unpack and eat breakfast. Right now, find your rooms, and boys, over to the dormitory. After you're done, let's meet back down here."

EIGHT

Camilla had speed-written a handful of news clips. Made quick calls to all the police districts in the country and gotten updates from their daily incident reports. All of it handed in before lunch.

Terkel Høyer had not been particularly impressed, to say the least, when she got back from Osted and had to admit she hadn't been able to get ahold of Trine Madsen, and therefore had nothing for the paper other than an interview with a guy from Susan Dahlgaard's class whose life had gone off the rails. Carsten Iversen spent most of his waking hours at the local hangout for drunks in front of the grocery store. She'd gotten very little out of him. He did confirm he'd been in the same class as the girl who had disappeared. And he did remember her.

He even remembered that she hadn't been in the class in first grade. Whether she'd joined in second, third, fourth, or fifth grade, he couldn't say. But she was okay, he claimed. She lived with foster parents out in Osager, and the teachers had always let her get away with anything she wanted at school. Nobody else in the class could so much as fart without getting sent up to the office, but for some reason Susan was special.

Camilla had tried to dig a little deeper. She knew that Susan had grown up in a Roskilde orphanage; much had been written about that back when she disappeared. She'd run away several times, hadn't always been easy to handle. But after she'd moved in with her foster parents, Inge and Lars, she seemed to have settled down.

Iversen didn't keep in touch with the others from the class. A few of the guys stopped and talked to him once in a while, but otherwise he kept mostly to himself.

Sad, she thought. She'd recognized him in the old class picture Louise had sent, and it was so depressing to see that young boy's happy, hopeful face, now that she knew how his life had turned out.

"I'm driving over to Osted," she said as she laid a copy of the picture down on Høyer's desk. "I'm meeting with Pia Bagger; she was in Susan and Trine's class, too."

Her editor looked up, annoyed at the interruption, but he nodded after he glanced at the photo. The other papers had also covered the story of the schoolgirl found in Echo Valley. And they all had speculated about whether the young girl had been alive when she was trapped in the cave under the tree, or whether someone might have killed her and then stashed her body inside.

"Pia was one of her closest friends. She and Susan shared a room at the hostel on the class trip, and she was one of the three girls who were the last people to see her." Camilla pointed to the circled faces in the photo. She didn't mention that she would have to stop by Pia's parents' place in order to try to get her current address. Camilla had done an internet search, but not much had come up and she hadn't been sure she'd found the right Pia.

Høyer nodded and asked if she could handle a full page. Which Camilla immediately confirmed, adding that she would let him know if the story needed more space.

. . .

She recalled that the Baggers lived on the other side of Osted, close to Jonstrupgården, the stables where she'd taken riding lessons for a short time. She passed through Kirkebjerg and looked out over the fields. The sight of the road sign pointing to Mannerup brought back a memory of biking out to see Søren, Pia's brother, back when they'd been dating. She slowed down and signaled a turn. He'd been in her older brother Lasse's class. She was fifteen when they'd started going out together, after Lasse's death. He and Lasse had been friends, and she had known him already because the two boys often met at their house before heading off to parties on the weekends. When she was fourteen, she'd started tagging along with them. But then the accident happened. Søren had been at the funeral, of course, but it wasn't until sometime later that they met again, at a party at the gymnasium. He'd ended up walking her home. They'd often seen each other at the gym, where he played soccer and she liked to hang out, but their romance had slowly fizzled out. And since then she hadn't thought much about him.

After passing several farms, she spotted the Baggers' house. Set back from the road past the curve, it was a red stone house with a tall hedge in the front yard.

She pulled into the driveway but stopped when she saw that it was full of cars. Four to be exact, taking up all of the small parking area in front of the house. For a moment she stared at the front door, thinking. If it was a birthday party or some family gathering, it would be awkward to barge in. But not seeing any other option, she grabbed her bag from the passenger seat and got out.

She averted her eyes from the living room window as she strode over to the side door and pressed the doorbell. A second later she heard someone moving inside, and she stepped back, ready to introduce herself. The lock clicked; the door opened.

Søren Bagger looked like she remembered him. Or perhaps it was more the way she'd imagined he would look. His wavy hair, combed back the same way he used to wear it. Tall and slim. His faded T-shirt. But the happy smile from back then was gone. His eyes were red-rimmed, his face ashen.

He looked surprised. "Camilla!"

"Hi."

Suddenly, she was at a loss for words. For a moment, they just stared at each other. She regretted not calling in advance, as his face showed nothing but sorrow. She thought about his parents, who were the same age as hers. Maybe one of them was ill.

"I'm sorry to just show up like this," she managed to get out. "I came by to ask your parents for Pia's address. I want to talk to her about back when we were in school. About what happened when Susan Dahlgaard disappeared. Do you remember?"

Søren nodded.

"I'm sure you've heard; they just found her body. On Bornholm."

She could see he wasn't interested.

"I can come back another day if this isn't the best time for your family. But do you know where Nina Juhler lives? Anywhere around here?"

He stepped back into the entryway and gestured for her to come in. When she was inside, he stood awkwardly. "She lives in Birkerød, the last house before the forest. But Pia's dead."

She stopped, stunned by his words. "Dead?"

She peeked into the living room and glimpsed the back of a large woman who had to be their mother.

Søren shut the door and pointed toward the round table in the kitchen. There was coffee, and without asking he poured her a cup and sat down across from her.

"The pastor just showed up." He nodded at the door.

He hid his face in his hands and dug his palms into his eyes, as if he were trying to dam up the tears inside. Then he shook his head and looked at her. "I don't understand it. I just can't believe she's gone."

"What happened?" Camilla wanted to hold him, comfort him. It was heartbreaking to see this man she'd once known so well falling apart. "Was she sick?"

"She drowned herself. Out at Dyndet lake. Someone working at the restaurant in Borup found her this morning."

His head drooped; his arms rested heavily on the table. He gazed at her with sad eyes and kept shaking his head. "The police came out at ten to tell my folks. They'd already pulled her out of the lake; they said there'll be an autopsy. She had on the coveralls she usually wears out at the stables, and she'd filled the pockets with bricks. And then she just walked out into the lake."

Camilla knew that lake. She unconsciously turned her head away at the sudden memory of a night she and Søren and several others had gone swimming there. The boys had mopeds, and she'd ridden on the back of Søren's. A few other girls had ridden along, too. They'd parked the mopeds close to the lake and run down the short slope in the moonlight, then they'd stripped off their clothes and jumped in. She and Søren had stayed longer than the others, and later they walked up the long stairway to the nearby ridge. They'd lain on their backs and gazed up at the stars. It had been her first time.

It was hard to believe she'd forgotten it. That she'd forgotten it had been with him.

"I drove straight out to her house after my parents called," he continued. "She has dogs, you know, and we weren't sure how long she'd been gone."

Camilla knew absolutely nothing about any dogs, or anything about Pia's life at all, for that matter. She took a sip of coffee and listened to him talk about his sister.

"She lived in Viby. She moved there right after she finished vet school." He looked up at Camilla. "You remember how crazy she was about animals? She was always saving frogs, pigeons with broken wings. She had her own little animal hospital here at home."

Camilla didn't remember, but she nodded enthusiastically, hoping he would continue. He didn't, though. He just stared silently out the window, as if the memories were still running through his head.

"Did your sister have kids?"

He broke out of his reverie and shook his head. "Just the animals. The dogs and also a cat, and then there's the two horses, but she keeps them boarded at a neighbor's stable. I've always thought she was more interested in animals than humans. She never got married, either."

Camilla glanced at his finger. A worn-looking ring told of a long marriage. He followed her eyes and tried to smile.

"I married Connie."

Her eyes widened in surprise. "My Connie?"

He nodded.

The "my" was an exaggeration. They'd been in the same class through ninth grade, and they'd been friends, but when Camilla and her mother had moved to Roskilde, they'd lost touch. And she hadn't really thought about Connie since then.

"We have three kids. Our oldest is a sophomore."

"Tell her hello from me. She was such a sweet girl."

"She still is. Actually, I think she's on her way here."

Camilla felt a sudden, unreasonable jolt of jealousy. It wasn't that she regretted not sticking with Søren and settling down in Mid Sealand. But the warmth in his eyes when he talked about Connie stung a bit.

She decided she would leave before Connie arrived. Quickly she moved on. "Did Pia leave a note or anything?"

"No, not really."

From the living room a female voice called, "Who's there with you, Søren?"

He stood up and opened the door. "It's Camilla, Lasse's little sister. She knew Pia, too."

It's so easy to be brought back into the fold, Camilla thought. She was their son's friend's little sister and had known their daughter, and that's all it took for her to be welcome. The feeling tugged at her again, a sense of belonging. Of being back with people who had known her for her whole life.

"Why don't you come on in," his mother said, but Søren told her they were still having a cup of coffee.

He shut the door. "Sorry. We just can't make sense of it. It doesn't seem real, that Pia would do something like this."

"Of course. I won't bother you anymore. I'm sorry to have barged in right in the middle of this."

"No, please, stick around a while."

It might help him, talking to someone who remembered his sister, she thought.

He pulled himself together. "How are you doing, anyway? I'm sorry I'm so bad at keeping in touch; it's so easy now with Facebook. Your brother was my best friend, and I'm not sure I ever really got over him dying."

It had never crossed her mind to look for Søren on Facebook.

"So you moved to Roskilde and went to high school there."

She nodded, then remembered that he'd been a blacksmith apprentice back when they'd gone out together.

Suddenly he smiled. "Do you remember the parties at Borup Bodega?"

She nodded and smiled back. Twiggy's Discotheque and lots of beer. She could easily have stayed here, remained a part of the community she'd grown up in. Who knows how her life might have turned out?

"What did you end up doing after high school?" he asked.

"I got into journalism school. And I worked at the Roskilde paper until I moved to Copenhagen. Now I'm on the crime desk at *Morgenavisen*."

"I remember Susan back then; she and Pia hung out. They would come home together after school and hole up in Pia's room. But they were a lot younger than me; I didn't really know her. Pia was in bad shape after Susan disappeared. It almost seemed like she was a different person afterward. Like she couldn't shake it. She was more serious, not so happy anymore. The impulsive girl who was always up for a spur-of-the-moment adventure—all that was gone. And she stopped hanging out with the other girls. She kept to herself, and the only thing she was interested in was the animals she tried to save. Our parents tried, but they couldn't get her to hang out with her old friends anymore. She just retreated further into her shell. Going to vet school was good for her, actually, moving away from home. She needed a new start. They really should have given the students crisis counseling back then after what happened with Susan."

"She didn't stay in touch with any of the others?" Camilla pictured a lonely and somewhat lost soul who had chosen to end her own life.

"No, but she did make new friends at vet school. It helped her some, going there; she became more outgoing again, and she loved playing with our kids. It's too bad she never had any of her own. The kids loved their aunt."

He choked up and cleared his throat.

"And she really didn't leave any sort of letter or explanation?" Camilla asked once more.

He shook his head and stood up. "Not that I know of. I found this on her dining room table, but I haven't gone through the house thoroughly yet."

He unfolded a sheet of paper. Even before he laid it in front of her, she could tell it was a copy of the old class picture.

On the back, written in bold, slanted letters, was one word: SORRY.

NINE

Louise kicked off her running shoes and stuck her head under the faucet in the bathroom. She'd run over to Søster Svenstrup, then along the back roads toward home, and now the sweat was dripping off her. It had been too long since she'd run. She'd meant to on their trip, but there was always too much going on. Now she had pushed her body to the limit, thinking it might help clear up the jumble of thoughts that made it impossible to concentrate.

She'd texted Jonas and told him again that his short hair looked great; she didn't want him thinking her curt message yesterday meant she didn't really care. She'd also texted Mik, who was looking after their dog in Holbæk while they were gone. She let him know she was back, but that it would be a great help if he could keep the dog a little while longer. And that was it. She didn't have it in her to explain everything, and as it turned out, it wasn't necessary; he'd answered her seconds later, saying it was fine. No questions. She hadn't written to Eik, but then he hadn't written to her, either. At first, she'd been angry that their breakup seemed so easy for him, that he could just turn around and put all his energy into building his relationship with his daughter, but now all she felt was the sorrow that had lodged inside her. If she didn't concentrate constantly on pushing it down, it would nearly overpower her, reminding her that she would never let anyone else hurt her this way again.

She wiped her face and walked into the kitchen, leaving sweaty footprints. Her pulse was racing, and a bitter metallic taste had spread inside her mouth. Hot, sweaty, and out of breath, she plopped down on a kitchen chair. It had been late, almost noon, when she'd decided she had to do something to regain control of her body. The morning sun had already beckoned many people out into their front yards. Her legs quivered when she stood up for a glass of water. Physically she was exhausted, but at least now her head was clear and she felt calmer.

Louise closed her eyes. For the first time in a long time, she didn't feel depressed. She felt liberated.

She drank another glass of water and decided to call Camilla, to find out if she'd managed to find any of the girls circled in the class picture. She went into the bedroom for her phone.

Her mother had called five times, and there was also a text—a very short one: "Left a message."

In the first part of the message, her mother was speaking so fast that Louise could hardly understand a word, but eventually her voice slowed down. Mikkel had tried again. During the night he'd hung a sheet up in the shower room and tried to hang himself.

Her knees gave out, and she dropped to the floor. She played the message over and over, and each time it felt as if her heart were splitting open. They'd found him just in time. The night-shift nurse had sensed something was wrong when she saw that Mikkel wasn't in his room or in the bathroom. She'd opened the shower room door and there he was, standing on a chair with the sheet around his neck.

Her mother's voice was weak and distressed. "He wants to die, Louise," she kept saying. "He doesn't want to be here anymore."

Louise wondered if the police had also contacted her parents. If they were aware of what could be coming. Surely her mother would have said something, though, if they knew that Mikkel could end up as the prime suspect in a criminal case.

For a long time, she sat on the floor, trying to get a grip on herself before she called back.

"How's he doing now?" she began.

"Your brother has been committed. As posing a danger to himself or others. He certainly is hurting himself; he needs help."

"Is he at St. Hans?" St. Hans, the sprawling psychiatric hospital out by Boserup Forest. She knew the procedure. First the hospital would make sure there was a bed available, then they would need to contact a judge to approve the involuntary commitment. Next they would call the police, who would be responsible for delivering the patient to the hospital. The police would stay until the patient was escorted to a room and the door was closed.

"No, it's called the Psychiatric Emergency Ward. It's close to there, though. They say he needs emergency care."

"I'm coming right now," she said.

She heard her mother talking to someone. "It'll be some time before he's admitted," she finally said. "Right now, he's waiting to talk to a doctor."

"I'm coming," Louise repeated, then asked when the kids needed to be picked up.

"They're home with your father; I drove up here the minute they called."

"Does he need anything? Or is there anything the kids need that I could bring with me?"

Her mother ignored the question. "I think your brother has depression. I feel like I don't know him anymore; he's never had dark thoughts like this."

Louise didn't answer her. All those sunny feelings she had after her run had been snuffed out by a rage that nearly took her breath away. She was angry at Mikkel, yes, but even more so at Trine.

"Damn you, goddamn you all to hell!" she hissed as she backed her brother's car out of the carport. She felt helpless, impotent. A sense of unease was growing in her; after having sifted through her sister-in-law's things the previous evening, she had found nothing whatsoever that pointed to Trine having planned in advance to leave her brother. All her things were still there. If she had fled, though, if she'd been frightened and forced to leave quickly, that would fit; she wouldn't have had time to grab more than a few clean clothes. Louise focused on other possible scenarios. Especially ones in which Trine hadn't left the house of her own free will.

Louise couldn't stand the thought that her brother might have been involved. And she couldn't imagine what had driven her brother so far into the black hole he was in. Something had snapped in his mind; that much she could understand. But a completely changed personality? She forced herself to cut off the loop of dark thoughts. No way; her brother could never have harmed the woman he loved. She felt guilty for even thinking about it. Her muscles still ached, yet right now all she wanted to do was run as fast as she could, to push herself to the point where her thoughts would stop fluttering around like crazy. Her brother was clearly deeply unhappy, and that was what she needed to focus on.

She drove up to the yellow building that housed the Psychiatric Emergency Ward. Two cars were parked in the small, fenced-in parking lot, and one of them was a police cruiser. She hurried up the stone steps. After walking through an automatic sliding door, she had to wait for it to close before the next door opened. She rushed over to the glassed-in reception desk, where a short-haired woman stood up. She told the woman that she was Mikkel's sister and that she wanted to see him.

The woman looked sympathetic. "I'm sorry, he can't have visitors at the moment. The police are here. They're waiting for the chief psychiatrist to determine whether your brother can be taken to the police station for questioning, or if they'll have to question him here."

Louise nodded and looked through the glass at the empty hallway behind the reception desk. It was also possible that the doctor wouldn't allow the police to talk to Mikkel at all. The welfare of a patient who had been involuntarily committed came first, and at the moment that was a consolation.

"I thought my mother was here," she said to the woman, who nodded.

"She's in the patient lounge, talking to your father on the phone."

Louise nodded and relaxed a little. She was surprised to realize that she was almost more concerned about her mother than about Mikkel. Louise could very well imagine how worrying about Mikkel must be tearing her apart. Louise was sure she'd also been shocked when the police arrived and asked to talk to Mikkel.

"Would you like a cup of coffee?" the woman asked. She pointed toward an area with chairs and told Louise she was welcome to wait.

Louise thanked the woman and accepted the mug. She'd barely sat down when the sliding glass door opened and a woman she recognized walked in carrying a plastic bag.

She'd put on some weight. Quite a bit, Louise noticed. Her distinguished, erect posture had sunk and ballooned out. But Louise recognized her face and the long, grayish-white hair that reached all the way down to her waist. She was also wearing the same type of loose harem pants she'd had on when Louise first met her. But now there was something sluggish about her movements, as if she were on medication. Or maybe she'd just lost her spirit.

It had been a long time since she'd had anything to do with Mona Ibsen. Three or four years. Louise tried to think back; she'd been in Homicide, working on a case with the negotiations unit.

"Hi," Mona said, a bit hesitantly. Louise had been so lost in thought that she hadn't seen Mona looking at her.

There was something delicate about Mona Ibsen. Something almost fragile, in stark contrast to her macabre hobby of collecting insects. She found them in the woods, then dried and pressed them before pinning them to her collection board. She was also supposedly psychic and a few times she'd helped the police with tough cases. Not that Louise was much of a believer in psychic abilities. But back then she'd felt it wouldn't hurt to hear what Mona had to say. They'd been searching for a little girl who had been kidnapped and Mona had pointed them in the right direction. After that they'd stayed in touch for a little while, but Louise hadn't heard from her in a long time.

"Hi!" Louise smiled at her. She couldn't help noticing the short, white scars covering both of her forearms. There was a cut that looked fresh under her left elbow. Mona saw her looking and jerked her arms down to her sides.

The sliding door opened just then and someone else Louise knew walked in. It was Mona's friend Gerd, a retired school psychologist. She was surprised to see Louise.

"Work?" Gerd asked her. She glanced over at the ward.

Louise shook her head and said that her brother had just been admitted. "I'm waiting for them to let me see him."

It felt strange to say the words, that her brother had been admitted to a psychiatric ward. Saying it out loud made it seem more real. Mona had a long history with psychiatric treatment herself, and Gerd had supported her since her schooldays. Gerd looked thin, but her sinewy arms were strong, and she seemed to have a calming effect on Mona. She'd been the one who'd first told Louise that Mona often had an intense emotional reaction when people disappeared. And now that Susan Dahlgaard's case was all over the news, Louise could almost have predicted they would meet out here. Mona was probably shaken up emotionally, and had come to have herself committed again.

Mona suffered from convulsions when she was emotionally overwrought, Louise knew. She became frightened and insecure, and she was prone to harming herself to fight off her anxiety. Louise hadn't noticed those scars before, though, and something in Gerd's eyes told her that things hadn't been going well for Mona. She seemed at peace at the moment, though. Mostly she stared at the floor, but she glanced up at Louise now and then. As Gerd took her arm, Mona told Louise that she hoped her brother would feel better soon. They walked over to the door to the ward together.

When Mona had disappeared down the hall, Louise called out to Gerd. Reluctantly the gray-haired woman turned back and took a few steps toward Louise.

"Is she here because of the girl they found on Bornholm?"

The former school psychologist shook her head. "The last few years have been very hard on her, I'm sorry to say." She spoke quietly to make sure Mona couldn't hear her. "There's not much left of our girl these days. She's in here more often than not, and sometimes she goes off into the woods to look for insects without telling anyone. That seems to be the place where she finds the most peace of mind. But it's her birthday today, and we've just been into town for cake and hot chocolate."

The first time she'd met her, Louise had sensed that Mona suffered from some sort of mental immaturity. As if she was stuck somewhere back in her teenage years. Her voice was girlish, and her expression seemed innocent.

"What about her parents, where are they in all this?"

Gerd shook her head. "They can't handle it. They've never been able to, and it's not that I blame them; not everyone has an understanding of mental illness. They used to stay in touch regularly, but that was before her condition became more permanent. I still think we can help Mona; it's just going to take longer this time. And the tranquilizers she's taking aren't doing her any good. You remember how well she looked the last time you saw her."

Gerd sounded sick at heart, and she looked discouraged. Louise felt sorry for her; suddenly she could relate to having someone close to you fall apart and not being able to do a thing about it. That feeling of utter helplessness. She asked Gerd to wish Mona a happy birthday from her, then she walked back to her chair and sat down. Moments later Mikkel appeared and was led to the counter by two uniformed police officers. One of them went up to the window while the other waited a few steps away with a firm grip on Mikkel's arm.

"Mikkel!" Louise cried. Her brother's head jerked up.

He took a step toward her, but the officer held him back and raised the palm of his other hand to stop Louise from approaching.

"What's going on here?" she asked, angry at the rough way Mikkel was being treated. "He's my brother, and I want to know why you're taking him away."

The officer at the window turned to her. "Your brother is being taken to the station for questioning."

"Is he under arrest?"

"At the moment he hasn't been charged," he said, though Louise could tell by the hard look in his eyes that they wanted to take him into custody.

"Trine Madsen's wallet is still in their house," she said. "What steps have been taken to implement a search for her?"

"Your brother has just given us permission to search his house. And also to check his phone and bank records. Right now, we're waiting on the search warrant."

"I didn't do anything to her," Mikkel whispered. He was crying, and he looked pleadingly at her as they led him to the door. He was wearing a white hospital gown over his jeans. He had obviously slept very little over the past few days; his eyes were glassy and he seemed disoriented. But the chief psychiatrist had determined that the police could take him with them, which eased Louise's very troubled mind a little bit. At least they felt her brother was well enough to be questioned.

They'd just walked out through the first glass door when her mother came rushing in from the other end of the ward. "What's going on? Where are you taking him?" she demanded.

Her mother was pale, and she was still wearing her potter's apron, which was covered with clay and variously colored splotches. When she reached the counter, she noticed Louise, who hurried over and hugged her. Together they watched the police escort Mikkel outside.

"I don't understand why they have to take him away," her mother whispered. "Why don't they just talk to him here? Like they said they would when they came."

"He'll be coming back."

"I want to take him home; I can't stand seeing him this way."

"He needs help," Louise said.

Her mother nodded reluctantly. "I know he does, but what if the police don't keep a close eye on him? What if he tries again?"

Her mother looked lost as she stared at the exit.

"They'll take care of him, I promise," Louise said.

She knew Mikkel would be under constant observation now because of the high risk of suicide. Later he would be checked every five minutes, and slowly the time between checks would be lengthened. Only when he began to disassociate himself from his thoughts of suicide would he be released.

"We have to trust that they know what they're doing," she said. She led her mother over to the chairs.

"Mikkel says the police think he killed Trine. Why would they say such a terrible thing? I think he's having delusions. Do you suppose he's hearing voices?"

Louise took her hand and spoke as calmly as possible. "The police are investigating whether Mikkel had anything to do with Trine's disappearance."

"But why in the world would he? He's completely crushed, heartbroken."

Louise kept hold of her mother's hand as they sat down across from each other. "Mom, listen. There's no sign that Trine planned on leaving him. She didn't take any of her personal effects with her, like her debit card or her driver's license or her passport, none of the things you'd expect her to take if she planned to leave."

Her mother pulled her hand away. "What is it you're saying?"

Louise kept her composure as she looked her mother in the eye. "I'm saying that I don't think she left him."

"And?"

"And if it's true, something might have happened to her; we all have to be prepared for that possibility. And we also need to be aware that the police might press charges against Mikkel if they find anything at all that points to his involvement in whatever it is that's happened."

"If . . ."

Louise nodded. "If it turns out that he did something to her."

Her mother exploded. "What nonsense! He absolutely did not! How can you sit there and say something like that? Listen to yourself! This is your brother you're talking about. Our Mikkel!" She leaned back in her chair and glared at Louise. "Do you really believe that? About your own brother!"

"No, I don't. But I'm trying to prepare you, because that's what the police suspect. And it doesn't surprise me that they're planning to search their house."

In fact, she wondered why they hadn't already done so. They had already been talking to all of Mikkel and Trine's friends, that much she was sure of.

"They want to know all about how he and Trine were getting along. If they were having troubles in their marriage. If they were fighting. If one of them had found someone else."

Her mother was still upset. "Mikkel hasn't, I can tell you that much."

"The police are talking to all of his colleagues at Volvo. And they're checking the bank for anything unusual about their financial situation."

"There's nothing unusual other than she ran off with all the money in the kitchen."

"Mom, would you please listen to me! I'm trying to tell you what's going on, what to expect."

Her mother raised her voice. "Listen to yourself!"

Louise let her blow off steam. Afterward, they sat for a few moments in silence, not looking at each other, then her mother said, "What about the kids? They need to be home, need to keep on with their routines."

Suddenly Louise felt overwhelmed by everything she was afraid would happen. The story would be on the front page of every paper in the country. Kirstine and Malte would be in the spotlight, too, no way of avoiding that. Everyone in town would know who their parents were. People would whisper about them. Point at them.

"Maybe it's best for them to stay with you," Louise said, after thinking it through. "At least for the time being."

Her mother wouldn't let it go. "But he didn't do anything to her."

Louise shook her head. "He didn't, no, and we have to find evidence to prove that before they decide to charge him. But we don't know what his mother-in-law told the police. They must have something on him that we haven't heard about. Something to base their suspicion on."

Her mother leaned forward and laid her forehead on Louise's shoulder.

For a long time, she wept quietly.

Louise put a hand on her back. She yearned to comfort her, but at the same time, after all her years as a police officer, she knew exactly what was going to happen. And it wasn't going to ease her mother's mind. Every part of Mikkel Rick's life would be examined down to the minutest detail. Everything would be turned inside out and upside down until they found Trine.

It wasn't easy being on this side of things. She had absolutely no experience with it, and the only thing that was crystal clear to her at this point was that she was much better at being on the other side. The police side.

TEN

Camilla's plan had been to drop by to see Nina Juhler after visiting Pia's parents, but when she pulled up to Nina's house in Birkerød, she couldn't go in. She parked down the narrow street and looked over at the white stucco house. There were clothes hanging on the line in the yard, and the door on the terrace stood open.

She was reeling, overcome by the profound sense of having once belonged here. And part of her still did belong. A large part of her had been formed by her childhood, by her friends back then. She realized that for many years she'd completely locked away her feelings about her brother's death. During her teenage years, directly following the accident, her grief had dominated her life and made her deeply unhappy, but as an adult, she'd seldom thought about him. He was the framed photograph her mother had on her dresser in Skanderborg, nothing more. Camilla didn't even have her own photo of him, and, truth be told, she wasn't sure Markus even knew what his uncle had looked like. Of course, she'd told him about Lasse. In fact, her son resembled her brother quite a lot—that thought had crossed her mind many times, but she always cut it off. She didn't want Markus to feel like he had to replace someone he'd never even known.

Seeing Søren again had made her think of her father, too. And her parents' divorce a few years after Lasse's death.

One day her father had simply taken the sign down from his used-car lot in Osted. The cars had been loaded up onto a trailer and hauled away, and that was that. He'd been a windbag and a pain in the ass, but he'd still brought a sense of life into their house with his swagger and his jokes, and that had all disappeared when he left them. She didn't remember her parents' breakup as traumatic, though. Sad, but not really a problem. Later, she'd wondered about her reaction and had come to the conclusion that Lasse's death had emptied her of emotions. Nothing could hurt more than that, no loss could be as great, so she'd experienced the divorce as mostly just a change in her everyday routine. She'd come to grips with it, had even had the thought that she might get more allowance money. That was when she started going out with Søren. Teenage life and parties seemed much more important to her than the consequences of her parents' ruined marriage.

She'd always been closer to her mother, so there had never been any doubt about where she would live. Camilla even refused to visit her father and his new girlfriend in Køge, which meant they saw very little of each other during the following years. She'd tried to rekindle their relationship when Markus was born, but her father had been too busy; it hadn't worked out. And that had hurt her. Later, when he moved to Præstø and took over his own parents' house, they more or less completely lost contact. And for many years it hadn't bothered her all that much. But now suddenly she missed him. Missed having a family.

She felt lonely, and over there in that house, Nina Juhler was living a life that easily could have been Camilla's. She impulsively texted her father, wrote that she'd bring over a cake if he'd make the coffee.

. . .

Her father's farmhouse looked out onto Præstø Fjord, with fields stretching out behind. He still had a few cars for sale parked out on the road in front of the barn, still kept his hand in the car business, but barely. His girlfriend had stayed in Køge when he'd moved here, and several times Camilla had thought he might be a bit lonely.

He drove a BMW that had seen better days, a wide vehicle with its rear bumper hanging. It was parked up next to the house, and she pulled in beside it. Her father came out the front door in his slippers and held his arms out to be hugged. She shut off the engine and grabbed the cake box beside her on the front seat.

"What a wonderful surprise!" he said as she let herself be swallowed up in his arms, her face turned away from the cigar in his left hand. He led her through the small portico in front of the door. She hadn't seen the house since her grandmother died, but it looked the same: the dim front hall jam-packed with stuff, the delicate lace curtains at the windows.

"Come on in," her father said. "Let's go out to the kitchen and see what's in that box."

When she was young, she'd hated his cigars. He embarrassed her in front of her friends by sitting out in the sunroom in a cloud of smoke, talking through the open door. When he was home, that is; most of the time he was out on Hovedvejen, selling and trading cars or, once in a while, a truck or camper van. Lasse's friends liked to come around, and he liked the company. Sometimes he let the boys scavenge old cars for parts, and they would tinker around in the garage behind his office. So once they got older, Camilla's friends had loved to stop by the lot, too.

Just as she set down the box of prune cream cake, her phone rang. A photo of Markus appeared on the screen.

"Hi," she said, happy he was calling on his own initiative. She was nearly always the one doing the calling these days. "I'm down at your grandfather's; just got here. Yes, I'll tell him hi for you, and, yes, I'll remind him you're turning eighteen next year."

She laughed and gave her father a look. He'd promised Markus he would pay for his driver's license. No strings attached, he'd added; Camilla had earlier complained to him about Markus starting to smoke. And it hadn't helped one bit to yell and scream and try to talk some sense into her son. Her father had told her to back off, that the boy would stop when he met a girl who got tired of kissing an ashtray. She recalled him saying this in a cloud of cigar smoke, but still he'd been right. When Markus had started going with Julia, he'd given up cigarettes. She knew she wasn't being fair, but she couldn't help the thought that at least something good had come out of their relationship.

"I'll be home for dinner tonight," Markus said. Without asking when she'd be back or if she had other plans. She held the phone for a few moments after saying goodbye.

"Problems?" her father asked.

Camilla shrugged. "It's not how he usually tells me he's coming home, not at all." She stuck her phone back in her bag.

"Girl troubles?" He took the pot of coffee and two dessert plates into the living room.

"Maybe." She nodded. On the practical side, she thought, if they had broken up, summer vacation would be no problem. Immediately she felt ashamed for thinking it would suit her just fine if Julia didn't go to Hawaii with them.

She told her father about their planned vacation. She also mentioned how she couldn't help but be annoyed with her son for apparently not being able to do anything without his girlfriend.

She opened a few windows to air the room out.

"You weren't a whole lot better," her father growled good-naturedly.

Camilla looked at him in surprise. "What do you mean?"

"That tall kid you were always dragging around. You refused to go to Kirsten and Erik's fiftieth wedding anniversary unless he was invited, too. Same thing when we stayed at the vacation house up in Rørvig."

He rattled off several other times she'd completely forgotten.

"A fiftieth wedding anniversary would have been pretty damn boring without someone my own age," she replied. She remembered that night at the community building. The songs that had been written for the couple, the three-course meal. But they'd danced with all the old people once the organist started playing. And the Rørvig thing, that had been true, too, but only because they wanted to go to the discotheque together; every summer several of their friends on vacation with their parents would meet there.

"That's what it's like when you're a kid," her father said. "You want to hang out with other people your age."

She smiled at him and scraped the last bit of whipped cream off her plate. She promised she would bring Markus down to visit soon.

"You know, you could come back to town with me. Stay a few days at my place. It'll be fun."

He instantly shook his head. "Got a guy coming to look at the big Mazda, and Thursday's bridge night; they'd feel awful if I went AWOL."

He didn't seem so lonely after all, she thought as he followed her out and handed her a five-hundred-crown bill to give to Markus. For ice cream, was how he put it. He thanked her for coming. It had been a short visit. Very short. But she was glad she'd driven down.

On the way home, Camilla dropped by Sticks'n'Sushi for take-out. She'd just set the food down on the kitchen counter when Terkel Høyer called.

"The Roskilde police have questioned a man in connection with a missing woman, Trine Madsen. And I just now realized that she's the one you drove over to talk to."

She could hear that he was angry, and she was about to defend herself, to explain that Trine had left her family before, but he wasn't in a listening mood.

"You're going to call over there, find out who's heading up the investigation, then you're going to look into what's happening. We published a short notice that the police are looking for her, but we haven't followed up on it. Send the article in as soon as you talk to them, and we'll get it on the website."

She stared into space for a few moments after he hung up, then she walked into her office, turned on her recorder, and dialed the Mid and West Sealand Police. She asked to speak to Captain Nymand in Roskilde. As she waited, she pulled up the *Morgenavisen*'s website and read the notice about Trine.

Police are looking for thirty-eight-year-old Trine Madsen, who disappeared from her home on Hovedvejen in Osted on June 19, sometime between 4 and 6 p.m. She was last seen earlier that afternoon. Trine Madsen is 169 cm tall and of average build. Possibly wearing a white T-shirt with a blue logo over the left breast and dark blue loose pants. If you have any information concerning her whereabouts, please contact the police at 114.

The Roskilde paper, the *Roskilde Dagblad*, had written:

Police suspect foul play in the disappearance of Trine Madsen. They would like to speak to anyone who has seen her since the time of her disappearance.

Nymand's voice broke in. "Yeah."

Camilla quickly identified herself and explained that she was calling about the new development in the Trine Madsen case.

"Development?" he said.

"You've questioned a man concerning the case. Have you pressed charges? Is he being held in custody?"

The captain was silent for a moment, then he cleared his throat and said he should have been expecting her call. "Normally I'd send you to our head of communications."

He sounded almost effusive now, which puzzled Camilla.

"Fire away," he continued.

Camilla asked him what he could say in general about the case.

"We've been investigating Trine Madsen's disappearance since we were notified about it, four days after she was last seen at her home in Osted. Trine's mother was the one who reported her missing. As the result of what we've learned, earlier today we brought a man in for questioning. The suspect's home has also been searched, and we're currently checking his telephone and bank information. We've also obtained some of the missing woman's personal effects, and they're being examined."

Cell phone and debit card, Camilla thought. "What leads you to believe there's a crime involved?" She could hear how tense she sounded.

"Several aspects of our investigation point in that direction. I can't get into details right now."

"Are you investigating this as a homicide?"

"Yes," he answered. Without hesitation. "A homicide investigation is underway."

Which only meant that the police were devoting more resources to the investigation than they would for a missing person case, Camilla reminded herself. She chose her next words carefully. "Do you know anything about where the presumed body of the woman might be?"

"No, we have nothing along those lines at present. What we can say is that she hasn't been found."

"Is the male suspect related to Trine?"

The silence on the other end was ominous.

"I thought that was why you called me directly. I assumed you'd heard from Louise Rick."

More silence. Camilla's thoughts raced, and suddenly she understood why Nymand hadn't immediately sent her to their communications office.

"You suspect Mikkel. I assume you questioned him, and I just hope the investigators who did the questioning knew that Trine had left her husband once before, left him holding the bag, with two small kids and all the bills to pay. I hope your people took the trouble to find out how it affected them back then, how hard Mikkel struggled to keep his family together."

She paused a moment to fight back her anger, but her voice trembled as she said, "You are wrong about him."

"It's always difficult to accept something like this when it involves people you know." Camilla couldn't stand his sympathetic tone. "I just spoke with Louise Rick; her brother has tried to take his life twice within the last forty-eight hours. That says quite a bit about our suspicion, I would think."

Camilla got a grip on herself. "Did you find anything when you searched the house? What evidence do you have against him?"

"I have no further comments at this time."

She heard a key turning in her front door.

"I'd like your paper to put out a notice," he continued. "We're asking anyone who might have seen Trine Madsen in—"

"Do you have something on Mikkel? Anything concrete to connect him with her disappearance?"

Nymand didn't answer. Camilla hung up. She was dizzy when she stood up to walk out and hug Markus.

She studied her son as he sat on the bench in the hallway, his hair tousled, taking off his shoes. She simply couldn't remember him ever inviting himself to dinner this way before. Usually, he just let her know at the last minute if he was going to eat at home, but this seemed planned on his part. Maybe there was something about boarding school and his final exams that he felt they should talk about before he showed her his grades.

She opened the double doors to the terrace and told him she needed to send something to the paper before they ate. It wouldn't take long, she thought. A few lines about how there was still no sign of the missing woman from Osted. That's all Nymand was going to get from her.

She couldn't quite read her son's expression. He seemed a bit nervous, but not as if he wanted to tell her something he was ashamed of, which was a relief.

It ended up taking longer than expected to find the right words. She didn't want to point a finger at Mikkel, but Terkel wouldn't let her get away with not revealing that the police had questioned a suspect in the case. She'd tried to get in touch with Louise several times, but either she was talking to someone else or her phone was set to go directly to her voice mail. Finally, she sent off the article and texted Terkel, then stood up to join Markus.

He was sitting in one of the sun chairs with a cola in his hand, looking out over Frederiksberg's roofs. She ran her fingers lightly through his hair.

"So are you enjoying summer vacation, or do you miss boarding school?" She tried to sound normal.

"It's okay." He told her about a weekend trip he'd taken up in Humlebæk with his friend Tue. "So it's not like I'm not seeing friends from school." He didn't sound particularly enthused about it.

"Let's go in and eat, okay?" Camilla said, even though she knew he probably wouldn't be able to get a single bite down until he got whatever was bothering him off his chest.

He followed her into the kitchen and watched her take out the plates and glasses from the cupboard. He looked like he wanted to say something, so she paused and waited for him to speak, but he only asked if there was anything he could do to help.

"Look in my bag," she said. "There's something in there for you from your grandfather."

It wasn't that her son didn't get a decent allowance. She felt that Frederik had been more than generous the last time they had set the amount, but still Markus lit up when he fished the money from his grandfather out of the front compartment of her bag.

"I invited him into town with me, but he couldn't get away." She put everything on a tray, then grabbed a few colas out of the refrigerator, set them beside the plates, and lifted the tray to take it outside.

"I'm going to be a father," Markus said.

The tray thudded onto the kitchen counter, knocking over one of the colas. "Father! What do you mean? You're can't be a father, you're a kid yourself!"

"I knew it," he mumbled.

She stared incredulously at him. "For chrissake, Markus! You just got money for ice cream!"

"Julia's pregnant. She went to the doctor this morning."

At least he didn't beat around the bush, you had to give him that.

Camilla turned away and counted to ten as she stared out the kitchen window. Then she turned back and as coolly as possible suggested they go into the living room.

They sat down on the sofas across from each other.

"She'll have to get rid of it," she said.

He shook his head at her. "You're incredible," he said, his eyes moist. "You've never welcomed Julia into the family or tried to make her feel she belonged. You've never taken an interest in her, never given a sign that you like her."

"That's not true," Camilla protested, but her voice lacked conviction; even she could hear that.

"It's like you've tried to push her away from the very start. Do you even know how bad it makes her feel? And it's really tough for me, too, when you act that way."

"That's enough!" Camilla snapped. "Practically all I ever do is let you know you're both welcome here, but she acts like she hates the idea. Like she'd rather the two of you stay at her parents'."

"Because you act like you don't like her!" Markus yelled. He was crying now. "She's my girlfriend. I've never had anything against Frederik, and did you ever even ask how I felt about him? I was nice to him because I knew you liked him, I could see it. I tried to make him feel welcome in our family."

"When the hell did you suddenly become the grown-up here?" she shouted.

"I have been for a long time," Markus shot back. He brushed a few tears away with an irritated swipe of the back of his hand, just like he'd done when he was a little boy.

She wanted so much to hold him, but at the same time she was trembling in shock. She tried to calm herself, but her anger, her uncontrollable rage at Julia for putting Markus in this position, wouldn't let go. She just couldn't stop herself.

"It's not very hard to understand why you like Frederik," she spat out, her voice shrill now. "I hear you get to borrow the boat this weekend."

Markus stared icy daggers at her, then stood up as if to leave.

"I'm sorry," Camilla whispered. "I'm really sorry, that was uncalled for. Please, just sit down, okay?"

Markus hesitated, then sat down again. His stare was still cold, though, and mature, in a way that bothered her.

"You've misunderstood me if you think I don't like Julia," she said, determined to convince him. "I do like her. But you're seventeen years old. You were sixteen when you started going out together. You're not even eighteen yet, and you have to understand, this is going to ruin your lives."

"You're wrong," he said quietly.

"You don't even know if she's the right one for you. I had a boyfriend when I was your age, I liked him so much. In fact, I just ran into him again. He married another girl from my class. That's what happens, other people come along. Julia is only the first girl you've had a real relationship with."

"I love her."

"This isn't going to work, Markus; you're going to regret it."

"So what are you planning on doing?"

"I'm going to talk some sense into you. Frederik and I are thinking of having a baby. Can't you see how strange it would be? Taking them to the same day care?"

He was screaming at her even before she finished talking. "So it's all about you? Again! About what *you* want! Well, this is about me and Julia and our lives, and we want our baby, and you don't have to have anything to do with it. Or with me. I can take care of myself without you and Frederik."

He flung the five-hundred-crown bill on the floor, then turned and strode out of the room, slamming the front door. She heard him thunder down the stairs.

Camilla sat for several minutes, trying to absorb what had happened. And then she realized she was shivering; a cool wind was blowing in through the open terrace door. She stood up and walked out to the kitchen, where she threw the bags of sushi into the trash.

ELEVEN

Fear exploded inside her as she struggled to wake up. The stench of piss and shit overwhelmed her, and a moment passed before she understood that the smell was coming from her. She felt the damp cold against her back, felt her heart hammering in her chest. Her body was tensed up, as if it had been in a state of alarm long before she'd been alert enough to realize how scared she was.

Slowly she blinked her eyes and tried to focus on the object in front of her. It was a red water bottle. For a long time, she stared at it; she was sure it hadn't been there before. She raised her eyes and let them rest for a moment on the wide boulder above her head, then she made her eyes slide over farther and farther, until finally she spotted an opening, a crack of light.

It took a while for her brain to process this, but at last she realized: It was a way out! She fought to reach for the light but found that she still couldn't move.

Her mouth was dry, her tongue felt like sandpaper; maybe she'd been drinking, she couldn't remember. She wanted to scream, but only a stifled moan came out. Someone must have been here; maybe someone knew where she was.

TWELVE

"Have you charged him?" Louise was in Nymand's office, determined to get an answer.

"No," the police captain responded.

"What evidence do you have to support your suspicion?"

Louise had driven over to the station in the hope that Nymand would still be there, even though most of the officers and personnel had gone home for the night. She'd waited at the hospital until Mikkel had returned, but she'd only been allowed to hug him before he was taken behind the "screen," as the closed ward where the patients received extra supervision was called.

"What do you have on him? Did you find anything when you searched the house?"

Nymand nodded. "We found her phone, in a coat pocket. It was dead, out of battery power."

She assumed they hadn't had time yet to go through the phone or the hard drive of Mikkel's computer, but she was fishing anyway, in case there was something else they'd found. And she was relieved that Nymand didn't mention anything more, because even though he wouldn't admit it, his silence made it clear: They hadn't found anything yet. At least not anything that would justify charging her brother.

But then he continued. "And the overnight bag, next to the desk in her clinic, packed with things for the Red Cross clothing drive. There was a pamphlet on the desk about a collection date."

"I assume you've talked to my brother's coworkers at Volvo," Louise said. She was annoyed at Mikkel for not having found the bag, but she kept that to herself. "Has anyone confirmed that he was away from work sometime on June 19? Do you have any witnesses putting him in Osted on that day?"

"I understand your position," Nymand said, "but you're professional enough to know we have to investigate those closest to Trine Madsen first. And we can't eliminate your brother until we've been through everything—his alibi, phone data, witnesses. He's attempted suicide twice now, not once but twice, even though he's responsible for two young kids."

"He feels like shit!" she spat. "He's hit rock bottom, and right now you could probably get him to say anything."

He shook his head. "We're not trying to get him to say anything. We just want to get an overview of what happened when his wife disappeared."

"Not wife, partner," Louise said.

"Partner. Anyway, he's not telling us anything. It would help if he'd at least try to defend himself, but he claims he didn't notice anything unusual in the days before she disappeared."

"There *wasn't* anything unusual." Louise told him about Mikkel and Trine's dinner with Louise's parents not long ago. "He's probably not even thinking about defending himself; he's devastated, he needs help. Trine is out there somewhere; you have to find her."

"That's what we're doing."

"But you aren't! You're all handling this like a pack of lazy dogs.

Why did it take so long to find her cell phone? If you'd taken the case seriously from the beginning, your first priority would have been to find that phone."

She'd been sure that Trine had taken her phone with her when she left and that the police had already checked her number and tracked her phone to map out her movements.

Nymand was about to reply, but she cut him off. "It's only now after Mikkel broke down that you're doing anything. You didn't raise a finger before my brother tried to kill himself the second time. You're taking his suicide attempt as a sign that he feels guilty. But let me tell you something."

She was leaning over his desk now. "If you'd done your job or sent the case to the Missing Persons Unit, you'd have known before my brother's suicide attempts that Trine's cell phone was still in the house. If you'd searched the house right off the bat, you'd have seen that nothing points to Trine having planned to leave him. You could have prevented him from trying to kill himself, if he'd known she hadn't left him. If he'd known that something might have happened to her. He wouldn't have ended up in this situation at all if you'd reacted the minute Trine was reported missing. But you didn't. You waited. And Mikkel kept thinking she'd left him."

"We talked to her mother."

"Oh, come on!" Louise closed her eyes for a moment to compose herself. "I get that you can't just take my word that my brother wasn't involved with Trine's disappearance. Fine. And I'm also aware that I'm too involved personally. But really, and I'm speaking objectively here, you have to keep looking around. My time at Missing Persons taught me that there can be all sorts of reasons for people to disappear. And yes, murder is one. But only one of many."

She couldn't stop herself from reminding Nymand that out of the sixteen hundred cases that came through the police department annually, only four or five ended up with the police believing that a crime had really been committed.

"Now that you've spoken to Mikkel and to Trine's friends and family, is there any indication that she was having an affair my brother didn't know about? And have you spoken to the patients who came to her clinic the day she disappeared?"

"We're looking into all that. Does your brother have a car?"

Louise nodded. "I'm driving it; it's parked outside."

"Does anyone else besides you have access to it?"

"Just Trine."

"We'll need to take a look at it."

Louise nodded and stood up to leave, but before turning away, she looked him in the eye. "You'd better pull out all the stops, Nymand. I'm going to be looking over your shoulder. If you'd been on the ball, my brother would be home with his kids now. He wouldn't be locked up in a psychiatric ward. And I'll never forgive this police station if he ends up killing himself. Because he's not responsible for Trine's disappearance."

Louise drove out to her parents' house in Lerbjerg. The tiny village, nine houses in all, was five kilometers outside Hvalsø, and on a warm summer evening, there weren't many other places Louise would rather go for a walk.

The crimson sun hung over the hideous Lerbjerg tower, visible above the trees. The old military-green TV antenna stood on a small hill behind Louise's childhood home like a long-forgotten landmark. An elevator inside led to the top; once there had been talk about making it into a lookout tower, a tourist attraction. She'd been up there, and it was true what the project's proponents claimed, that you could see all of Sealand.

Her father had just started making meatballs. Kirstine and Malte were outside, and her mother was taking a nap. Louise walked her old bike out of the stable connected to the farmhouse and started riding through the woods and down toward the Avnsø.

She stopped at the lake and sat with her back to a tree, staring for the longest time down over the dark, mirror-like waters. Swarms of mosquitoes buzzed low over the surface. Though she was in the shade, she didn't feel cold; the golden sunlight tossed coins down through the leaves of the trees.

She tried to gather her thoughts. She missed Eik, missed his arms around her. She missed talking to him.

Ripples spread out in concentric rings several meters from the bank as a fish bobbed to the surface, but by the time she looked over, it was already gone. Maybe she should get in touch with Rønholt and ask his advice. He was her old boss, the man who had brought her in to head up the small Missing Persons Unit where she and Eik had met. And where, after they'd become a couple, it had been necessary for one of them to leave and find another job. She'd chosen to be the one to leave.

For quite a while, Louise deftly avoided the unbearable thought that she would have to confront if she had any hope of helping Mikkel: What if he *was* behind Trine's disappearance? What would June 19 have looked like?

She leaned her head back against the tree trunk and closed her eyes. Her brother had been gone before Trine and the kids got up. He left the house at six-thirty to get to work at seven though he could easily have left at a quarter to seven and still made it to work on time. And Trine could have woken up earlier than usual that morning. Could they have had an argument before he left for work?

The police would know soon if they had been in touch with each other later on that day, if there had been any phone calls other than the one her brother had mentioned. They would be able to trace

Mikkel's movements from the information provided by his cell phone carrier. By checking the location data, they would find out if he'd been home in Osted sometime that day, even though he denied it. Provided he'd had his cell phone on him, that is.

Louise imagined Trine's day. She'd seen patients in her podiatry clinic—the thought irritated Louise, because if Nymand's people had been doing their jobs, they would already have spoken with everyone who'd had an appointment with Trine on June 19. But maybe the police *had* spoken to them, she told herself. Her thoughts were flying all over. She was finding it hard to focus the way she usually did on a case. She realized it was because she wasn't used to being a part of the family involved. She just couldn't see it, couldn't sketch out how it might have happened if her brother had done what the police suspected. Maybe it was because she was too close to it to see clearly, but she just couldn't come up with a scenario that fit the facts she knew.

Trine had picked up Kirstine and Malte, that much was certain. She'd driven them home, and the kids had watched TV until Mikkel got home at five-thirty. What had happened between four and five-thirty? Who or what had caused Trine to leave her children, her wallet, and her phone in an unlocked house?

If Kirstine had noticed anything strange when her mother disappeared, she would definitely have said so. She was old enough now, and she was smart. And Malte was always overexcited to meet new people. If someone else had been at the house that day, those two kids would have noticed. The only person they wouldn't have paid any attention to was their father.

"What did Kirstine and Malte tell the police?" she asked her father when she returned from the lake. "When were they interviewed?"

Her father looked tired. He tossed a tea towel aside and leaned against the kitchen counter. He didn't seem surprised by her question.

"I think it was the day Trine's mother reported her missing. The police contacted Mikkel that day; they asked him to pick Kirstine and Malte up at school and bring them home so they could talk to them there, in familiar surroundings. That's what Mikkel told us."

Louise nodded. The next time the kids would be taken down to the station and videotaped by someone from the district. Standard procedure.

"Was Mikkel allowed to listen when the officers spoke with them?"

"He was told to wait out in the kitchen. Why do you ask?"

He turned toward her and leaned back against the countertop.

Louise shrugged. "I'm just wondering how they experienced their mother disappearing. Kids can get things turned around time-wise, you know, so it might be hard for them to say if she'd disappeared right before Mikkel got home or if she'd been gone longer."

Suddenly Kirstine and Malte burst through the back door, both holding their hands cupped together in front of them. They immediately ran to Louise, and she bent down to give them a hug. They both opened their hands at once and two big toads stared up at Louise. After a moment, one of them hopped over onto Louise's thigh. Malte shrieked with joy.

She laughed, too, as they told her the toads' names: Hansel and Gretel. The other toad hopped out, too, but instead of stopping, it sprang down onto the floor and hopped back toward freedom.

Louise looked at her niece and nephew. She didn't have the heart to ask them about the day their mother disappeared. Instead, she helped them make up a story about the two toads while they set the table.

After dinner, and after Kirstine and Malte had gone upstairs to watch TV, her mother came back to the table with coffee. Louise had noticed her mother studying her in silence during dinner.

She poured a mug of coffee for Louise. "And what about you?" she asked. "How are you?"

That's all it took. Everything came pouring out. She told her parents about her breakup with Eik, and though she tried to hold back, she couldn't help crying. In an attempt to distract her with a happier topic, her father asked about her job at police headquarters in Copenhagen, but she told them she wasn't at all ready to go back.

"I have another two months of leave," she reminded them.

"But if you're not going to do anything in particular for the next two months, maybe it would be good for you to get started, to have something else to think about while the others are gone. Especially after everything with Mikkel."

Louise shook her head. She had absolutely no desire to start back at work. She wasn't ready; she couldn't even keep her mind focused on her own brother's case. All she wanted to do was curl up and hide until everything was okay again.

She noticed her parents exchanging glances.

"What does Camilla have to say about all this?" her mother asked, clearly hoping Louise's best friend could talk some sense back into her.

"And Suhr?" her father added.

Hans Suhr had recommended Louise to succeed him as head of Homicide in Copenhagen after he'd retired. The plan had been for him to stay until Louise got back, but when she said she'd be gone for six months, a colleague, Thomas Toft, had been named temporary head of the department. She'd left the Missing Persons Unit to become the leader of the Homicide Department in the nation's capital, and now she couldn't even solve her own problems.

She answered curtly, "Toft can handle things."

After a pause, her mother said, "You have to try to see it from Eik's side, too."

"I do, I can definitely understand him." *I understand him one hundred percent,* she thought to herself.

"And Jonas, he's doing okay?"

"He is, he's doing fine. They get along great together. He's having a wonderful time, and he's gotten close to Steph, I think. That's good for both of them."

They managed to get through the rest of the evening without talking directly about Mikkel. Just before she left, she told them about her meeting with Nymand.

"If it becomes necessary, I'll get ahold of John Bro," she said.

She told them that she'd already called the well-known defense attorney to let him know they might need him. Bro was one of the best in the profession—and most feared, in the eyes of the police. "But right now the police have nothing. They'll need a lot more to charge Mikkel."

Thoughts buzzed in her head as she drove back to Osted. They had tried to talk her into staying overnight. She'd sensed that all of them being together under one roof meant something to her parents, but she needed to be alone, to sit quietly in the kitchen nursing a beer, waiting for the Thai sleeping pill to kick in. She'd planned to stop taking them when she was over her jet lag, and that morning she'd decided to quit. But after everything that had happened today, it felt different now. She sat down at the kitchen table and washed the pill down with a beer, knowing she would wake up feeling leaden and woozy the next morning. But right now it seemed like the only way she could make it through the night.

THIRTEEN

BORNHOLM, 1995

They waited until the light had been off for half an hour, then they opened the window as quietly as they could. Susan crawled out first, with the others right behind her. They ran as quietly as they could through the darkness. When they finally reached the street, they giggled in relief, then looked around for the boys.

Trine tightened the scarf around her neck and shivered, but then she heard the mopeds coming and forgot all about the cold wind blowing through her clothes. The girls ran toward the private school. Earlier that evening, after dinner, they'd walked down to the harbor to the convenience store, and that's where they'd met the boys. Susan had casually walked over to them and asked if there was anything going on tonight, and that's when they'd all made plans to meet up later at the school.

Trine clung to the boy in front of her, her hair whipping in the wind as they rode out toward a stretch of woods close to the shore. She'd shared a cigarette with him down at the harbor. Skipper, he was called. The boys were in the ninth grade except for the tall one, who had dropped out of school.

The night was luminous and clear when they reached the shore, and the moon cast a silver sheen over the water. Suddenly the quiet seemed overwhelming in the sudden absence of all the noise from the mopeds. Trine and Nina helped gather up branches for a bonfire. They'd brought a bag full of beers, and Pia had bought cigarettes.

"Anybody want to swim?" one of the boys yelled. Trine held back, but Susan and Pia ran down to the water and stripped off their clothes. She heard them laughing and shrieking as they jumped into the water, and she regretted not going with them. It would be weird now, though, to stand there and take her clothes off all alone. Tonny, a skinny boy in a denim jacket, tried to get the fire going. He'd pulled out a length of small hose from his back pocket and siphoned gasoline from one of the mopeds. Nina brought an armful of twigs and small branches and threw them down at Tonny's feet. Then she picked out the shriveled leaves from her short hair, which had somehow gotten everywhere, as if she'd crawled around on the forest floor to gather up the twigs.

The gasoline-soaked wood burst into flames when he put a match to it.

A boy named Daniel handed her a beer. He seemed nice enough. They sat together and kept the fire burning without speaking. The swimmers got out of the water. Susan giggled loudly, and when the tall one they called Stretch said something, they all laughed.

"Where are you girls from?" Daniel asked.

"Osted," Trine said. She wished she were with the others.

He shook his head and said he'd never heard of the place. "What's it like there?"

"Think of it as Denmark's longest town," she said, trying to sound bubbly, bright. "There's one long main road, and the whole town is strung along it."

"Sounds boring," he said in a bored yet melodic voice, with his singsong Bornholm accent. She was about to snap back, but she held her tongue when she saw the others coming back. Susan was holding Skipper's hand. Even though he and Trine had only shared a cigarette, and they hadn't really talked, it still stung a bit to see how Susan already had her claws in him; he was clearly the best-looking of the bunch, with his blond hair and the way he smiled.

She looked at him and asked, "Was it cold?"

Skipper had let go of Susan's hand. He shook his head and said it was nice. "But I wouldn't mind getting warmed up a bit."

Trine felt herself blushing, and she looked away.

Sparks flew high from the blazing bonfire. They sat in a circle and shared the beer the boys had brought. Daniel tossed on a few bigger chunks of wood and began telling them about an old abandoned house just outside of town.

Pia clapped her hands and exclaimed, "We have to go see it!"

Trine kept an eye on Skipper, who was sitting beside Susan. Pia nudged her and held out a cigarette. Trine wasn't used to smoking, but she took a long drag and managed not to cough.

"How about you?" She held the cigarette out to Daniel, who she thought looked a little bit like Joey from *Friends*, though maybe it was just the moon or the flames from the bonfire.

"Who wants more?" They had three bottles of beer left, and Trine took a long slug as they were passed around. She was drowsy and a bit dizzy from the cigarette, but she didn't want the night to end. Susan lay with her head in Skipper's lap. Trine tipped the bottle once more before passing it on.

Pia asked when they could all go out to the abandoned house.

Trine smoked another cigarette. Her throat felt sore, and suddenly she was tired and wanted to sleep. The sky was growing lighter.

"Shouldn't we get back?" She looked around the circle. No one answered her; they'd started singing an old Kim Larsen song. She asked again, louder this time, reminding them they had to get up at seven. In three hours.

"I'll take you back," Daniel offered. But Trine wanted the others to come, too.

She asked them one more time, tried to get Pia's attention, but Pia was whispering back and forth with Tonny.

Finally, Trine took Daniel up on his offer. She could barely stay awake. When she stood up, Nina said she wanted to go back, too, and finally Susan and Pia joined them. Before they left, they made plans to meet the boys again the next evening.

They got caught. The four of them stood lined up in Kirsten's office while Lena and Steffen chewed them out. Their parents were notified, and they wouldn't be allowed outside anymore in the evenings. But for some reason they weren't sent home.

Nina cried her eyes out after her father called the hostel and yelled and screamed at her. He threatened to come and get her, but Lena talked him out of that. He made it clear, however, that his daughter would be grounded for a long time when she got home. And her friends knew what that meant; several times Nina had shown up in school bruised and battered after her father had gotten mad at her. They did what they could to make her feel better.

The day felt endless. They were ordered out onto the bikes, then the whole class rode out to Echo Valley, where they stumbled around among the fallen trees and rocks that shifted under their feet. They were given assignments, and when they stopped to eat, it started raining. They all huddled together in a shelter. Even though Trine had been bone-tired while being lectured that morning, the excitement from the night before still rolled through her veins, and she and the other girls whispered to one another about the Bornholm boys every time Lena and Steffen were out of sight. Pia had a sore throat after her swim, but she just laughed and said it wasn't anything a little alcohol couldn't cure.

Trine asked Pia what had happened between Susan and Skipper while they were swimming, but Pia hadn't really noticed. And they talked about Stretch, who had been kicked out of school, and Daniel, whose father owned a trucking business. Skipper's father was actually a skipper and owned a fishing boat, but that was all Pia knew about him.

After dinner the dining hall tables were cleared, and Kirsten came out with a large pan of dream cake, which Lena cut into twenty-two exactly identical pieces and placed onto paper plates.

"Quiet," she yelled. She told them that before they left, they had to hand in their assignments from that afternoon and write two pages in their diaries.

All Trine could think about was when they could run off again. Daniel had told them the abandoned house was somewhere in the middle of the island. It had been empty since 1974, when the owner, an old artist, had died. Except for several places where it was falling apart, the house was exactly the way he'd left it. All his things were still there, down to the toothpaste in the bathroom.

"I need to talk to you," Lena said when Trine and her three friends had finished eating and were leaving the dining room. "Trine, you and I are switching beds tonight. You take my room and I'll sleep in your bed in the room with you three girls."

"No," Pia said, "it's really not necessary, we're not going anywhere. We promise. Come on!"

"Remember, a deal is a deal," Susan said. Trine nodded enthusiastically.

"The decision has been made," Lena said, turning away. "And remember, you're not allowed to leave the hostel. And no talking on the phone."

Several of the others in the class were already heading for town. The girls sulked as they watched them leave in small groups. Only Mona stayed behind; she was engrossed in writing in her diary and didn't seem interested in going anywhere.

Susan began whispering, telling them about the plan she and Skipper had come up with the night before: the boys would be at the private school half an hour after lights-out at the hostel, and they would all go out to the abandoned house together. But Susan thought it was too risky to try to sneak out with Lena in their room—she was afraid of being sent home.

"You have to go over there and tell them we can't come," she said, pointing at Trine.

Pia thought that was a great idea. Nina was the only one who took Trine's side when she said she didn't want to, that she didn't want to get sent home, either.

Susan wouldn't give in. "You'll have the room to yourself; it'll be easy to get out without anyone seeing. Just tell them we can't get out tonight. Tell them to come back tomorrow at the same time, and if we don't show up in a half hour, it's because they're still keeping an eye on us."

"Let's just forget it," Nina said. "They're not *that* important, they're just some boys. We don't even know them."

Susan and Pia ignored her. "Tell them we'll be there tomorrow if we can," Susan repeated. "Or else we'll try again the day after tomorrow."

Finally, Trine gave in and promised to talk to the boys.

At a quarter to midnight, she climbed out of the window. She peered around and shuddered; the night seemed murkier, creepier now that she was alone. Just before reaching the trees on the other side of the parking lot, Trine spotted someone sitting up against the bicycle shed and froze. For what felt like ages she strained to see who it was, but it was too dark.

A high voice called out, "I won't say anything."

Chills ran down Trine's spine, and her voice shook when she said, "Mona? What are you doing here?"

"I won't say anything," Mona repeated.

"It's the middle of the night. Why are you here?"

Mona didn't answer, and Trine walked over to her.

"Go on," Mona said. "They're here; I heard the mopeds. They're parked up there waiting."

Trine didn't know what to do. She didn't believe that Mona wouldn't tell on her, but she couldn't just let the boys wait. Susan would be furious if she didn't let them know, and the girls might never see them again, too.

"Will you stick around while I run up and tell them the others aren't coming?" Trine asked.

Suddenly it seemed best to pretend she wasn't a part of it, that she was just the messenger.

"Wait here." Trine leaned in closer so they could see each other. "I'll be back in a minute."

Mona nodded silently, and Trine took off running.

FOURTEEN

The doorbell woke her again. The cheery melody chimed into the guest room and caught her fast asleep.

Slowly Louise rolled over and lay still for a moment while she stared into space. Her mouth was dry, but she savored the tranquil hum in her still-slumbering body. The doorbell chimed again. She shook herself awake and swung her legs out of bed, then stretched and walked over to the window and opened the curtains. Immediately she jumped back, knocking over the small table beside the bed. But when she tried to scream, no sound came out.

Mona was standing right outside, her face pressed against the glass, staring blankly in at Louise. Her nearly white hair hung down over her shoulders. Louise's heart hammered as she stared back in shock.

The doorbell rang again, and Louise staggered out into the hall and opened the door.

Flemming Larsen raised his eyebrows at the sight of her messy hair and crumpled nightgown. She'd worked for many years with the six-and-a-half-foot-tall forensic pathologist, and they had become good friends.

"Hello? Did you just see a ghost? Or get shocked?"

A few moments went by before she processed the sight of him standing there. "Both." Suddenly she needed to feel if he was real, and she reached out.

"I heard you were home." He held out a bottle of Calvados and a pack of cigarettes—their standard survival kit. "I also heard about your brother. Why didn't you call?"

Louise was overwhelmed by the fact that he'd showed up there. She imagined everyone in the Homicide Department, all the forensic technologists, and the people in the Department of Forensic Medicine gossiping about how her brother had been committed and was suspected of knocking off his partner. But at the same time, the sight of Flemming made her feel calm. He was a familiar presence, a sturdy rock. Several times they'd been close to becoming more than just friends, but it had never happened. And she'd always told herself it was for the best. Flemming was one of the people she trusted the most. And suddenly she didn't understand why she hadn't called him.

"Just a sec." She slipped her sneakers on.

"What's going on?" he asked as she elbowed past him and ran toward the corner of the house.

"Go on in, I'll be right there," she yelled over her shoulder.

She darted past the four lilac bushes at the end of the terrace, then out to the backyard, but there was no sign of Mona. She ran back to the driveway and up to the road, but she saw no sign of the pale woman. Confused now, she hurried over to Trine's clinic and walked around it. Mona hadn't waited for her, that was clear.

Louise felt a bit dizzy. Had she really seen the woman? It was embarrassing, but maybe she'd been dreaming. Maybe the Thai sleeping pills were affecting her. Then a bright reflection caught her eye. There was a white piece of paper sticking out of the bush just outside the bedroom where she'd been sleeping. Like a little flag waving among the yellow flowers.

It had been folded several times, and when she smoothed it out, she recognized the old class photo. In addition to the rings around Trine, Pia, and Nina on Trine's copy, this one had another face circled, with a name written beside it: "Mona."

For the first time Louise recognized the girl's pale face. Her hair had been the same back then, long and almost white. She stood for several moments studying the old photograph of the young faces from the class 7C. Happy and open faces, except for Mona's.

She felt queasy as she walked back to the front door holding the class photo. Flemming had made himself right at home and was brewing coffee, though he'd never been in Mikkel's house before. The bottle of Calvados and the cigarettes lay on the table.

"Where are the mugs?" He said nothing about her escapade outside.

She pointed. "In the cupboard." She pulled a chair out and sank down into it, allowing him to do the honors with the coffee. "Who called you?"

"Mik."

Louise nodded. Her ex-boyfriend, who was now the head of the Serious Crimes Unit in Holbæk. The two men had been talking about her, and with only good intentions, no doubt about that. They wanted to protect her, show her they cared. Right now, though, she felt like she was being suffocated. Knowing they were talking about her. Knowing they had realized what had happened, before she even really understood herself how serious the situation was.

The doorbell rang. It sounded hostile to Louise, even though the bright melody did what it could to seem happy. Flemming turned to her, his face a question mark, but Louise stared out toward the hall without moving a muscle.

"I'll get it," he said.

She nodded. Heard the lock being turned, heard the mumbling of several voices, and then Flemming's deep, firm voice cutting through. "No comment."

So. The news was out. The press had tracked down Mikkel's name. Louise cursed the sources in the police department who were more loyal to reporters than to the people involved in the case.

"Thanks," she said when Flemming came back in. He shrugged.

Her phone rang. "His name's out," Camilla told her. "Somebody leaked it to the press. They know he was brought in on reasonable suspicion and questioned, and they know his house has been searched."

"I know," Louise said.

"They also know he's your brother. Maybe you should move in with me for a while, get away from that house out there."

Flemming placed a mug of coffee in front of her and asked if she wanted milk. She shook her head.

"Is that your dad, is he helping?" Camilla asked.

"Flemming's here; the first journalists have already shown up."

"Assholes!"

Louise laughed. *"You're* calling them assholes? You'd be here, too, if you didn't have my number and know I'd talk when you called."

"They haven't even pressed charges; he's only been questioned." Camilla sounded indignant, as if it were her job to defend Louise's brother.

"But they're hoping to get something on him. They're going to go through his computer and phone and Trine's phone, which will probably happen today."

Louise knew she wasn't letting herself be comforted, but she had way too much experience with this type of case to not be worried;

Mikkel could very well be held in custody if they found anything that could convince a judge they had enough to press charges.

They heard a vehicle pull up outside, some sort of truck, and when the doorbell rang again seconds later, Flemming was already on the way out to the door. Louise promised to call Camilla back and hung up.

"Forensic techs," Flemming said when he returned. "They want the keys to your brother's car."

Louise stood up. *Of course,* she thought. They would take the inside apart, look for blood in small creases and cracks. They'd brought along a tow truck in case they found anything at all that needed to be examined closer. She hadn't even looked in the trunk.

She went out to the hallway for the keys. She crossed her fingers, hoping that the press wouldn't still be hanging around when the techs started their work. In truth, she wished they would just take the car in to the station. All the neighbors would be watching them inspect the car.

"How was the trip?" Flemming asked, after she'd handed the keys to the two techs. He'd suggested they sit out on the porch and enjoy the weather, now that summer was here, but Louise didn't want to be on display for the neighbors and onlookers.

She felt Flemming's eyes on her, and she glanced up.

"You think he had something to do with what happened," he said. He'd read her like a book.

For a moment she stared straight ahead, then slowly she shook her head. "I don't *think* he did. But it's hard for me to understand his way of dealing with all of this. He should have contacted the police when Trine disappeared all of a sudden. He should have done everything he could to look for her. I don't understand why he didn't. Why he just seemed to accept that she'd left him again."

"But maybe she *has*? I mean, left him."

Louise nodded.

Flemming had poured Calvados into two egg cups he'd found in the cupboard. He toasted her to get her to take a sip. Louise took a drink before reluctantly admitting that she wasn't so sure anymore.

"Mikkel thinks so." She set the egg cup down. "He's totally devastated, broken up over it. I really think he's afraid of being left alone with Kirstine and Malte. Afraid he can't take care of them, with how heartbroken he is. And he's trying to sneak out the back way, I guess you could say. But the tragic part is, he's blind to how it would be the absolute worst thing he could do to them. He's truly hit rock bottom."

She shook her head sadly, then emptied the egg cup. She couldn't remember the last time she'd downed liquor so early in the morning. She hid her face in her hands.

"You know what? You need to get your ass in gear!"

She looked up; sure enough, he was angry. "You need to find every single person who might know something about your sister-in-law. What's going on here? Where's the Louise I know? You have an entire investigative unit behind you. And the whole Homicide Department, for that matter. And you're sitting here doing absolutely nothing. Come on, get going!"

Louise stared at him and he glared back at her; she felt as if she was letting *him* down. Slowly she shook her head. "I can't." Her voice sounded so small.

Flemming leaned over the table. "What does that mean?"

"It means, I'm not working right now. In fact, I won't be for quite a while. I have two more months of leave."

"Okay, yeah, you're on leave," he said, calmer now. "And I'm not saying you should go back to work to help your brother. But you could easily put together your own little investigation; you could find your sister-in-law yourself, if you wanted to. Where's your energy, though? Where's the fighter I know is inside you?"

He sank back in his chair and studied her for a moment. "Where are you, Louise?"

Again, it all began pouring out of her. In one long stream, she told him about the breakup with Eik, about how the others had left Thailand without her.

"I stood there waving at them, and it was like my life flew away, the life I thought I had. It moved on without me. Like I got sent straight back to the time right after Klaus died."

She'd never have thought she could say something like that to anyone except Camilla, to open up in such an embarrassing way, but there was no stopping now.

Flemming didn't seem embarrassed or sidetracked by sympathy, however. He shook his head and snapped: "That's enough of that. When your boyfriend died, it had nothing to do with you. It was those asshole friends of his, letting you live with all that guilt for so many years. You've got to let go of this and move on. You have every right to blame Eik; I get that. He's a self-centered, egotistic little twat, sticking his tail between his legs like that when the going gets rough."

Louise looked up, a bit confused at the way her self-pity tirade was being interrupted.

"To hell with him!" he said.

"We were going to be married," she said a bit pathetically.

"Maybe you two still will, when he gets back. But it's goddamn wimpy of him to turn his back on you, just because all of a sudden he thinks he can't handle two kinds of love."

Flemming wrinkled his nose in disgust.

They sat in silence for a few moments before Flemming leaned forward again. "You've got to pull yourself together," he implored.

"Get ahold of Mik Rasmussen, get going, so you can find out what's happened to your sister-in-law."

She should be glad he cared enough to yell at her, she thought, but right now it all seemed so overwhelming. After a few moments, she straightened up. "We're not getting anyone else involved in this."

"You might need help from the police," he countered. "You'll need to talk to friends and family."

"We are the family!" Louise reminded him. "Trine's mother flew up from Spain; she's the one who reported Trine missing."

"So go look her up."

"I don't know if she'll speak to me, since she also pointed the police toward Mikkel."

"Follow the money," he said, undeterred.

She explained that Trine's debit card had been left behind in the house.

"Then find out what your brother was doing the day she disappeared. Is it possible he was here at the house earlier? Was he in contact with her anytime that day? Were they going to meet somewhere?"

"The police are already looking into all that," she said, annoyed now. Her thoughts began moving away from all the obvious things the police would investigate.

"Maybe it's worth looking in a different direction," she said. She told him about the class photo, which made her wonder about Trine's past. Something or someone might have popped up. An old friend, maybe, someone who needed help and had reached out to her. It might explain why she'd left the house in such a rush. Someone outside their current circle of friends, someone neither Mikkel nor the police knew about.

"If that's the case, there's still no way she would have been gone for a whole week, though, not without letting someone know," Flemming said.

"But something could have happened to her after she left." Louise chewed on that a moment. She recalled a tragic news story about a man who had died from an accident at work. When his wife was notified, she rushed to the hospital and was killed in a traffic accident, leaving behind two small children.

"We have to assume the police have checked all the hospitals and emergency rooms," Flemming said.

She agreed; of course they had.

"Who was that woman who nearly scared you to death right before I showed up?" he asked, after refilling their egg cups with Calvados. He reached over and picked up the wrinkled photocopy of the class picture.

"Mona. I met her in Roskilde several years ago while I was on a case. She has this thing about people who have disappeared. Then we ran into each other again at the psychiatric hospital when I went out to see Mikkel. Ever since she was young, she's had emotional problems; she has a reaction when missing persons cases come up in the media. I didn't know before, but apparently it goes back to this class field trip on Bornholm. She was in the same class as the girl they just found in Echo Valley, the one who disappeared on the trip. Mona probably hoped I had time to talk to her."

"It's a sad story, tragic." Flemming said he'd flown to Bornholm with a team of techs shortly after the body had been found and they'd taken Susan Dahlgaard back with them to Copenhagen.

"Mona's nice enough, that's not it. She's just a bit odd; she's on a different wavelength from most people." She told him about Mona's obsessive and somewhat creepy interest in insects.

"Insects." Flemming described how Susan's body had been covered by a thick, crawling sheet of insects when he'd arrived at the cave. The first ones to find her had laid eggs, and new generations had hatched out in the mummified shell of her body.

He grabbed his tiny cup and emptied it.

"Did you do her autopsy?" Louise asked.

Flemming nodded. "What was left of her. It was relatively dry in the cave, and the ventilation was good enough to inhibit decay. I've seldom seen a cadaver this well preserved. The skin was hard and leathery, as expected, but there was still quite a bit left of her clothes. We knew right away we'd found Susan."

Louise had seen it before. The brown skin, hard as the table separating her and Flemming. Fingernails that looked long and bent because the fingers had dried up and shriveled. She visualized the photos of the young girl that must never be released to the press.

"Had she been injured? Did you get any sense of what had happened?"

"It's hard to say, but the Bornholm police are treating it as a crime. I found a fracture in her left temple that caused brain damage."

Louise was surprised. "Could you really see that after so many years?"

Flemming explained that about a third of her brain remained.

"But how did she end up in the cave?"

"My best guess is that she suffered an epidermal hematoma from the blow to her head."

He explained in layman's terms when he saw he'd lost Louise. "There was bleeding between the tough outer membrane of her brain and her skull. There's an artery right here under the temple." He pointed with a finger. "After a sufficiently hard blow, the artery starts to bleed, but there's a period of time until death occurs. It's what happened to the wife of Liam Neeson, the actor, when she fell while skiing. She walked away from the accident without help. But within an hour or two the bleeding causes pressure on the brain, and then you feel sick, you might get a violent headache and throw up, and finally you lose consciousness. If that's what happened to Susan, I can't say how long it took from the time she was hit until she died. She could have felt okay and been completely conscious for several hours."

"You think she hid in the cave after being hit?"

Flemming pushed the empty egg cup away, as if he wanted to keep himself from filling it up again. He hesitated a moment. "Probably. The police didn't reveal everything I found to the media, to be respectful to her foster parents and others who had been close to Susan. But I found several large wooden splinters in both her hands and in one of her shoulders. She was also missing the fingernail on the fourth finger of her right hand."

"So Susan was alive when she was trapped inside the cave," Louise said.

He nodded. "I'd say so. The tree trunk blocking the entrance has rotted away, there's no bark left on it, so we can't check for marks. But the techs found a fingernail beside her body. And that section of the tree was cut out and taken in for more tests. The remains have been released to the foster parents. I don't know when the funeral is, but I bet it'll draw a crowd, don't you think?"

Louise nodded. A silence fell between them.

"Talk to Mik," Flemming said softly, his eyes pleading with her.

She winced. It was touching, the way it was clearly hard for him to see her struggling, not asking for help from the people around her.

"I'll think about it," she said, just as softly.

Even though she and her ex-boyfriend shared a dog, asking him to help was difficult for her. If it had been for work, there would have been no problem. But this was personal; it was a different story. Mik was a lieutenant detective in Holbæk, part of the Mid and West Sealand Police, and there was no doubt he could get information about the case. Still, she was hesitant to ask. And the truth was, she was glad about the police investigation. Now that they were treating it as a possible homicide, the Roskilde Police would prioritize it, put more people on it than if it had just been a missing persons case. Hopefully they would find out the truth, with enough digging. Right now, she was more concerned about Mikkel's mental state. Worried that they weren't keeping a close enough eye on him, that he might somehow try to kill himself again. That was what seriously scared her. He'd been there for her, back when she'd been desperate, and now she had to at least try to help him pull through this.

A text came in from her father: "Hi, honey. Am with Mikkel, he slept well last night. Apparently, Liselotte was the one who convinced the police that Mikkel harmed Trine. Mikkel said it was obvious from questioning yesterday. He doesn't know why she's so mad at him. Can you talk to her and ask her why she's doing this to him? Hugs, Dad."

The doorbell rang again, and Flemming answered it. The techs were finished with the car. They hadn't found anything to justify taking it in for further examination.

"You can use it again," Flemming said. "I left the keys in the hallway."

Louise thanked him, then read her father's text out loud.

Even before she finished, he said, "Go. You want me to come along? I'm on call, so I don't have to get back to Copenhagen, not until they need me."

She shook her head; she'd rather tackle her brother's mother-in-law by herself.

Outside, before saying goodbye, he pulled her close and held her, so long that she began to relax. "Promise me you'll call," he ordered, though in a whisper. "At least once a day."

She nodded.

"All right then. I'll talk to you this evening, at the latest."

She smiled and nodded again, overcome by his protective instincts.

FIFTEEN

Camilla parked at Osted School. She'd managed to set up a meeting with Steffen Dybvad. She stood for a moment and looked around; there was something strangely distant and yet also so familiar about being back at her old school.

The lobby was empty and quiet, and her heels echoed as she walked in. The school was closed for summer vacation.

At first, Dybvad had resisted, but finally he'd agreed to talk with her. It turned out that he'd started teaching biology at Osted just a short time before she left, so he was relatively new when he went along on 7C's field trip. Camilla didn't remember him, and she'd hoped she could get in touch with Lena, who had been her history teacher. But Lena had moved to Greenland and was now working at a school in Nuuk.

They shook hands. "Follow me," Dybvad said.

Something in his voice told her he might be more affected by the case than he'd led her to believe over the phone. He'd also told her he didn't remember the details of the trip—it had been too long ago, he claimed. And there had been so many field trips since then.

Camilla could see that, but surely some details must have stuck from a trip where a girl disappeared and was never found.

"My theory was always that Susan ran away," he admitted, after they sat down across from each other and Camilla set her phone to record the conversation. "I truly didn't believe anything had happened to her. But I was wrong."

He carefully folded his hands in front of him and looked up at her. "In a strange way it's a relief finding out what happened, but it's also horrible to think she's been lying there all this time."

Camilla nodded, hoping he would go on. He kept weaving his fingers together, in and out.

"The police came by last week, wanting to know if I'd thought of anything not in my statement back then. They asked me when I saw her last and if anything significant happened during the days before she disappeared. But I couldn't really help."

"Would you be willing to go through the whole story one more time? Even though you've already told it?"

He obviously wasn't thrilled with the idea, but after a few moments he relented.

"They were a bunch of holy terrors, those kids. One of the first nights, several of the girls crawled out the window after lights-out. We found out, and they were put under supervision. Susan Dahlgaard was one of them. At that time, she'd already been given several warnings. She was ahead of her classmates, more mature both physically and mentally, and she had this invisible magnet some kids have. The others were attracted to her, and not only the boys. The girls flocked around her, wanted to stick close to her, but it seemed like she wasn't aware of her magnetism. It wasn't like she used it, she just had it. Lots of times a class has a leader the other girls have to live up to. Susan was like that. She did well in her classes, too, even though she didn't always do her homework."

"These warnings you mention, what were they about?"

"She played hooky sometimes. Susan was a nice girl, but she was always pushing it, seeing what she could get away with. She grew up in an orphanage in Roskilde, and things weren't always easy for her, to say the least. She had an older brother, he was at a boarding school for troubled kids on Amager, and once in a while she ran off to Copenhagen to be with him. He was a few years older; he hung out with the kind of boys most parents want their teenage girls to stay away from."

Camilla nodded.

"I thought she ran away because of the brother. She seemed restless, like she was looking for something. I thought of her as a stray, and I figured she'd run off from the other girls, caught a ride to the ferry, made it to Copenhagen before the police even started searching for her."

He seemed weighed down by a guilty conscience. "I thought she went to Copenhagen."

"What happened the first night when the girls ran off? Were they alone, or did they meet up with anyone?"

He looked up. "They met up with some of the local boys. You'd think they had jungle drums over there, every time a new class arrived on a field trip. The kids always managed to find one another. They still do. And that goes for both boys and girls."

Camilla nodded again.

"In fact, it was the running around at night that got all the attention. Right from the start, we and the police thought Susan had run off. Of course, they organized a big search for her, but it was like every trace of her ended down at the Svaneke harbor, where Susan left her friends."

Camilla had read up on the case before coming. The four girls had snuck out and taken two of the youth hostel's bicycles at eleven that night. Down at the harbor they met the boys they'd been with the first night. The three other girls claimed that Susan wanted to stick around with the boys, so they biked back to the hostel. Without Susan.

"The boys were a rough bunch," Dybvad said. "They broke into places, stole cars. They claimed Susan wasn't with them that night, though they did admit meeting the girls at the convenience store at the harbor, and they'd talked about meeting up later. But it didn't happen. Instead the boys stole a car and wrecked it."

Dybvad paused and watched Camilla, who was scribbling down notes.

She knew from articles back then that the boys had long been suspected of being involved in Susan's disappearance. But the police had found no evidence of their guilt. They'd been nailed for other things, though, when the police started investigating them. No trace of Susan was found in the stolen car the boys wrecked between Svaneke and Rønne, but it was filled with stolen goods and alcohol from a break-in in Aakirkeby.

"The boys were punished; the boy driving the car was even sent to prison."

"What happened earlier the day of her disappearance?" Camilla asked.

He needed only a few moments to bring back the memories of that day. "After breakfast we biked out to Østerlars Church to see the murals from the Middle Ages; we spent about an hour there. We ate lunch there, too. And we went on to Almindingen, where we started out at Sydmasteren—it's a giant Norway spruce uprooted in a storm, and seven new trees sprung up out of it."

Camilla nodded quickly, hoping to head off more of his lecture.

"Then we biked to Basta marsh and then on to Echo Valley. It always takes a little longer than you think—someone either falls off their bike or wanders into sting nettles, that sort of thing. But we lucked out on the weather that day."

So he remembered the details after all. Lucky for her.

"Naturally, all the kids had to yell to hear their voices echo at Echo Valley. After that we rode on to the highest point on the island, Rytterknægten, and climbed up the lookout tower. The kids had time to buy candy there, then we finished the day's ride at Rokke-stenen, where they all tried to rock the boulder. We biked almost fifty kilometers that day, so the kids were bushed when we got back. After dinner they were free to do whatever they wanted until bedtime."

"So Susan had been to Echo Valley earlier," Camilla said.

"Yes, and she was at Brændesgårdshaven, the gardens, and the castle ruins at Hammershus. That Thursday the plan was that we'd bike down to Dueodde. When we discovered Susan was gone, we decided Lena would stay behind and wait for Susan to show up, and I'd take the kids by myself."

He leaned over closer to Camilla. "We thought she'd come back, we really did," he emphasized, obviously upset. She nodded.

"But when we got back from the ride, she still wasn't there. Lena had already called Susan's foster parents, and they all agreed that Lena should contact the police, even though it could have had serious consequences for Susan. She was happy living with that family, and she liked school. They all knew there was the risk of the district putting her under supervision if the police got involved. But Lena felt we couldn't just do nothing, and I agreed one hundred percent. A schoolteacher can't take responsibility for something like that, even though we thought it might only be a few hours before she showed up."

"But the three other girls didn't say anything?"

Dybvad shook his head. "At first they told us they hadn't seen her leave the hostel. When the police came around and talked to them that afternoon, though, they broke down and admitted they'd all snuck out the night before and taken the two bikes. And they said they last saw Susan down at the harbor."

"Did any of you go out to look for her?" Camilla said.

"The police asked us not to; they didn't want us ruining her trail if they had to call in the dogs. And then we rounded up all the kids, told them the police wanted to talk to them. We made it clear that they had to tell the police everything they knew or had seen up to the night Susan disappeared."

"And that convinced the girls to talk?"

"Right. They weren't exactly thrilled about their parents knowing they'd snuck out again. Nina especially was scared of her father finding out, but like I said, they talked to the police, and they pointed out the last place they saw Susan. The next morning, they brought in police dogs, the Bornholm boys were questioned. I can't remember now how many days before the police went public, but anyway that's when things got rolling."

Neither of them spoke for a moment while Camilla looked over her notes.

"Have you been in contact with Susan's friends, the three girls, since then?"

"It was hard for everyone later on, obviously, because she didn't come back," Dybvad said, evading her question. "They tried to find her brother, but he'd left the boarding school, and the social authorities lost track of him. The police finally located him several years later; he'd died of an overdose on Vesterbro."

"So none of you ever found out that she hadn't gone to her brother." Camilla was beginning to get the picture of a young, rootless girl who didn't fit in, an outsider even before the class field trip. A girl who was no stranger to trouble.

"Her foster parents took it hard. They were grieving; they truly cared for her, even though she wasn't their biological child. They kept in touch with the police for years, always wanted to hear if there was anything new."

One of the other papers had just published a long interview with the foster parents, who no longer lived in Osted. It was true, they'd taken the loss of Susan very hard, and she had been the last child they'd taken in, according to the article.

"I've looked for Susan on Facebook several times. It was so long ago, so many years, but something like this sticks with you. You keep hoping she'll show up someday. Like I said, I thought she left the island. Just like how she ran away from the orphanage and some of the other foster homes. I thought she'd be okay; she was a tough girl. And definitely not dumb."

"But the other girls, have you had contact with them since then?" Camilla asked again.

Dybvad's expression shifted; the question obviously annoyed him. He shook his head as if he didn't understand where she was going with this. "All the kids were shaken by what happened. They felt terrible. Maybe we should have cut the trip short, but we ended up staying the last day, partly because we hoped she would show up."

"But you never talked to them about that night, when they split up with Susan? Did any of you hear them when they came back without her?"

He stared down at the table for several moments before shaking his head. "No, we didn't. Lena and I were sleeping together, and we were more involved in each other than in making sure the kids were in bed. Of course we told the police, but the parents didn't find out, and I'd appreciate it if you kept it to yourself."

Camilla took note of what he said, but she didn't promise him anything.

"The only one to say she saw them come back was Mona Ibsen.

She thought they got back early the next morning, but according to the girls it was around midnight."

"But that was checked out, right?"

He shook his head. "Mona was a special girl; she imagined a lot of things. Had visions and dreams—I don't know what to call that sort of spiritual stuff. She was a sweet girl, active, happy, she just had a lively imagination, and once in a while she got carried away by these visions and premonitions. I thought she might have just wanted the attention. Earlier in the year I hadn't really noticed her sticking out, but then she started acting strange; suddenly she didn't want to go on the trip. She was afraid something was going to happen. Something bad, she said. A few weeks before we left, she came to me in the teachers' lounge and insisted we cancel. Luckily her parents backed us up when we said everyone had to go—after all it was still school time, even though we weren't at home. In fact, I thought it would be good for her to get away. But then all this happened with Susan, and things really went downhill for her. We told all the kids that they could talk to the school psychologist when we got back, but it was a lot more complicated for Mona. She struggled with it the rest of the time she was in school."

"So her witness statement wasn't taken seriously because she was a little bit different?"

He leaned forward again. "That's not true; we did listen to what she said and the police talked to her. I'm sure her witness statement was part of the case, but to be honest, the three girls who'd been with Susan were more credible."

SIXTEEN

Liselotte Madsen's small one-story house in Dåstrup stood in a neighborhood where the hedges were tall and the fruit trees old. The summer heat shimmered above the asphalt of the quiet street as Louise climbed out of her car and walked up the driveway.

Her brother's mother-in-law was short and agile and very tanned. When she opened the door and saw who it was, she looked uncertainly at Louise and stood as if she were trying to block the doorway.

"Hi," Louise said. "I came by to see how you're doing. Could we talk for a bit?"

"We've got nothing to talk about," the woman said.

"Why do you say that? I need you to tell me why you're so sure that Mikkel has done something to Trine. What is it you know that the rest of us apparently don't? I'm not here to accuse you of anything; you did the right thing to report Trine missing. I just want to understand why you believe my brother had something to do with it."

Mikkel's mother-in-law stared stubbornly down at the sidewalk.

"The one thing we all want is for Trine to be found," Louise pleaded. "And that's why we should all work together and help one another out."

At last, the woman looked up. "Are you here as a police officer?"

"No, I'm here as family. But I've been with the police long enough to know how to be objective. If my brother had something to do with Trine's disappearance, it will come out. But right now the important thing is that we find her. If she's been hurt, we have to find out what happened."

"Come inside." Liselotte stepped aside to let Louise in. "*Something's* happened to her, I know that much. She would have told me if they were having trouble or if she was planning to leave. She didn't leave him."

"No," Louise said. "I don't think she did, either."

The woman looked startled. "You don't think she just left him?"

"No. But why do you suspect Mikkel is involved?"

"Who else could it be? Who else would want to hurt her? I read somewhere you should always look for the guilty person in the family."

Louise peered at her. "So that's the only reason you suspect him, because the nearest family is the most logical place to look for the guilty party?"

The woman shrugged. "He's the only one who could want to get rid of her."

"But why in the world would he do it?" Louise said. "The day she disappeared, they'd just talked to each other. They'd made a plan for him to buy groceries on the way home. They were going out to Malerklemmen for doughnut holes if the kids weren't too tired. What makes you think he was planning to get rid of her?"

"Okay, then, who else could it be?" Liselotte stared at her defiantly.

Louise took her hand and spoke calmly. "My brother loves your daughter. He would never hurt her. Do you know he's in a psychiatric hospital, that he's attempted suicide twice now? He's absolutely crushed."

"Likely he feels guilty," Liselotte answered, though she didn't pull her hand back.

Louise shook her head. "No, his heart is broken. He's grieving."

They sat for a moment looking at each other.

"But if it's not him, who is it?" Liselotte sounded desperate, as if she were willing to accuse anyone. Louise couldn't blame her. She blamed herself for not coming over to talk to her right away. Suddenly Louise understood how lonesome Liselotte must be feeling, all alone with her suspicions and fears.

"We'll find out," Louise promised. "But we have to help each other."

Several moments passed before Liselotte nodded slowly and squeezed Louise's hand. "Maybe I was too quick to believe Mikkel did something really bad. He is such a sweet boy. But I know something has happened to my daughter."

"You might be right." Louise told her that Kirstine and Malte were staying at her parents' house in Hvalsø. "We need to protect them while all this is going on."

Their grandmother nodded and said she'd thought about offering to take care of them. "But they know your parents better; we're not so close anymore, now that I spend so much time in Spain."

"I think you should go over there and spend some time with them. Fear has a way of growing when you're alone. My parents would be happy to have you come."

She knew she was speaking for herself; her mother would have to seriously grit her teeth to let Trine's mother inside the door.

"And I guess I'd better warn you. Journalists are probably going to show up; they'll want to talk to you about Trine. My advice is not to say anything right now. Of course, it's up to you. I'm not trying to stop you; it's just that it's smartest to wait until we know what's happened first."

She felt that was the best she could do to keep Mikkel's mother-in-law's mouth shut.

Liselotte nodded. "How is Mikkel doing? I saw him for a moment at the police station. If he really had nothing to do with it, he must be feeling terrible."

Louise nodded. "More than terrible, I'm sure."

"And it's all my fault," Liselotte said. She rubbed her forehead.

"No. It's not your fault. The police are thinking the way you did, that the obvious place to start is with those closest to Trine. The vast majority of homicides in our country are domestic homicides, where the victim and the killer know each other."

"Homicide," Trine's mother said, shaken now. "You think she's dead."

"No! That's not what I'm saying, but I'm sure the police have opened a homicide investigation, and we should be grateful for that. It means that they'll prioritize it. If it was still a missing person case, nothing much would happen, not until there was some indication of a crime. Right now, the police are working twenty-four/seven on this. I'm just sorry my brother is their prime suspect, because I don't believe he did anything to Trine. That's why I'm trying to find out what happened."

Louise could hear herself spewing out all these professional platitudes. And she reminded herself that she was talking to family.

"I'm worried about him," she admitted. "I hope he's strong enough to make it through. Anyway, I can't figure out Trine leaving the kids before he got home. Something must have happened, right before she disappeared. What do you think, what could possibly have made your daughter leave the house and leave the kids alone that way?"

"Trine is always helping other people," her mother said. "She's always been that way."

Louise nodded. "When she left, she must have been thinking she'd be right back. Otherwise she wouldn't have left the kids."

"Could it be the neighbors?" Liselotte said.

"Mikkel already spoke with everyone living around there. He also talked to her friends. It's plausible she would have left if one of them had needed her."

Liselotte nodded.

"Did she mention anything at all to you about any old friendships, anyone she'd recently started seeing again? Former colleagues, someone she went to school with? I mean, people she knew before she met Mikkel. People he wouldn't know."

Liselotte sat thinking for a long time before she shook her head. "But then I'm not the one to ask, I haven't been around."

Louise had to agree; the woman hadn't been involved all that much in her daughter's life the past several years.

"She used to see her old girlfriends from high school once a year, but it didn't last. When I talked to her, honestly, it was my impression that she'd rather just stay home with Mikkel and the kids. Look, they saw other people, but if she did take up with some of her old friends, I don't know about it."

Louise stood and said she had to be going. "Come out to Lerbjerg, have dinner with us tonight. The kids will be happy to see you. And it would be good for all of us to pull together on this."

"Don't you think you should talk to your parents first? I might not be welcome anymore."

"You are absolutely welcome. We're a family. And you haven't done anything wrong. Except that you could have been a little quieter about your suspicion," she added, trying to make light of it. As if it were just a dumb little mistake, and now they should put it behind them.

But, of course, it was more than that. It was a betrayal, a completely uncalled-for accusation, and it was also possible her mother would have a hard time keeping her opinion of Liselotte's behavior to herself. But right now they had to stick together.

SEVENTEEN

The first thing she perceived was the sound of fabric shifting. Then a faint touch, a sense that there was someone close by. She fought to clear her head, then took a breath and began screaming as loudly as she could. It sounded frightening and all wrong in the paralyzing silence. Then a rough hand suddenly covered her mouth, abruptly cutting off her scream. She shrank back as far as she could.

"Quiet," a hoarse voice snarled in the dark. She turned and twisted her head, freeing it enough to catch a glimpse of the person leaning over her. Terrified now, she screamed again and again, wildly, into the dark, gasping for breath, her throat aflame. Out of the corner of her eye, she noticed the person backing away, and for a short second she thought it had helped to yell and fight back. Then she felt the prick in her shoulder, and again she slowly lost control of her body as she passed out.

EIGHTEEN

"I'm on my way to Bornholm," Camilla tapped out in a text to Louise. She was sitting at the airport, waiting for her flight to Rønne. She'd started to call her friend to tell her about Markus and the pregnancy, but she'd changed her mind. She hadn't heard from Louise since telling her that Mikkel's name had been leaked to the press, and no doubt her friend had enough on her plate at the moment.

The flight was delayed for forty-five minutes because of some technical problem. During the delay, she'd managed to both curse out the Danish airline employees and fight with her son's father. She'd tried to get ahold of Tobias the day before, and he'd left a message saying he would call back, but he didn't. Camilla knew he had a full plate, too, with his young twins and new wife, a woman who was very unhappy about him working full-time while she stayed at home and took care of everything.

Camilla was still waiting at the boarding gate when she got ahold of him at last. And maybe that was for the best, she later thought. Because if she hadn't been on her way to Bornholm, she probably would have tracked him down and clobbered him with something cheap and heavy. When she told him their son was going to be a father, the first thing he said was that it was great news, that Markus could take care of the twins since he'd be at home with his own kid anyway. She got it, he was trying to make it sound like he was joking, but she could hear that he meant it. She blew up and yelled some very nasty things into the phone before hanging up on him.

She was still angry as she started the rented Fiat and floored it, even though she knew she would be late anyway for her meeting at the Rønne police station. She had an appointment with the investigator in charge of the Susan Dahlgaard case. He'd told her on the phone that he'd joined the force right before Susan disappeared and had taken part in the search, had spent weeks afterward knocking on doors and speaking to people.

The GPS led Camilla to Zahrtmannsvej. She'd planned to pick up something at a bakery to butter him up, but instead she roared up to the station with sweaty hands and red splotches on her neck.

"Welcome to the island," Steen Wiinberg said.

Camilla smiled and shook his outstretched hand. Police usually thought talking to reporters was a waste of time, and usually they hated to see her coming. But once in a while she ran into an officer who believed the press and the police were on the same side. He had even made coffee and set out cups.

"I understand a couple from Viborg found her," Camilla said, after they'd sat down and she'd set her phone to record.

Wiinberg nodded. "They were walking through Echo Valley with their two kids. One of the kids had to pee, so her mother took her behind a few boulders beside the trail, and that's where she noticed the cave in which the body was lying."

"But why did it take so long? It's been almost twenty-five years."

"Susan was behind a big fallen tree, and the trunk was blocking the cave. It took time for the tree to rot away enough to see the entrance."

"Are you any closer to determining if her death was a homicide?"

Camilla had gone through the press releases from the Bornholm police, but there had been little information regarding a possible crime.

"It's hard to say exactly what happened. She suffered a head injury, but right now my theory is that she went into the cave for shelter, and somehow she hit her head when the tree fell. The forensics report showed no other injuries. I spoke to the pathologist who performed the autopsy. I wanted to hear what they'd been able to see, since the body was basically mummified. He explained that with strangulation, sometimes they could see a fractured hyoid bone or thyroid cartilage, even though the body is dried up. But all they found was the fracture above the left temple."

"So for the moment you don't think her death resulted from a crime?" Camilla said.

He began rambling again. "We had heavy rain the night Susan disappeared. It's possible she fell and hit her head, and then looked for shelter. Or like I said, it could have happened when the tree fell. The cave is more like a crevice; it's too narrow to hold more than one person, but it's possible there were others around. Someone could have knocked her in the head and hid her in the cave. But it was nature that uprooted the tree that blocked Susan's way out. Humans could never have done that."

Wiinberg pointed toward her phone. "Let's keep these theories private. It's still too early to come up with any official statements."

He pushed a map of Echo Valley across the table and pointed to a spot above the brook running through the canyon. "What's hard to understand is what she was doing alone out there."

Camilla nodded.

"If we assume she was alone, it's possible she was on her way to Rønne, to catch the ferry to Copenhagen. It would take her about three and a half hours to get to Echo Valley from the hostel. So time-wise, it fits. The canyon is on the way from Svaneke to Rønne. But why she would go all the way out there, we don't know."

With his pencil he traced a dotted line from the highway exit to Echo Valley and farther up the cliff to where Susan was found.

"It's not like it's totally inconceivable, as it wouldn't take more than twenty minutes to walk there from the highway, but why duck into the forest if she was going to Rønne?"

He looked up thoughtfully at Camilla. "It's also possible she stole a bike down at the harbor; she could have biked that far in less than an hour. We can't know now if there was a stolen bike out there; anyway, there was no report of one. But . . ."

Camilla waited for him to go on.

"Or someone could have picked her up and driven her out there. We looked into that at the time, but we couldn't find any witnesses to support that theory."

"Could it have been the weather?" Camilla said. She added that Susan and her class had been in Echo Valley a few days before her disappearance. "If the storm hit as she passed the side road into the canyon, she might have tried to find shelter. She did know the place a little bit."

He thought that over for a moment. "Maybe. I just think it's strange, such a young girl walking into those dark woods by herself, just because of a storm."

They sat for a few moments in silence.

"I talked to one of the teachers on the field trip," Camilla said. "He said the girls met some boys from over here. And even though they got caught the first night they were together, the girls still snuck out to meet them again. The boys were involved in some minor crime. Do you know anything more about them?"

Several stacks of case files lay on the desk in front of him. He thumbed through them until he found a yellowed folder with dog-eared corners and pulled it out.

"We could never prove Susan was with them the night she disappeared. And we came down on those boys hard."

Camilla checked to see if her phone was still recording.

"At first, we mostly wanted to know if Susan had hung around with them, after leaving her friends down at the harbor. And it's possible she did, but she wasn't in the car the boys wrecked that night. So we still have that unexplained time gap from when her friends left her until she reached Echo Valley."

"Where did the other girls bike to after leaving Susan behind?"

Again, he leafed through the old witness statements. "Over to the smokehouse. The place has tables and benches outside, where you can sit and look out over the water. They admitted during questioning that Susan went down to the supermarket after dinner. The four girls had chipped in for a bottle of rum and a pack of cigarettes, and they sat around drinking and smoking."

Camilla thought for a moment. "So they must have been quite the drinkers, huh?"

She tried to remember how much booze a thirteen-year-old can handle. At that age, she'd drunk her first horrible white martini at a youth club party and had thrown up in the bushes the rest of the evening.

He raised his eyebrows.

"What I mean is, the girls said they got back around midnight," Camilla said. "If they left the hostel at around eleven, met the boys down at the harbor, biked over to the smokehouse, drank and smoked and rode back to the hostel, all within an hour . . . they must have downed that rum pretty fast."

"Or left it behind."

"Possibly. But it's also possible they were out longer than they claimed."

"Why would they lie about that?" he asked.

"To cover up something? Make themselves look more innocent than they were?"

She thought about it before shaking her head. "It doesn't make any difference now, anyway. But another girl did say the three girls didn't get back until very early the next morning. She claimed she saw them come in."

Wiinberg nodded slowly. "I remember her. We actually questioned her again later on, after the class went home. A colleague from the Roskilde Police looked her up. There was something interesting about her statement, but as it turned out, it didn't add up. She thought the girls got in about four-thirty, shortly before the sun came up. But there were thick rain clouds that morning; you wouldn't have been able to see the sky lighten so early."

"So you're saying her witness statement was ignored because it was cloudy and gray?"

"It didn't jibe with what the other girls said, either. Back then we had reason to believe she just wanted attention. Nobody else in the class heard her get up or noticed she'd been out. And if what she said was true, she would've been sitting outside in that terrible weather most of the night. There was no reason to believe she had. All three girls said they got home before the storm got bad, which happened around one that night."

"But what if she was right?" Camilla said.

"If she was, all it means is that the girls might have drunk more than they claimed, been more drunk."

"Yeah, or lied about what happened after leaving Susan. Maybe they didn't want her along when they were supposed to meet the boys."

"Listen, we took the girl's statement seriously, and we also talked to the other girls several times," he said, a bit cooler toward her now. "We pulled out all the stops on the search. The mobile unit came over, we had tons of police reinforcements, the Home Guard helped. Our entire focus was on finding Susan."

Camilla changed direction before he dug his heels in. "Tell me about the four boys. They wrecked a car after meeting the girls at the harbor, right?"

He nodded. "They lost control of a stolen car in the heavy rain, hit a tree. They were nothing but trouble back then."

"What happened to them?"

"They were just kids, but two of them had already been arrested for vandalism and theft. Thomas Krogh, the one who was driving the car, was sent to juvenile prison in Jutland. I believe Daniel Axelsen and the others got suspended sentences and community service for larceny and selling stolen goods, vandalism, too. They still live here on the island; they've been on the straight and narrow a long time now."

"They all still live here?"

"Three of them. We just finished questioning them again, after Susan's body was found."

"And the fourth boy?"

"Thomas Krogh. He's dead. A few years after his release, he had a hashish-related psychotic episode and he jumped off a cliff into the ocean, got crushed on the rocks. He never cleaned up his act after prison, was still involved in crime here and there."

"How old were the boys back then?"

Wiinberg pulled out another file folder and read. "Fifteen, sixteen years old. They were in ninth grade, except for Krogh; he wasn't in school back then. Stretch, they called him."

"I want to try to piece together what happened on the class field trip over here. Was it usual for these boys to hang out with students on field trips?" She recalled that several kids from her own class had met some of the island's locals, and had kept in touch with them long after returning home.

He nodded. "Times were different back then; it was before cell phones and social media. Young people still hung out with one another, and when these new exciting kids came over, the island kids had their eyes on them. A lot of relationships started out that way. I was young once myself." He showed a glint in his eye as he smiled. Camilla smiled back. He could have been one of the boys she'd been interested in. Blond hair, broad cheeks, a look she would have noticed back then.

"I'm from Hasle, so unless you stayed there, it probably wasn't my moped you rode behind."

Got me, she thought as she shook her head and chuckled at his teasing. "Svaneke. So there's no way we would remember each other."

He turned serious again. "We're questioning several of the witnesses from back then. Right now, we're focusing on whether anyone saw Susan in the vicinity of Echo Valley, but we want to speak with everyone who remembers anything from the days leading up to her disappearance."

"That abandoned house where the boys hung out, is it still there?"

He shook his head. "They tore it down a long time ago; it was caving in. But back when we were looking for Susan, we turned the old place upside down. We found a bunch of stolen goods, but no sign that she'd been there."

"What about the other girls?" Camilla asked. "Did you find any sign they'd been there?"

He studied her for a moment before shaking his head. "They were irrelevant, as we were only looking for Susan."

"So you don't know if the three girls could have been in the house the night of Susan's disappearance?"

Again he studied her before answering. "No. Why do you ask?"

"Just a thought," she said, nodding casually yet dismissively. He dropped it.

Camilla thanked him for his time and asked for the names of the boys still living on Bornholm. He hesitated before writing down their names and addresses.

"Everybody talks to everybody here," Wiinberg said. "So instead of you going down to the harbor and asking about them, which would mean everyone will know the press is looking for them, I'm giving you their names. Just go easy, they went through a lot back then. And they have families now, at least two of them do."

Camilla checked the names. Two of them lived in Svaneke, the other in Nexø.

"It might be a good idea to call Daniel Axelsen before going out there. He's a truck driver, so he's gone a lot. The other two you can probably catch now."

NINETEEN

It hadn't been easy to get a room; the tourist season was in full swing. First Camilla had called the Melsted Seaside Hotel and tried to talk them into squeezing her in, but all the rooms were reserved. Then she used every ounce of her charm on the receptionist at the Hotel Siemsens, and she'd managed to snatch the last vacant room in all of Svaneke. Which suited her fine, because two of the now-grown men lived in town.

Most of the tables outside the café were taken up by guests drinking coffee or beer. Summer was in the air, in the carefree buzz of conversation, the sunhats, the children running around playing, and there were no customers inside the restaurant. Two men and a woman wearing chef jackets and checkered pants were eating at the table in back. A young waitress walked up to Camilla.

"Hi. The kitchen isn't open until five, but we're serving drinks outside."

Camilla thanked her and said she would like to talk to Finn Kofod. The young woman looked confused and she started to shake her head, but then one of the cooks leaned back and pushed open the kitchen door.

"Skipper!" he yelled.

The young waitress looked over at the others and laughed. "His name is Finn?"

The man's hair was slicked back, his sunglasses pushed up above his forehead, and he was tanned. He'd already looked Camilla up and down before she could get an impression of him. She walked over and introduced herself, then asked if he had a few minutes to talk.

He glanced over at the others before nodding and placing his hand on the small of her back to lead her away. "Let's go upstairs."

Without asking, he grabbed two colas out of a cooler and opened them. The bottle caps clattered on the floor.

"Susan Dahlgaard," he said, after they'd sat down in a small party room with a view over the town's pedestrian street.

Camilla looked into his blue eyes. "Do you remember her?"

He nodded. His hair was almost white, and at first glance the contrast with his tan made him look healthy, but close up he looked tired. *Haggard,* she thought. She asked him how long he'd owned the restaurant.

"Ten years. I worked for my dad until he sold his fishing cutter and retired back in 2008. I bought this place the year after, and I also run two pubs in the summer, in Gudhjem and Allinge."

No wonder he looked worn out, Camilla thought. "I know the police have already talked to you again. I've just come from Rønne. Wiinberg told me where I could find you. I went to the same school as Susan Dahlgaard, a few classes above her."

He was leaning back now, sizing her up, waiting. Despite his exhaustion, there was something guarded in his look. But her bringing up the old case didn't seem to bother him.

"Do you remember how you met the girls?" Camilla said.

He nodded and told her that he and the other boys had usually hung out down at the harbor. "Once in a while the guys earned a little helping my dad. I worked for him after school, and they lent a hand when they were needed. When we had money in our pockets, we spent it on cigarettes and beer, and if there were girls in town, sometimes we invited them to party. It was a lot more exciting with girls from off the island."

"And what do you remember from the night Susan disappeared?"

He leaned forward and scratched his temple, then reached into his shirt pocket for a pack of cigarettes.

"She was a live one," he said, after lighting a cigarette and pushing open the window behind him. "And good-looking. I had my eye on her when we met the girls that first day. She was different from the others. More mature. I remember her saying that her brother lived on Amager, that he was a musician and took drugs. I didn't believe her, at least at first. She said she grew up in an orphanage and she'd run away from foster families several times. It was like she made everything she said sound bigger than it was, like she was making herself out to be a star or something. And we lapped it up. She had a spark. She was more daring, had more spunk than the others. I liked that."

Camilla couldn't help noticing how engrossed he was in his story, as if the memories were still fresh. "But that night . . ."

He nodded and leaned all the way forward. Stuffed his cigarette butt down into the cola bottle and knit his fingers together, stared straight into Camilla's eyes. "That was a shitty night. We wrecked the car and they caught us with all kinds of stuff. We were a bunch of little hoodlums back then."

"But the girls, you met them down at the harbor. What do you remember about that?"

He stared down at the table for a moment, as if he'd suddenly blanked out, but then he nodded. "We met them, but we didn't really talk to them; they walked off, and we had other plans."

"You were planning a break-in," Camilla said.

He looked up and nodded. "Stretch had stolen a car in Nexø, and we had our eyes on this house in Aakirkeby; nobody was living there. We were going to empty the place out."

"What happened down at the harbor? Did you see the girls split up, or did they stay together?"

He avoided her eyes, but he slowly shook his head. "We left before they did. I remember seeing them standing in front of the convenience store with the bottle of booze they'd bought."

He looked up. "I wanted to stick around and hang out with them. I liked chasing girls back then, and I was sort of a lightweight; all the other shit we ran around doing wasn't really me. I went along with them mostly because I wanted to be part of the gang."

Liked chasing girls. She could imagine that. "So the four girls were together when you drove off?"

He nodded.

"Did you see the other girls again—Susan's friends, I mean? Before they left the island?"

There was a shout from the kitchen. "Skipper, that party's here. They're waiting in the restaurant."

He stood up and shook his head. "We never saw them again," he said, ending the conversation.

That suited Camilla fine. Her thoughts were darting off in every direction as she tried to put the pieces together. The more she learned, the harder it was for her to blame the teachers for supposing that Susan had disappeared on her own. Her need to dramatize everything, her difficult childhood—it made sense. And she could easily imagine the local boys falling for her.

She emptied her cola and set it on the table, then walked down the staircase. She smelled food; the three cooks who had been eating were in the kitchen now, getting ready for the evening crowd. It was almost six when Camilla walked back to the hotel.

"What, you ate with Markus?" she exclaimed. Her father had called. The waiter had just cleared her table, and she'd been checking the addresses of the two men she planned on seeing the next day when her phone rang.

Tonny Nielsen lived in an apartment down at the harbor in Svaneke and Daniel Axelsen's address was in Nexø. When she'd googled their names, two newspaper articles showed up about Daniel, the truck driver, but there was nothing on Tonny Nielsen. Wiinberg had said that he was on early retirement benefits and she should be able to find him easily enough.

"He called me this afternoon and said he had something to tell me," her father said. "So I drove into town."

Camilla thought for a moment. "I thought you were playing bridge this evening."

"No big deal to miss it once in a while. It was great to see Markus. The kid's got a lot of common sense. Can't believe how grown up he is."

Not grown up enough, Camilla thought. She was annoyed by how they'd met—behind her back, it felt like to her. And her son wasn't grown up enough to know that if he needed to have a man-to-man talk, it wasn't the smartest move to pick his grandfather, who had no idea what it meant to be there for someone else.

"You've raised a very responsible boy," he continued, his voice warm now. "You can be proud he's mature enough to live up to his responsibilities at such a young age. You two talked about that, I hear."

Camilla was momentarily speechless. Finally, she pulled herself together. "I explained to him that it wasn't going to work. He shouldn't be a father, not now. You're right, he's a good boy, he's responsible. But he's still a boy, seventeen years old. Think of everything he's going to miss out on."

"Yes, or everything he's going to gain. Having a kid is the greatest gift you can ask for in life."

"For chrissake, Dad!" she yelled. "You could at least try to be on my side. He doesn't know what he's doing, doesn't know what it means to have a baby. The responsibility. And how the hell could he know? He's still getting an allowance. He's going back to high school after summer vacation. His frontal lobes aren't fully developed, his thinking is spontaneous, he can't really see the consequences. He's not even old enough to drive. It's totally unrealistic to think he can understand what this will mean for his future, having a baby now."

"He's very happy with Julia. And she also seems to be a very nice girl."

"What, she was there, too?"

"Yeah, we all three went out to celebrate. These two young kids are so happy about it, and I felt we had a really good talk. Seems to me they know what they're getting into."

"I have to go," Camilla said, and she hung up before he could say anything more. Her cheeks were burning, but her fingers felt ice cold. Her little son. The one who only yesterday, or so it seemed, was always having to be driven to his break-dancing classes or to playdates with friends. Her skin crawled; she shook inside from anxiety. She felt an overwhelming loss of control, loss of her son's love. There was no one she felt closer to or loved more than her son, and right now he was slipping through her fingers. He was heading in a different direction and didn't need her to be the rock in his life anymore.

It took her a moment to notice the waiter standing by her table, asking if she was okay. Camilla blinked a few times and listlessly ordered a double whiskey.

It was misting outside when Camilla left the hotel the next morning and walked down Havnebryggen to Postgade, the street where Tonny Nielsen lived. There was no buzzer or speaker for apartment 12G, but the building's green door was open, so she stepped into the entryway and stood for a moment to get an idea of the kind of person who might be living there. Nielsen was on the ground floor. On the nameplate on his door, his first name was missing the *y*. He'd probably lived there quite a while, she thought. She pressed the doorbell and listened for footsteps behind the door. She'd waited until ten to make sure he was up. She rang the doorbell again; the shrill buzz pierced the morning silence in the stairway. She was about to hold her finger down on the button when the neighbor's door opened. A young woman holding a baby came out and nodded politely at Camilla.

"Do you happen to know if Tonny Nielsen is away from home, on vacation maybe?" Camilla asked.

The woman strapped her child into her baby sling. "I doubt that very much," she said in a melodic Bornholm accent. "Try down at the harbor; they're usually sitting on the bench out on the wharf or in front of the convenience store."

"They?"

"Him and the others." She edged her way past Camilla. "He was home last night, anyway; he pounded on the wall when Lykke started crying."

Three men sat at the end of the wharf with their backs to her, looking out over the Baltic Sea. Every town probably has a beer zone, she thought. In Svaneke it was at the harbor, with a much better view than the one in the small downtown square in Osted.

For a second Camilla wondered if she should grab some beer for Tonny, but she decided instead to invite him over to the hotel's outdoor terrace. She would need to lure him away from the others to get anything out of him.

She walked up beside them. "Tonny?"

The three men turned to her, but only one of them nodded. He was perched on a mobility scooter to the right of the bench. His longish dark hair was sharply parted on the side to cover his bald spot on top—or at least to try to; it was obvious to anyone behind him.

"Who's asking?" he snapped, as if it were a scene in a Western. He clearly enjoyed the attention.

Even though the summer drizzle hung in the air, the harbor was lively. Sailors were working on their boats or stocking up on provisions; others were just lounging for the vacationers on the wharf to watch.

"I'm Camilla Lind, I'm a reporter at *Morgenavisen*. I'd appreciate it if we could talk."

Tonny's face was blank as he looked her over and slowly drained his beer. He stuck the empty bottle in his scooter's front basket.

"It shouldn't take long," she added, unnecessarily as it turned out, for he was already zipping up his red Adidas sweatshirt. He nodded shortly at his pals and signaled to her that he was ready when she was.

Camilla suggested they sit up on the hotel's terrace, but he preferred a café farther up Havnebryggen and to the right. She realized he might not want people to see him talking to her.

"Fine. It's up to you."

"I figured you people would show up, now that they've found her." They sat across from each other; a woman in her sixties had served them coffee in white cups, and without asking she'd set a plate of freshly buttered bread between them. Most likely meant for Tonny.

"Had a little chat with Skipper yesterday," he said, "about how they were going to put us through the mill again, never mind it was years ago, and none of us knew her."

"I'm not here to put you through any mill," Camilla hurried to say.

"Once you're in the system, you're marked for life."

Camilla let that pass.

"Just look at Stretch, he sure as hell didn't make it. He didn't do nothing, and people still figured he was mixed up in that business with the girl, just because he was the one who ended up in jail. But that was for something else. People forget. He was our buddy, and we tried to help him, but nobody listened to us. Like I say, you're marked."

"I just want to talk to you about that night you met the girls down at the harbor."

He snorted. "Met! We didn't meet them; they came running after us. We didn't ask them to come. They were all wild about Skipper."

There was no mistaking the bitterness in his voice, as if he still felt rejected.

"Do you remember Susan Dahlgaard?"

"Oh yeah, oh yeah. I remember her stripping and jumping in the water." His smile bordered on a leer.

He smelled of days-old booze, and his sweatshirt was stained. But she studied his face, noticed the long lines, the handsome features. He'd been good-looking before all the drinking.

"Were you and the other boys in the same class?" she asked, to help get him started.

"Stretch wasn't in school. I was in the same class as Daniel. Skipper was the same grade, different class."

"And Stretch—that's Thomas Krogh, right?"

"*Was*. He's dead." He bit his lower lip without looking at her.

"How did he die?"

"Threw himself off the Helligdomsklipperne, into the water. They say he had a hashish psychosis. I don't know if he thought he could fly, or if he was just sick and tired of people suspecting him all the time. Everybody figured she was in the car with him."

There was nothing sentimental about this man. Things were what they were, no more, no less.

"Happened a few years after he got out. He met this woman inside; they were living somewhere outside Copenhagen. When that fell apart, he moved back here."

Camilla checked her phone to see if it was recording. She hadn't asked permission, and he looked like the type who might get angry if she told him. He knew she was there to get a story, though.

"I didn't see him much after he came back. Prison changed him. I never much liked him, anyway, but he was the one who got the money and knew how to get more. His mom is my mom's cousin; we knew each other from way back."

He sat silently for a moment. "He was a little older than us, but I think he looked up to Skipper. His dad was rich; they lived over in this big house."

He pointed somewhere behind Camilla.

"Stretch wanted to be like him. It was fun and games when the classes showed up on their field trips. We almost always got to know some of them, and we kept our eyes peeled for any good-looking ones."

He looked a bit surprised when he smiled, as if he'd forgotten there were also some good times back when he was young.

"Of course," Camilla said.

The aproned woman walked over and grabbed their cups, then

filled them up behind the counter. Camilla couldn't help but notice her tipping up a bottle of aquavit several times. After the woman returned with their coffee, Camilla took a sip. Not that she was surprised, but hers wasn't the one that had been spiked.

"And that night?" she said.

"We had a job to do, but we said we'd drive out to the house afterward."

"The house?"

"Yeah, we hung out in that house out there."

Again, he pointed vaguely at a spot behind Camilla, and she realized it was just a gesture. Somewhere out there.

"Nobody lived there, hadn't for a long time," he said.

"Were the girls supposed to ride out there and wait for you?" Camilla eagerly leaned over the table, suddenly spotting a possible connection.

He slumped a bit and stared out the window for several moments, then turned back to her. "We didn't get that far. I broke two-thirds of the bones in my body, and the others wound up in jail."

She persisted. "But you and the girls agreed to meet at the abandoned house?"

That annoyed him. "We didn't agree to do shit. We said we didn't have time to play, we had other plans. We were on our way to hit a place and then take everything out to the old house. That's all we told them."

"What about Susan? Did you see her and her friends split up, or did they all leave the harbor together on their bikes?"

He stared at the table and shook his head. "I don't know. I was over siphoning gas for my moped, and when I got back, the girls were gone. I don't know if they were together or not. That's what I told the police, too."

He paused for a moment. "I wish to hell we'd been with them that night, so all that shit never would have happened. A lot of things would have been different."

They sat in silence. He was right, Camilla thought. His body wouldn't have been ruined in the car accident, and Susan might not have disappeared.

"But you're sure you told the girls you were going out to the abandoned house later that night, after the break-in?"

He nodded. She felt sorry for him. It wasn't hard to imagine how he'd clawed his way through his teenage years by hanging out with the guys who had money. By stealing gas from other mopeds for his own. Break-ins, stolen goods. She guessed he was the poorest one in the gang, the one who picked up the crumbs that fell. And the one who had been crippled by the accident. It could hardly be sadder.

He was about to say something else, but then he stopped and shook his head. He'd drunk his coffee and now he kept his eye on the door to the kitchen.

"Refill," he said when the woman came over.

"None for me, thanks," Camilla said.

"Do you think the girls might have gone out there to wait for you?" she said after the woman left. "And then left when you didn't show up?"

He shrugged. "I was in the hospital for over a month. I had plenty of other stuff to think about. My folks had enough problems, they just wanted it all to go away. And I didn't talk much to the other guys. They stopped by a few times, but they all had plenty going on, too. The cops said we were lying about Susan, but we didn't know anything, that's the truth. And I don't know nothing now, either."

Camilla walked over to the bar and paid their bill. She handed the heavyset woman five hundred crowns extra and asked her to set them aside for the next time Tonny dropped by.

The woman took the money and nodded to Camilla. "Now I can let him put a little on his tab again." She slammed the cash register shut.

Camilla ended up spending several hours waiting for Daniel Axelsen. Their noon appointment got delayed until one o'clock, then two o'clock. Each time he apologized profusely and promised to be there as soon as he could.

She'd thought about driving out to Echo Valley and using the map Wiinberg had given her to find the cave, but instead she decided to stick around the neighborhood. She didn't want to be floundering around looking for a cave out in Almindingen when Daniel called and said he was ready to meet her. After seeing what there was to see in Nexø, she camped out at a café and read up on the area where Susan had disappeared, including Echo Valley:

> Bornholm's largest rift valley can be followed all the way to the coast, southwest of Gudhjem. Flanking the valley is an oak forest (mostly Cornish oak), a national preserve with hornbeam and linden, and a meadow where in the spring the lily-of-the-valley blossoms are exceptional. Hikers can head down into the valley at Jægergrotten, the most beautiful section of the meadow, or up onto the cliffs as far as Fuglesangsrenden, which was formerly known as Styrtebakkerne, The Diving Hills. Some believe the name comes from the human sacrifices performed here, where people were cast off the cliff.

At just before two-thirty, Daniel Axelsen called and said he was back. Camilla had ordered nachos and a large cola to pass the time, and now she could feel the sugary beverage coating her teeth.

He lived in an angular yellow house on a residential street. His semi was parked on a large asphalt slab along one side of the house.

A swing and a colorful climbing wall stood in the front yard. Camilla parked in the drive, and as she started up the sidewalk, the front door opened and revealed a large, stocky man with a barking dog in his arms.

Axelsen was everything his friend Tonny Nielsen wasn't: healthy, happy, successful. His life hadn't slipped away from him, and there was no bitterness in the eyes that met Camilla's. He shifted the white terrier over to one arm, then shook her hand and greeted her warmly.

"Come inside. My wife and kids will be back later; they drove down to the harbor for ice cream so we could talk in private."

"That's great!" Camilla said. "It won't take long. I really appreciate you taking the time to talk to me. I'm sure you know I'm writing a feature about Susan Dahlgaard. I spoke with one of the teachers who was along on the class field trip, and I also stopped by the Svaneke Hostel. I stayed there myself when I came over with my class a few years before Susan disappeared. I'm also trying to get in touch with Susan's friends from back then. The ones you met in 1995."

She didn't mention Pia's death and Trine's disappearance.

They sat in the living room, which had large plate-glass windows with a view of the backyard. A small wooden gazebo stood between the well-kept beds of perennials.

"And I spoke with Tonny Nielsen earlier today; he told me what he remembered from that evening."

She also didn't mention Tonny saying he was off stealing gas when they split up from the girls. She wanted to hear Axelsen's version of the story.

He nodded seriously and folded his hands. After sniffing up and down Camilla's bare leg, the little dog had curled up in a basket by the window.

Unlike with Tonny, Camilla made sure it was okay with Axelsen if she recorded their conversation before she set her phone down.

"How did you meet Susan and her friends?" Camilla said.

She knew both men were around forty, but Axelsen looked at least five years younger than Tonny Nielsen. His full cheeks were rosy, he was tanned, and he seemed energetic as he leaned forward.

"We used to hang out in front of the convenience store at the harbor. When the students on field trips showed up, it was the natural place to meet."

"Did you boys usually try to get to know the kids when they came to town?"

"That depended on who it was, of course," he said without having to think about it. "Some schools send sixth-grade classes over; we weren't interested in them. But seventh- or eighth-grade classes, we always looked them over pretty good."

"And you remember Susan's class? You met four girls the first day."

He thought for a moment. "That sounds about right; there were four or five of them. We rode out to Hullehavn that first night."

"Hullehavn?"

"The little beach on the other side of the hostel, on the Nexø side; it's a good spot to swim. We made a bonfire. The next night we waited for them up at the school, until one of them ran up and said the others couldn't make it because they got caught the night before."

"Do you remember which one of the girls it was?"

He looked as if he was trying to remember her name, but he couldn't come up with it.

"But it wasn't Susan?"

He shook his head. "No, it was one of the others. A nice girl, I was sort of interested in her. We made plans for the next night; she and the other girls would try to sneak out, and we'd meet down at the harbor. And if they didn't show up at a certain time, we'd know they'd been caught again."

Even though she was recording, Camilla jotted down a few notes so she would remember what to return to when he was finished.

"So Stretch showed up with the car the next night, and the party started."

Camilla looked at him in surprise. "Party?"

"Yeah, the car meant we could drive out and buy from the back door." He explained about a small grocery where you could wake up the owner and buy cheap beer at night.

"I understood from Tonny that you met the girls at the harbor before leaving." She watched him closely.

He nodded. "The plan was for them to ride out to the house and we'd pick up the beer on the way."

"We are talking about the abandoned house out by Echo Valley, right?"

He nodded again. "We told them they could borrow our mopeds, but they wanted to bike. I doubt they'd ever ridden a moped alone before."

Camilla tried to picture them.

"But then Stretch wanted to break into that house on the way, and he's the one who had the car, he was in charge. And yeah, we never made it out there."

"So does that mean you saw the four girls leaving on their bikes?"

He thought for a moment. "Susan wasn't with us, definitely not, if that's what you're getting at. The police searched the car, too, and they could see she hadn't been in it."

"No, no, I'm just asking if you saw Susan biking off with the other girls when you split up."

He nodded. "We all took off at the same time. They biked; we drove out of town in the car."

"So they didn't leave Susan behind?"

He was getting annoyed with her; she could see that. Or he might have thought she was trying to trick him into saying something she could use against him.

"I'm only asking because the story up to now has been that the three girls split up with Susan at the harbor," she said. "And now it sounds like all four of them were going out to meet you at the house."

He stared a few moments at his folded hands. "I think some people here on the island still think we did something to her. Especially now that they've found her. Nobody comes out and says it, and the police did say publicly she hadn't been in the car, but I can feel people's eyes on me. I don't want to say anything here to get people riled up again. But I really do hope they find out what happened to her. Mostly because it might mean people will finally believe we're innocent."

Camilla nodded; she could see his point.

"Skipper and I stood down at the convenience store and gave them directions to the house. Stretch was in the car, in the parking lot behind the hotel; he wanted to get going. Tonny was with him when we got there. The four girls took off on two bikes, but I can't say whether or not they split up after we left for the car. I didn't see it happen."

She tried to visualize the situation again. "Did Susan ask if she could come with you instead of biking?"

Quickly he shook his head. "There wasn't enough room for her, or anybody, for that matter."

Camilla sensed that the interview was over, and she stood up. "I'm not out to rile things up again," she said, as a sort of apology for her pointed questions. "I just want to find out what happened to Susan. How she ended up in that cave."

Which was very close to where you boys hung out, she thought. She followed him out to the hallway, where they said their goodbyes.

· · ·

A tourist bus and a row of cars were parked in the gravel parking lot in front of the candy store, toilets, and Echo Valley House, which had the reputation for serving the best and biggest tartlets in the country. On the way, Camilla had stopped by the abandoned house— or rather, where it had been; nothing was left of it now. A gravel road led from there to the parking lot. She stood looking in the direction of the place Wiinberg had marked as where Susan's body had been found.

Slowly she walked into the forest, a steep cliff in front of her. For a moment she paused to take it all in, trying to imagine what it had been like for the young girl, out there alone in the middle of the night, with cliffs all around her. In the wild storm and rain.

A cool breeze was blowing, but though it was late afternoon, the sun was still warm enough for her to leave her jacket in the car. Camilla followed the trail Susan must have taken twenty-five years ago.

She stared up at the jagged cliff visible between the trees. Several fallen trees with long, thick roots hung off the steep slope. With the map in one hand, she headed for a small bridge spanning the picturesque stream trickling down the ravine.

On the other side of the bridge, she stopped before clambering up out of the forest floor and onto the cliff; the lush green beech forest stood in stark contrast to the rugged, moss-clad rocks. Trees with exposed, wildly tangled roots hung threateningly over her head. The craggy rocks on the slope provided a bit of footing to help her climb. She reached a small forested plateau and leaned up against a tree for a moment, then she turned the map around to see if she needed to climb farther to find Susan's cave. A well-beaten path led through the dead leaves, but it looked like she should stay close to the cliff.

The X on Wiinberg's map wasn't far from the path. It looked like a place where someone who needed to pee and wanted a bit of shelter would go. It was hard to see anything other than boulders and outcroppings jutting out of the forest floor, but she was determined to push on. Suddenly she stopped. Another fallen tree lay like a stranded whale in the summer-green growth. The hollow, dark yellowish tree was old, the bark long gone. Camilla brought out her phone and began taking pictures of the cliff and the tree that twenty-five years ago had trapped Susan, though today it didn't look at all imposing.

The opening in the cliff wasn't much more than a small fissure, a cleft in the rock. Camilla had imagined a broad, half-round cave mouth. She walked over and peeked inside at the narrow floor. The walls were rough, with sharp edges that made it impossible to move around. There was just enough space for a young girl to lie down.

Wild horses couldn't drag Camilla into that minuscule dark cave. Not even with death on her heels. She didn't dare imagine how claustrophobic it would feel, being trapped inside. A stone coffin.

Camilla sat in her car in the parking lot, staring out over the green treetops. She couldn't shake the stony cold that had crawled under her skin, along with an emotion she didn't care for one bit: fear.

Susan must have been frightened out of her wits. Terrified, anxious, fleeing from something, she thought. Otherwise, crawling into the crevice in the cliff made no sense. Or else someone had forced her into the tiny cave. Camilla's thoughts milled around, yet when she tried to picture what had taken place, nothing made sense.

Wiinberg called. "I just met with the chief; we're reopening the case."

"Good. Maybe it came out back then, but it sounds like the boys had planned to meet the girls out at the abandoned house, before they split up at the harbor. And there are obvious discrepancies in their explanations of what happened."

"Where are you going with this?" He added that they would check the witness statements thoroughly. "But they didn't say they'd planned on meeting later."

"If they'd agreed to meet out there, that could be why Susan was in Echo Valley. The abandoned house is right by where she was found. Like I said, the boys' stories differ a bit, but two of them told me that was the plan."

After a few moments of silence, Wiinberg cleared his throat. "I'll call when I've compared the witness statements."

TWENTY

"Trine, Pia, and Nina are lying. Talk to Mona Ibsen." Camilla's text woke Louise up just before eight. She'd conked out at nine-thirty the evening before, in the wake of a Thai sleeping pill and an irrepressible urge to sleep for a hundred years. The dinner with her parents and Mikkel's mother-in-law had been a catastrophe. As she'd expected, her mother had put up a chilly front and hardly said a word all evening, though her father had handled the situation a bit better. Luckily Kirstine and Malte had gotten them through the dinner, which ended when Louise offered to drive Liselotte back to Dåstrup after they'd eaten.

But something good had come out of it, she thought as she lay in bed, trying to drift back to sleep. Every fiber of her being struggled against getting up and facing a new day. The previous evening had made her wonder if a person's emotional state could cause a physical collapse. Her body felt numb, as if all her nerves had been clipped, and she was exhausted, unable to concentrate.

After taking Liselotte home, she'd bought some comics and driven over to visit Mikkel. She waited for over an hour before a doctor came out and said he was asleep and might not wake up before the next morning.

"You're welcome to sit with him," the doctor said.

Mikkel was in a small room behind a locked frosted-glass door. The narrow room had a small stool beside the bed, which had no sheet or duvet, only a small pillow and a cotton blanket. He lay fast asleep on his back, in a white hospital gown, and he didn't react when she spoke and touched his hand.

She cried. He wasn't sleeping naturally; he'd been given medication and was far, far away. After she'd sat for forty-five minutes, a nurse came in to check him.

"He's not going to wake up tonight," he said. "Come back tomorrow. You can call in advance—we don't have regular visiting hours, so you're welcome anytime."

"I'll be back tomorrow," she said. She'd left the comics beside Mikkel's bed.

The worst part was the uncertainty. The lack of access to the police files. The silence. And the thought of what she herself would have put her brother through if she were one of the officers investigating his possible guilt in Trine's disappearance.

She still hadn't called Mik in Holbæk to ask if he'd find out what the Roskilde Police had on her brother. But it had eased Louise's mind a bit when Liselotte repeated that there was nothing specific behind her suspicion of Mikkel. And during the dinner at Louise's parents' house, Liselotte had promised to tell that to the police. In a state of suppressed rage, Louise's mother had squeezed the promise out of Liselotte while Louise and her father stared down at the table.

Louise read Camilla's text again before answering. "What are they lying about?" She wriggled around and managed to push a few pillows underneath her neck.

"They say they split up with Susan down at the harbor. But lo and behold, it turns out they agreed to meet the girls at a house near where Susan was found. The girls said they were back at the hostel just after midnight, but I don't think that's true. Find Mona Ibsen; she did see them coming back."

The class picture Mona had left out in the bushes lay on the bed table. Susan, Trine, Pia, Nina, and Mona. Louise studied the young faces. *Kids,* she thought. And yet there was something in their eyes. Something challenging, not in any sexual way, but more like "look at me." A streak of mischievousness and impudence. Except for Mona. She stared straight into the camera, expressionless, making no attempt to look happy.

An old familiar feeling suddenly hit Louise, making her hop out of bed. An instinct. Susan, Trine, Pia, Nina, and Mona. Two of them dead, and one of them gone without a trace. She thought of Mona's face outside of the window. That morning she'd been too shocked to read her expression, too surprised, confused, still too affected by the Thai sleeping pill to react quickly enough. But she had to find out more about the group of friends.

She smelled coffee as she stepped into the psychiatric hospital's reception. While she was approaching the counter, a shrill scream ripped through the silence.

"No, no, no!" The woman sounded desperate, and immediately several personnel ran past Louise and down the corridor toward a closed glass door. An alarm beeped, and several more people appeared. Shortly after, the yelling faded away and the alarm was shut off.

After the screaming stopped, two women and a man returned to the reception area. When they noticed Louise, one of the women walked over to the glassed-in cubicle. Seemingly unaffected by the situation they'd just dealt with, she smiled and said good morning.

Louise introduced herself as the sister of Mikkel Rick. She apologized for showing up so early, just after breakfast. But the nurse smiled and said she wouldn't be bothering anyone by visiting her brother.

"The dayroom is crowded now, but if you don't mind staying in his room, I'll tell him he has a visitor."

Louise followed her down the hallway toward the glass door. Six or seven people sat in the dayroom, where there was a TV and a shelf with board games and books. She stopped for a moment at a message board. "To the personnel" stood in crooked letters, and someone had drawn a colored square with a nice "Thanks to all of you" inside.

The nurse knocked on the door of room 3 and called Mikkel's name.

"Yeah." Louise felt both heartened and uneasy at the sound of her brother's voice.

The nurse opened the door and told him his sister was there. "Can she come in?"

"Sure, yeah." The tone of her brother's familiar voice sounded different, deeper and a bit slurry. He'd been in a deep, deep sleep the night before; she knew they were starting him on drugs and realized he might not be himself, that it took time before the doctors found the correct dosage. But his drugged state shielded him from a world that was severely difficult for him. That included her.

He was sitting up in bed with his back against the wall and his legs crossed. A comic book lay on his lap, and he was holding a bowl of corn flakes. It took him an extra moment to react, but then he smiled. Louise stepped into the room.

Mikkel was standing before Louise even reached the bed. He spread his arms, and they stood holding each other for several moments. He was still in there, and his expression was alert and aware, even though he moved a bit clumsily and sounded sluggish.

He pointed at the comic books. "Thanks."

She pulled the stool over and sat down. "How did the questioning with the police go?" She skipped the part about asking how he was. It was up to him if he wanted to talk about that.

Mikkel sat back on the bed, laid the bowl of cornflakes on the floor, and leaned back. "I answered the best I could. It's like they think I came home earlier than I did. But Dennis up in Storage confirmed that I didn't leave work during the day. I called Trine when I left Roskilde. The call went through the Bluetooth in the car, it's in their system. But they still kept after me. They didn't tell me what Dennis told them until right before they drove me back. My whole time there they let me think nobody at work said I was there all day. That was the worst part. Because I knew I hadn't left. And I knew the others had to know I was there. But then at one point I wasn't sure about it."

He shook his head, and Louise nodded. She would have done the same in a similar questioning, but now it angered her. They'd put the screws to him, which was standard procedure. Seen from the other side, though, it seemed cruel.

"What else did they have?" she said.

He pulled his legs up underneath him. "They asked when was the last time we had sex." He raised his eyebrows and shook his head. "What kind of sex we have, if we get rough."

Louise nodded. "It makes sense that they ask about that."

"About our sex life! They should be fucking concentrating on finding the mother of my kids."

She couldn't help but smile, and quickly she agreed with him. "Sex games can be rough, and they can get out of hand. And it wouldn't be the first time a husband or wife tried to hide such a thing."

He stared at her, a bit wavery and out of focus, but she could still see the amazement in his eyes. "You mean, like maybe I tied her up and fucked her to death, or what?" He kept staring at her with that fuzzy look as she nodded.

"Or put a mask on her. Hindered her breathing. The type of eroticism that uses oxygen deprivation up to the moment of climax. It intensifies an orgasm; I've heard it's really popular. It's not surprising they ask you about those things. That's what I mean."

"But how? So the moment I get home, I meet Trine at the clinic and have some sort of bizarre sex with her and then leave her there and go up to the kids and ask them about their mother? Are the police stupid or what?"

"If only you knew what some people do at home." She leaned forward. "Do you know Pia and Nina, the girls Trine went to grade school with?"

Her brother had picked up the bowl of cereal from the floor and begun to eat, as if all this talk about sex had made him hungry. He chewed for a while before nodding slowly.

"Once in a while she ran into an old grade-school classmate when we were out shopping or up in Roskilde. But I don't think she actually got together with any of them; she wasn't friends with any of the girls, nothing like that. She's never talked much about school. And I never asked much about it, either."

Louise leaned closer to him. "Could she have been in contact with any of them recently? Did you two happen to run into anyone in the week or so before she disappeared?"

He stared into space. "I don't think so. There's Carsten Iversen from her class. He hangs out down in front of the grocery, but she only says hi when we walk by. They don't talk. Or if she has, I wasn't around. Sometimes she shops before I get home, though. And you do run into people."

Someone knocked on the door, and they both turned. The nurse who'd led her in said that the doctor was ready to talk to Mikkel. She sent Louise an apologetic look.

"That's fine," Louise said. "Thank you so much for letting me interrupt his breakfast."

She leaned forward and kissed her brother on the cheek. She noticed a change, as if he'd retreated into himself the same way as he had at the hospital, turned his back on everything. For a moment she'd been so absorbed in her own thoughts of motives and possibilities that she'd forgotten he was still grieving. She laid her hands on his shoulders.

"We are going to find her," she whispered.

"But they still think I'm the one who did it."

"I don't think so. But you need to try to remember if Trine mentioned anything recently. I have the feeling she's carried a secret around for years, and now it's coming out. It's important you tell me if you remember someone she's been in contact with."

He nodded. On the way out she stopped in the doorway and looked back at him. He was a prisoner of his own sorrow, which was on his mind much more than going over Trine's comings and goings in the time leading up to her disappearance. It was amazing how little people noticed in their everyday lives. Telephone conversations, running into people—they all faded and disappeared.

Louise stood out in the hallway and gathered her thoughts before calling Nymand and asking to see the list of calls from Trine's phone.

"Incoming and outgoing calls," she said.

She was told that the list hadn't shown up yet.

"I just need a copy of the list. Or a screenshot of the calls she made in the days leading up to her disappearance."

She'd been prepared for him to blow up and refuse to release anything. But he promised to send it, and he even asked her to stop by the station sometime that day.

They don't have shit on Mikkel, she thought. She took satisfaction in realizing that; it was almost a physical feeling, being a step ahead of them.

After Louise closed the frosted-glass door behind her and heard the lock click, she walked down to the office and asked a nurse if it was okay to visit Mona Ibsen.

"Yes," the nurse said, somewhat surprised at the question. "She'd like that. It's seldom she gets visitors other than Gerd. Just a moment."

She ducked into the office for a few minutes. When she returned, she asked Louise to follow her down the hallway in the opposite direction from Mikkel's room. She stopped and knocked on a door, and after waiting a moment, she knocked again.

"Go on in and sit down, I'll find her for you."

Louise opened the door to a room the same size as Mikkel's. She stopped in the doorway; on every surface—on the bed, floor, windowsill, nightstand, walls—lay and hung clippings of newspaper articles and colorful, glittery pages from weeklies. All concerning Susan.

The nurse glanced at her before holding out her hand to indicate all the clippings. "She's enormously interested in this case," she said with a hint of apology. "She always gets very involved in missing person cases, she has folders full of old articles, but as I'm sure you know, she was in the same class as Susan Dahlgaard. She's followed that case with particular interest, I think you could say." She smiled hesitantly.

Louise nodded and said she knew that Mona reacted strongly when people disappeared. She recognized some of the old articles, interviews with classmates and with Susan's foster parents. Many of them had been written just after the girl's disappearance, back when the papers were full of reports about the intensive search. Louise also spotted smaller notices and follow-ups on the case. Statements from various people, photos. A journalist from one of the weeklies had been on Bornholm and had interviewed people from the Svaneke Hostel, the woman selling ice cream at Hammershus the day Susan's class was there, and other Bornholmers who cared to talk about the case. There were several photos of the police from press conferences. Many of the clippings were crumpled and dog-eared, with creased pieces of tape at the top, as if they'd been taken down and hung up again many times.

The most recent clippings lay on the bed. Susan's school photo. The newspapers' grainy aerial photo of the Almindingen forest, in which Echo Valley was marked. Camilla's stories were there, too. Louise stood lost in thought, studying the extensive collection. She started at a noise behind her, and when she whirled around, Mona was standing stock-still in the doorway. They stared at each other for a moment, then Mona turned on her heel in fright and fled back down the hallway. Louise hadn't had time to say a word.

Louise wished she'd been more awake and alert the morning Mona had shown up outside Mikkel and Trine's house. Maybe Mona had wanted to talk to her then, but obviously she didn't now. She looked terror-stricken.

TWENTY-ONE

Louise left the hospital and drove directly to Svogerslev. In the car she called Gerd to tell her she was on the way. Maybe she should have asked if it was a convenient time. Or if she could pick something up for them to snack on with coffee. But when the hospital's glass doors closed behind her, she was in no mood for pastry or verbal niceties. She was shaken that Gerd hadn't told her about Mona's condition. That she hadn't mentioned this bizarre and disturbing obsession with Susan's case when they'd met on Mona's birthday.

The cluster of houses lay behind low, well-trimmed hedges in a residential area of the small suburb of Roskilde. Louise was barely out of her car before Gerd came rushing out of the house.

"Has something happened to Mona? When I got your message, I tried to contact her, but I was told she couldn't come to the phone. Has she been hurt?"

Gerd was out of breath when she reached Louise.

The woman seemed deeply concerned, and Louise shook her head. The first time she met Gerd and Mona, she'd had the impression that out of the goodness of her heart, the retired school psychologist was acting as a type of guardian, even though Mona was an adult. But over the years, maybe she'd become more of a daughter to Gerd, who'd once told Louise she couldn't have children.

"Maybe you're not here because of Mona?" Gerd sounded hopeful. She rushed to move a wheelbarrow off the sidewalk so Louise could get by. "Is there something else you need to talk to me about?"

"Nothing's happened to Mona," Louise said. She reminded herself that Gerd thought of her as a police officer; no wonder the woman had feared the worst when Louise called and said she was coming without explaining why.

"We need to talk about her, though," Louise said, after they'd walked into the house.

Gerd was pale. She'd always struck Louise as a calm, loyal, and steadfast supporter for Mona, her rock, but now she seemed nervous, unsure of herself.

"She's not well," Gerd said. "Her mind is tormented, and she can't handle so much at one time. That's why I'm trying to take care of her. Mona is a very sensitive woman; she has a terrible time dealing with anxiety and fear."

"I'd like to talk to you about what happened to her on Bornholm, back when Susan Dahlgaard disappeared," Louise said in a neutral tone of voice.

Gerd nodded; she understood.

"I think you'll agree that Mona seems abnormally obsessed with Susan's case," Louise continued. "And as I understand it, she started seeing a psychiatrist right after coming home from Bornholm. Has anyone spoken to her about her involvement in what happened back then?"

They walked into Gerd's living room. Several of Mona's framed insects stood on one of the shelves along the wall. The last time Louise had visited Mona, it had seemed bizarre and brutal to watch how intently she focused on sticking the needles through the dried insects. It was just a hobby, Gerd had explained.

"She felt horrible back when her classmate disappeared," the woman said. "Mostly because she feels she could have prevented it."

"How could she have done that?" Louise sat down in the chair Gerd pulled out for her.

"All these years she's blamed herself for not making the people in charge listen to her. Did you know she didn't even want to go on the field trip? Before they left, she told her parents she wanted to stay home. I believe in the omens she saw. She knew something tragic was going to happen." Gerd looked solemn.

Louise felt there wasn't time for that sort of nonsense, but she held herself back. "My sister-in-law was on that field trip, too," she said. "Trine was in Mona's class."

Gerd nodded absently.

"She's disappeared. At first we thought she'd abandoned her family, but I'm beginning to think it's somehow connected to Susan's body being found. I wanted to talk to Mona about what happened back then, but she ran away when I stopped by at the hospital. She doesn't want to talk to me."

"We have to take care of Mona," Gerd said, as if she hadn't heard Louise. "What happened on Bornholm damaged her irreparably. It distorted her relationships with others, destroyed her trust. You can blame her parents for that, of course, but also her teachers, for not listening to her."

"Is Mona dangerous?" Louise asked.

"Good God, no! What in the world makes you say that? She wouldn't hurt a fly."

Louise glanced over at the bookshelf, at the framed insects.

Gerd followed her eyes and smiled wryly. "All right then, she wouldn't hurt a cat."

"What is it about Mona and these insects, what's that all about?"

"She started collecting them after the class field trip. First it was only a few she caught and dried. She'd sit with them for hours, smoothing out their wings, adjusting their legs, folding the pages of a notebook before placing them inside to be pressed and dried."

"So her hobby started after the field trip?" Louise asked.

"Yes, but it might be more accurate to say that her hobby began as a phobia. Mona developed an anxiety about insects after the field trip, and it's grown stronger since then. But even though she's very sensitive, she's also strong, she's managed to control her fear and turn it into an interest. She's handled it incredibly well. It's something we talked a lot about in the difficult time after the Bornholm trip."

Gerd leaned in close to Louise and spoke very quietly. "When Mona got back, she suffered from horrendous nightmares. She dreamed that Susan lay in a dark place, buried in insects slowly eating her body. And when she started collecting insects, I interpreted it as her way of coming to grips with the nightmares. Embracing her anxiety and owning it. Can you imagine how horrible it must be, watching a classmate being eaten by thousands of tiny crawling animals? Can you imagine the images in your mind's eye?"

Gerd was shaking her head.

"But why?" Louise was gripped by the ominous, bleak mood the woman had created.

"Imagine what it does to a person, living an entire life knowing you tried to do something, but you couldn't make people listen. That you tried to warn the adults, that maybe you could have prevented a tragedy if someone had believed you."

"But nobody could have known," Louise said. "No one knew that Susan's body was lying there in the forest. They thought she'd run away when she split up with the girls that night."

"Mona knew." Gerd sounded absolutely convinced.

Louise was losing patience. "How can you be so sure? Did she see what happened?"

Gerd shook her head somberly. "She wasn't with them when Susan disappeared. But she knew the other girls lied about what happened, she saw them when they came back without Susan. And she told her teachers, but they believed the other girls instead of her. Those girls are part of the reason Mona is in the shape she's in today. And we're still dealing with the unfortunate consequences of being shut out, of not being believed. Mona was a happy girl before this terrible episode. She played handball; she was talented and could have gone far with it. Several weeks before it happened, her team won the Sealand championships. But she stopped playing after Bornholm. She lost interest, gave it up, even though we tried to talk her into playing it again. She dropped her friends and turned inward. Mona became an entirely different girl."

Gerd looked bitter.

"But what about her parents? If she really was doing so badly, why didn't they put her in a different school? Her parents must have heard her."

"They don't believe in that sort of thing," Gerd said. "Not even the police took what she told them seriously. People like Mona are sensitive in a different way than most of us. They sense things, have premonitions. She has abilities that are hard to understand if you don't share them, or if you're not open to them."

Gerd's hands were folded on the table, as if in prayer.

"Okay, but what exactly was Mona trying to say back then?"

"That Susan's friends were lying. Susan and the other girls were running around the night before she disappeared, too, without getting caught. Mona saw them leave and come back drunk, but they got away with it. Their teachers were a lot more interested in each other than in keeping an eye on the students, making sure they stayed in their rooms—the girls had been warned already when they got caught the first time. After Susan's disappearance, Mona told the police what she'd seen the evening before, but the girls denied it. And they stuck to their story."

Louise finished up by asking if there was any reason to believe Mona was involved in what had happened to Pia Bagger and Trine. If she might have snapped when Susan's body was found.

Gerd looked sick at heart as she slowly shook her head. "Mona's the victim here," she said, her voice soft now. "We need to do everything we can to take care of her. And protect her."

As they said their goodbyes at the door, Gerd laid her hand on Louise's arm. "One day the truth will come out. And it'll be very good for Mona."

TWENTY-TWO

BORNHOLM, 1995

Mona kept her word. She didn't tell the teachers she'd seen Trine sneak out the window to tell the boys the others weren't coming after all. After Lena slept in the girls' room for one night to keep an eye on them, she went back to her own room.

All along Susan had said that Lena and Steffen were screwing, and now she was sure that was why Lena had moved back to her own room after only one night. Trine had been watching them, and she thought Susan might be right.

Everyone was tired and even Carsten was quiet after a wild day of running around at a Bornholm amusement park, Brændesgårdshaven. They'd gone on the rope slide, paddled the rowboats. Mona, though, had kept to herself most of the day. Several others in the class had given the girls a hard time about sneaking out at night. They were glad the girls had been caught, but they were mad, too; the teachers were pissed off about the girls breaking the rules, and the whole class was paying for it. But the girls agreed with Pia when she said the others were just jealous, that they wished they'd snuck out, too.

After dinner, not much was said around the tables as they wrote in their diaries. Someone had left their denim jacket on the bus, someone else had forgotten their bag. Trine didn't really listen. She was resting, because now that Lena would be sleeping in her own room, they were planning another night of adventure.

The night before, when Trine had talked to the boys, they had told her they could communicate with each other by hanging notes on the advertisement pillar down at the harbor. When the class got back from the amusement park, Pia had biked down with a message: "11:30—Private School."

They'd drawn several hearts and a barely recognizable moped. But when Pia got to the harbor, among the private ads from people wanting to sell lawn mowers or give away kittens, there was a message already waiting for the girls: "Meetup: Sports Arena. 11:30. Bring the booze."

They all contributed, and because Susan looked older than the others, she borrowed a bike and bought the bottle of rum, plus a pack of cigarettes. They hid everything underneath a mattress.

Trine had told the others about Mona sitting out by the bike shed the previous night, how creepy it had been. They agreed to take the other way around the hostel, so Mona wouldn't spot them if she was out there again.

"Is she spying on us or something?" Nina whispered. She scowled at Mona, who was sitting alone at the back of the room, hunched over her diary.

"Who cares, to hell with her," Susan said. "She's nuts, no one believes all that stuff she goes around talking about. We'll just lock our door so no one can get in after we're gone."

"But you don't have a key!" Pia said.

"Sure I do. The one to Kirsten's office works on our door, too. It probably opens all the rooms."

"Did you take it?"

"Borrowed it."

Nina and Pia had fallen asleep after the lights were turned off. The girls had run into a bit of a delay, due to noise from the room where the boys slept. Several times Lena and Steffen had gone down to yell at them, but now it was finally quiet.

While the others opened the window, Trine grabbed her jacket off the bunk bed and listened a moment for signs of anyone in the hall. Pia and Susan crawled out and shivered as they held the window open. Nina swung her legs out over the windowsill and ran her fingers through her short hair. Seconds later Trine hopped out and pushed the window shut.

All the hostel's windows were dark. They stood still and listened in the silence until they were sure the coast was clear. Trine felt giddy and light from nervous excitement, wild, exhilarated, knowing they were breaking the rules. They'd gotten away, and they were alone.

They hunched over and scampered down a series of paths and past several identical reddish-brown vacation houses, laughing all the way as they tripped and bumped into things in the dark. At long last, they reached the end of the cluster of houses and spotted the corner of the large sports arena.

"Can you hear anything?" Trine whispered; the darkness made her nervous.

They stopped, and for a moment they were swallowed up by the immense stillness of the night. More careful now, they headed for the front of the arena, Susan leading the way. Trine linked arms with

Nina, squeezing hard as they neared the end of the building. No voices. No mopeds.

Disappointment swept through Trine when she realized they were too late. The boys had left. She'd been fantasizing, trembling in anticipation of sitting around the fire with the boys. She'd even quietly hoped that Susan had forgotten about Skipper, but if not, she'd go after Daniel, he was good-looking, too. She'd fallen a bit behind the others, and tears begin welling up; suddenly she couldn't cope with the thought of never seeing them again.

"To hell with them!" Susan said, after they'd walked around the arena and returned to the vacation houses. She resolutely screwed the lid off the rum and held her hand out for one of the colas Pia was carrying. "If they're gone, we'll just—"

But suddenly they heard the mopeds up on the street, then the darkness was broken by their headlights. Trine ran after the others, laughing as the lights blinded her. She shielded her eyes with her hand.

"Let's go," yelled one of the boys from out of the dark. The other girls were already hopping up on the backs of the mopeds, and Trine hurried now, happy to put her arms around Daniel's broad back.

The boys had already started a bonfire. They sat on the small beach at Hullehavn and looked out at the swimming pier. Trine took a long hit of the rum and cola Susan had mixed, and she watched as Skipper walked over and put his arm around Susan.

"Truth or consequences," Pia yelled out, sending a challenging look around the circle. Their faces glowed amber in the light of the flickering fire. Trine sat beside Daniel, who held a bottle similar to the ones Trine's mother used when making elderberry juice.

"Small Gray," he said, flipping the lid off, "homemade, vodka and hot licorice."

"Is it real strong?"

Daniel smiled wryly and assured her it was good for her. Healthy.

The shot of vodka cut through Trine's throat, but she fought back the pain and smiled when she gave the sticky bottle back to Daniel.

"Truth or consequences," Pia yelled again, now insistently pointing at Susan, who sat between Skipper's legs, leaning back against his chest with her legs crossed. "Truth or chug it!"

The vodka reached Susan, who sat up a bit and grabbed the bottle. There was a natural quality to all of Susan's movements, to everything she did. As if she were sure that getting whatever she wanted was a law of nature. That *of course* Skipper, clearly the most interesting of the boys, would put his arm around her waist.

Trine watched her, and though her head was already spinning, she realized she would never have Susan's self-assurance when it came to boys. She would never think it natural to be chosen by the best-looking and nicest boy. But Daniel was okay, too, she thought. She leaned against him.

Suddenly Susan spoke up, loudly and clearly. "Where and when was your first time?" She stared across the fire at Trine, her head tilted. With her gaze locked onto Trine's eyes to provoke her, Susan smiled at her maliciously as she sipped her beer.

Trine felt Daniel's arm shift off her back as he turned to her.

She realized she was holding her breath, caught in the sizzling tension around the fire. But then a couple of the boys started laughing.

"Come on, come on!" they yelled.

Susan's smile didn't let up. Her long, honey-colored hair fell smoothly around her tight sweatshirt. Skipper lit a cigarette for her, and she lifted it slowly to her mouth. Tonny reached over and shut off Nirvana, which together with Pearl Jam had driven off the stillness of the night, surrounding the talk around the fire with a hectic curtain of sound.

"My first time was . . ." Trine's voice was hoarse in the sudden silence. She looked pleadingly at Nina, the only one not staring at her. All the girls knew Trine hadn't been with a boy yet. Desperately she leaned forward, grabbed the bottle, and took another long hit as she stared back at Susan.

"Nooooo," Stretch cried out, "we want to hear about that first time."

"Details," Tonny howled.

Pia came to the rescue. "It's my turn now," she yelled, drowning out the others. Trine's cheeks reddened in shame as the vodka and crushed hard candy burned her throat.

"Truth or consequences," Pia said. She leaned forward and fixed Susan with a stare. "Which would you choose: strip naked or talk about your childhood?"

Trine was startled. Now the silence around the fire was serious. Even though the boys knew nothing about the orphanage or foster families, they sensed something major was going on. Something much bigger than the way Susan had humiliated Trine.

For what seemed like an eternity, Susan and Pia stared savagely at each other. Then Susan stood up, stepped behind Skipper, and unzipped her sweatshirt. Slowly she pulled her blouse up over her head and unfastened her bra. She stood for a moment, naked from the waist, her breasts shining in the cold light of the moon. Goose bumps rose up on her arms. The boys were speechless, and Trine shifted uncomfortably, but she couldn't help staring when Susan unbuttoned her jeans and wriggled them down off her hips and legs. She kicked them away, took another step back, quickly peeled off her panties, swung them around her head, and yelled almost lewdly, "Last one in the water is a loser!" She ran down toward the black water, with all the boys eagerly trailing her. They whistled and clapped while rushing to get their clothes off.

Trina, Pia, and Nina were left sitting at the bonfire.

"I think I'll go back now," Nina said. She stood up, and Trine joined her. She felt dizzy, confused.

Pia was still seated. "Shouldn't we wait for her? We can't just leave her here."

"No," Nina said. "We're leaving now."

Trine agreed; they were leaving. She and Nina and Pia had been in the same class since first grade. Susan had come later, so she wasn't one of them. Not even close, after what had just happened.

TWENTY-THREE

Camilla pulled off the road. She was acutely aware of how easily she could say something wrong or something that could be misunderstood, so she concentrated on the conversation, tried to sound upbeat, tried to be accommodating and understanding.

"Honey. I know it's your life. And I respect you; you know I do. And it's great that you're happy with Julia. But you're seventeen years old. Both of you have to think of the future. Your education, job possibilities. You haven't even finished high school yet."

Markus jumped in. "We've thought about that. Julia's going to take a year off and stay home with the baby; she'll start high school when the baby's old enough for day care."

"Maybe it doesn't sound too complicated now," Camilla said. "But it feels different when you're in the middle of it all. You don't sleep at night, and none of the life you know now will be the same. Everything's going to be about the little one. I remember so well how it was. There were lots of days I didn't even take a shower, I hardly had time to eat at first."

She stopped herself. She didn't at all mean to make him feel guilty about how she nearly couldn't handle the first few months after his birth. But she remembered clearly how she'd walked around like a zombie, dressed in soft jogging clothes. She also remembered having to call Markus's father at a work seminar to get him to order a pizza to be delivered to her. That was after she'd been pacing the apartment for nine hours straight with Markus over her shoulder. Whenever she stopped or tried to do something else, he began screaming.

Camilla pushed the memories aside. She loved her son more than anyone else on earth. He was the most important person in her life. She'd been alone with him for so long that they'd become a team; they belonged together, and so she had to back him up. She knew that. She surrendered.

"Markus, you are the best thing that ever happened to me. I couldn't love you more, and I'll support you one hundred percent if you two decide to go through with this. I'm sure we can find you a small apartment, and I'll help as much as I can. But I'll be gone once in a while, to be with Frederik, at least as long as he's living in the States. So you'll have to be able to get by on your own, too."

Suddenly Camilla realized how unwilling she was to give up the freedom that comes when your children grow older. She hadn't actually felt all that great an urge to split her time between Denmark and California, even though Frederik was working there. But now that the option was threatened, that she might not be able to just fly over to be with him whenever she wanted, it felt claustrophobic.

"We can handle it ourselves, no problem. I've read about teenage parents. More than five hundred girls a year here become mothers before they're twenty. So we're not the only ones. And I read an article in *Berlingske* that a young father wrote about how he and his girlfriend had a kid after getting home from boarding school, where they met. She was sixteen, he was seventeen, just like us. They had another kid, and their first one is starting school now."

Camilla couldn't help smiling. Of course he would have read up on it, to have his arguments ready. But he didn't mention how teenage mothers are themselves often the daughters of teenage mothers or that girls who had grown up with a single parent were twice as likely to become a young mother. Daughters of manual laborers, daughters of parents without jobs, and daughters with at least one parent with a criminal record were twice as likely to have a baby while still a teenager. And she realized she didn't know anything about Julia's parents. She hadn't even met them.

Camilla had also done some reading, had read several articles. She knew she'd focused more on the passages her son had skipped over. Of course there were girls who simply wanted more than anything in the world to become a mother at a young age. But the studies she'd had time to dig up on the internet showed that most teenage girls who got pregnant chose to have an abortion.

"When is it that you can see if it's a boy or a girl?" Markus asked.

"There's something else you have to think about, Markus. Because you're not of age yet, it's your parents, your dad and I, who are your guardians. So legally speaking, we're the ones responsible for the child until you turn eighteen. We'll also be held responsible when it comes to your financial situation. It's expensive to have a child. Day care, diapers, clothes—"

"But the food's free, as long as she nurses."

"True. And you know Frederik and I will help, too."

She intentionally didn't mention his father; after their last conversation, it was abundantly clear that Tobias had all he could handle with his own twins.

"There's also another legal aspect to this you need to be aware of. If you break up, you'll have to pay child support until your child is eighteen."

"We're not going to break up! We wouldn't be having a baby if we were thinking about breaking up."

Camilla turned and looked out over the golden fields of grain. A tiny sliver of sorrow sank inside her. She missed Frederik. Missed having an adult to talk this over with, someone else who would dare to insist that it wasn't as easy as her son made it sound, because he had no way of foreseeing the consequences of what he was throwing himself into.

The door out to the terrace was closed that day, and no clothes were hanging on the line, but a small white Toyota was parked outside in Nina Juhler's driveway. Camilla pulled up behind it and sat for a moment gazing at the front door. She tried to gather her thoughts, shake off the phone call with Markus. It was slowly dawning on her that the hardest part about genuinely sharing his joy was the knowledge that his relationship with Julia wouldn't last. *You're a cynic,* said a voice in her head. *A realist,* said another.

The front door opened and a woman with short blond hair stepped into the doorway, folded her arms, and stared out at Camilla, who immediately got out of her car.

"Hi," she said as she walked up to the house.

Camilla recognized Nina from her photos on Facebook. She'd looked her up and read that she was a project coordinator at Save the Children. Recently she'd been in Sierra Leone, helping to rebuild a birth clinic in a slum.

Camilla introduced herself, and before Nina could say a word, Camilla explained that she'd like to talk to her about Trine Madsen. "I know Trine, and I know you two were in the same class."

Nina let her arms fall. She hesitated.

Obviously she hadn't expected this, Camilla thought. "I've tried to contact her, but apparently no one knows where she is. I'm wondering if you've spoken to her recently."

Nina slowly shook her head. "We don't really stay in touch. She lives out in Osted. On Hovedvejen, not far from the school."

Camilla nodded. "I know, but she's been missing for more than a week."

"What do you mean?" Nina glanced at Camilla's car in confusion, as if she were looking for an explanation there.

"What I mean is, she's gone. Could I come in for a moment?"

Trine's old schoolmate nodded and stepped aside to let her in. A suitcase stood in the hallway, along with a jacket on the floor.

"I just got home from Africa; I landed this morning." She stuck her hands in her front pockets.

"So you haven't been following the news lately?" Camilla thought about the open terrace door and the laundry on the clothesline that she'd seen on the day she'd stopped by but couldn't bring herself to go inside.

Nina nodded quickly. "I have, yes. My mother called while I was gone; she said they'd found Susan. But it wasn't easy to get onto the internet while I was away. And I just walked in a few minutes ago."

She showed Camilla into her living room. There were freshly cut flowers in vases around the room, and a stack of folded clothes lay on the table next to some unopened mail.

"My mom." Nina stopped in the middle of the living room. She kept fiddling with her rolled-up shirtsleeves while discreetly looking over at Camilla. "She's a sweetheart; she looks after the house when I'm gone, and she always sets it up like this in here so that it's nice for when I get home. Would you excuse me a moment?"

Before Camilla could answer, she disappeared down the back hall and closed a door behind her.

Camilla stood for a moment, thinking back to when she'd been parked outside Nina's house the first time, the emotion sweeping through her as she imagined Nina's life here, a life she herself might have led if she'd stuck around Osted. But this wasn't the idyllic traditional family she'd imagined.

She tiptoed out into the hall. She could hear water running behind the closed bathroom door. Silently she listened; was Nina talking to someone in there under cover of the noise?

Camilla heard a beeping sound from the living room and hurried back to see that it was a phone on the coffee table. She sat down in an armchair with a view of the yard. The lawn had recently been mowed, but the potted plants on the small terrace needed watering.

Nina came back into the room and Camilla saw that her cheeks looked freshly scrubbed and her short hair had been combed back close to her head. Nina sat down on the sofa, carefully crossed her legs, folded her hands, and looked at Camilla.

"So you wanted to talk to me about Trine?" Nina seemed more accommodating now. "It has to be several years since I've seen her."

Camilla laid her phone on the table and set it to record.

"Back then she'd just left her husband and was living somewhere in Havdrup. But I heard they got back together."

Camilla studied Nina as she spoke. "You two drifted apart after grade school?" she asked.

"Actually, we went to the same high school, but we only bumped into each other once in a while. Sometimes we did take the bus together, but it seemed like we just didn't have as much to talk about anymore. Isn't that often how it happens?"

She raised her eyebrows at Camilla. "I know she had kids, but other than that, nothing. We were never that close."

"I thought you hung out together in school," Camilla said. "That you were best friends in the lower grades."

Nina nodded. "We played together," she said, her version of the friendship succinct.

"Did you start drifting apart after what happened on Bornholm?" Camilla asked, trying to prod more details out of her.

Nina glanced up, but she shook her head. "We just plain drifted apart. Like people do when they get older."

"What actually happened on Bornholm back then?"

Nina leaned forward. "Is that why you're here? To dig around in that old story?"

"I'm not here to dig around. Actually, I feel like I have a pretty good idea of what happened. I've just been over on Bornholm, and I talked to the boys you hung out with back then. So I already know about how you met them at the harbor, the nights with the bonfires on the beach before Susan disappeared. But right now I'm most interested in finding out where Trine is. I don't know if you realize this, but she disappeared right after Susan's body was found in that cave. The police are searching for her."

"For Trine? They're searching for her, really?"

Camilla nodded. "And her family is very worried, obviously. I went to grade school at Osted myself, a few classes before you. Trine is married to the younger brother of a friend of mine. It's not just a story I'm working on here, it's important to me personally that she's found."

She tossed out these details in the hopes of getting Nina to open up, to see if she could find cracks in her facade, and it looked like it might be working.

"Would you mind if I opened the door?"

On her way to the terrace door, Nina grabbed a pack of cigarettes from the bookshelf. She stood at the door with her back to Camilla and smoked for a few moments, then she asked, "Who did you talk to on Bornholm?"

"Skipper, Daniel Axelsen, and Tonny Nielsen. Do you remember them?"

Nina nodded faintly and turned around.

"And the police," Camilla added.

"I wouldn't recognize the boys now, but I remember meeting them. It affected all of us, deeply, when Susan disappeared."

Nina was obviously upset, and Camilla let the silence hang for a moment.

Nina walked back and sat down. "What did they tell you?"

"What they remembered. They went through the last night you were all together."

Nina looked as if she wanted to turn back the hands of time. "We didn't understand anything when the police came to talk to us."

"But you girls told the police you all biked together from the hostel, including Susan, and then she stayed with the boys down at the harbor while the rest of you rode away."

Nina nodded. "She was flirting with one of the boys, and when we wanted to leave, she said she was staying, to go on without her. We promised to leave the window open so she could crawl in when she got back. We rode out to the smokehouse and sat there a while before going back to the hostel. But she never made it back."

Camilla watched her intently. There wasn't a single crack in her story. She spoke a bit mechanically, almost as if she was reciting something memorized.

Nina leaned back on the sofa with her hands on her lap. She had short, unpainted nails.

"So that's what you believe happened?"

Trine's old friend nodded.

"But it can't be right," Camilla said.

Nina froze, then stared back at Camilla without blinking as she nodded. "It is. We got back just after midnight."

"A witness says you didn't get back to the hostel until early the next morning. That you were gone for several hours."

"Mona." Nina seemed relieved. "No one believes Mona, she sees things that aren't there."

"That might be. But you and the boys had planned to meet at the abandoned house where they hung out. You just never told the police. And that fits timewise, if you biked out there and waited for them to show up. And then biked back to the hostel early in the morning."

Nina's face still showed no sign of emotion. "We didn't ride out there," she said, her voice quivering slightly. "We stayed in Svaneke and got back early. Mona is lying; I'm not even sure she saw us that night. She's making this up, exactly like everything else she said back then, to make herself seem important."

Camilla held her hand up. "I'm not really interested in who's telling the truth. That's police business. I just want to find Trine."

Nina sat up straight, on the defensive.

"Did you know," Camilla continued, "that the police were still watching the boys long after Susan disappeared? I don't think they've ever been totally cleared of suspicion."

Nina lowered her eyes, stared at the floor.

"Have any of you been in contact with them? Ever hear from them?"

Nina shook her head without looking up. "Not that I know of."

"And you don't know either if they know your full names or have your addresses?"

Nina looked up abruptly. "No. Why?"

Camilla shook her head. "Just a thought. Did you know that Pia Bagger committed suicide a few days ago?"

Nina's mask fell. "Pia?"

She sounded shocked. Camilla nodded and said, "She drowned herself in Dyndet lake, out by Malerklemmen."

Nina covered her mouth with her hand and began to cry.

"Pia's dead, and Trine's disappeared," Camilla said sympathetically. "I think it's time you told the police what really happened on Bornholm the night Susan disappeared."

TWENTY-FOUR

They'd been there before. From the borderland of consciousness, she'd felt them moving over her face. On her hands and arms. Like a crawling miniature parade, they marched over her. She heard the faint bumps when she managed to gather enough strength to shake them off and their tiny, hard shells hit the ground. And now they were back. They crept incessantly over her skin, over her entire body, like a living, crawling blanket. She tried again to shake them away. Tried to pull her hands up to brush them off, but her arms wouldn't move. Her eyelids were too heavy to open. She remembered the stinging stab of pain in her shoulder, but she'd lost all sense of time long ago. She'd tried to get her bearings from the strip of light behind the jagged rocks, but she couldn't see a thing. The small insects were working their way over her mouth and into her nose, and she felt their small stinging bites all over her body. One last time she tried to move her hand to stop the unbearable crawling, tried to shake herself free of it all, but she couldn't find the strength. Desperate now, filled with revulsion, she understood that all she could do was lie there on the ground, alone in the darkness, and surrender to the small creatures overtaking her body.

TWENTY-FIVE

Louise had spent both the night before and all morning with Mikkel at the acute psychiatric hospital. After she'd spoken with Gerd yesterday, he'd called and asked her to come right away, saying that he wanted to talk to her. He'd sounded subdued, which tied her stomach in knots; on the way to the hospital, she prepared herself for the possibility that he might be wanting to confess something. But a completely different Mikkel, an almost jubilant Mikkel, was sitting in the dayroom waiting for her when she walked in. He got straight to the point.

"So you don't think Trine left us again; it's not the reason she's gone," he said, more a statement than a question. "She didn't leave me!"

His combed-back hair was still wet from his shower, and he wore a clean hospital gown. A warm feeling spread through her when she saw the look in his eyes: full of hope and a new determination. Several sheets of paper lay on the table in front of him, and he sat with a pencil in his hand.

Louise sat down across from him. "No, I don't think she did. But I'm afraid something might have happened to her. I'm afraid she could be the victim of a crime in connection with the old case from—"

Mikkel shoved two sheets of paper across the table. "Here are the people I know she's been in contact with. But there've been a lot of people at the clinic I don't know. You can find them in her online booking software."

"It's more old friends, male and female, that I'm interested in hearing about." She knew the police were already contacting Trine's clients and the people they'd found on her phone. "I'm thinking mostly about people from her grade-school or teenage years. Do you know anything about Mona Ibsen? She was in Trine's class."

Mikkel didn't recognize the name. But he began spurting out a stream of other names, people they knew. Parents from the kids' school and day care, women she occasionally went running with. He also mentioned a group of women she met up with every other month; they ate dinner together and then went out to see a movie.

He'd made quite an effort, she had to give him that. He still seemed weak and sluggish from his meds, yet it was as if his renewed sense of hope burned strongly enough to break through the chemical fog and help him think clearly. He talked about the vacation house they had rented. About going on vacation, about the future. About everything except the fact that Trine was gone. As if everything was going to work out as long as she hadn't left him.

At first Louise had tried as gently as she could to make him aware of the possibility that Trine would never come back, even though the police were doing their utmost to find her. But it didn't sink in; the only thing he seemed to care about was that *he* wasn't the reason she had disappeared. She hadn't left him.

That morning he'd called and asked Louise to come back again. She'd had a horrible night; after a serious conversation with herself, she'd stopped taking the Thai sleeping pills. She had to stop sometime, that much she knew. But being unable to sleep was no good, either, if she was going to help her brother. She'd argued back and forth with herself while lying in bed, struggling to fall asleep. Suddenly she was overcome by how terribly she missed Eik. And Jonas. She missed having a family, people she belonged to. And in the darkness the feeling grew and grew until finally she got up and found Mikkel's whiskey in the living room. It had burned her throat and had done nothing to corral her runaway emotions.

Mikkel pushed another sheet of paper over to her, the list of what he and Trine had done over the last month. He'd described their comings and goings for each day in meticulous detail.

Louise read through it. Studied the names and places. Looked for connections, but all she saw was a logbook of a family's everyday life. Shopping, picking up and dropping off kids, visits to the doctor. Leisure activities. Nothing that stuck out, nothing out of the usual. Just everyday life.

Louise was leaning against the wall in front of the Roskilde police station when Nymand returned. He led her inside, past a small group of people at the back of the room waiting to apply for temporary driver's licenses, then up a stairway to his corner of the shared office space. He asked her to sit down.

"Thank you," he said.

Louise looked at him in puzzlement.

"I hadn't linked Trine's disappearance with the suicide out in Viby," he continued. "I wasn't aware that Pia Bagger and your sister-in-law knew each other, and I probably wouldn't have figured it out if Camilla Lind hadn't brought it to my attention. I assume you two came up with the idea together, that these recent events might be connected to what happened on Bornholm back then. I'm sending two officers out to speak to Nina Juhler later today."

Louise was about to say that he should be thanking Camilla, not her, but she simply nodded. He didn't need to know she'd been stumbling around by herself in desperation and hadn't contributed much of anything. Nymand added that the three men from Bornholm would be brought in for a new round of questioning, too.

He glanced at his watch. "Presumably Wiinberg is picking them up now, all three of them. We don't want to give them a chance to coordinate their stories."

"But nothing points to them being with Susan the night she disappeared," Louise said.

"No, but we need to know where they were when Trine disappeared, and also during the time leading up to Pia Bagger's suicide."

"You suspect them." She nodded; she'd had the same thought. But what motive could any of them have for taking the lives of the girls who had been on the field trip, one after the other, after so many years? "Have you spoken with Mona Ibsen? The one who saw Susan ride off with her friends?"

Nymand nodded. "Mona has looked me up several times over the years. And I admit it, she's always insisted that Susan was lying hidden somewhere in the forest. She also talked about insects. 'A forest' doesn't narrow it down much, but maybe I should have taken her more seriously. I'm open to these sorts of things, believe it or not. At least when we have the time. But a forest—"

"I was wondering more about whether you're afraid she could be in danger, too?" It was also possible they suspected Mona was behind what was happening now. She'd already told Nymand about Mona showing up outside her brother's house. And the class picture she'd left behind.

He shook his head. "I'm sure she's been very upset by everything that's happened. But we have no reason to believe she's ever been in contact with those boys, back then or now."

Louise told him about her talk with Gerd, how she was more

worried about Mona now than ever before. "It sounds like Mona's condition has worsened. Maybe your people should look into a possible link between Mona and what's happened with Trine and Pia."

She saw at once that she'd gone too far. And she reminded herself that on this case she had no official standing, she was just another woman with her own feelings and opinions about it.

He stood up to get Trine's phone records. "Mona told us she called Trine, Pia, and Nina after Susan was found, but none of them answered or called back, even though she left a message."

"What did she want to tell them?"

Nymand sat back down. He looked tired. Worn out even, though it was early, still an hour to go before lunch.

"She said she only wanted to talk about what happened back then. And it looks like Trine called Nina and Pia around that same time, too." He handed her the records, underlining Mona, Nina, and Pia's numbers for her.

She opened her bag and pulled Mikkel's papers out. She slid them over to Nymand.

They sat for a moment, then he asked, "Have you seen Mona lately? I mean, besides the glimpse at your brother's house."

Louise nodded and said she'd run into Mona when she was visiting her brother at the hospital.

"You would agree that Mona can barely take care of herself, that it seems unlikely she could somehow be involved in the deaths of two of her old friends, doesn't it?"

"'Friends' is an exaggeration," Louise said. "Mona was the only one back then who was making an effort to talk to the police. I'm just saying it might be worth finding out what she had to say."

"But we *have* found out." He sounded even more exhausted. "She says she saw the four girls ride away on bikes and only three of them return early the next morning."

"What about the other nights, what did she see then? Did you ask her?"

"I'm sure the Bornholm police did a thorough investigation back then, but you have to remember, Mona wasn't with the other girls. She was at the hostel the entire time, which limits what she could have seen."

He paused for a few moments before leaning forward. "I get it, you're trying to find an explanation. And you want to help your brother. But you also have to understand, we're doing the best we can, we're doing *everything* in our power to find your sister-in-law. You have my word on that."

"Yeah, and don't stop," she said without smiling. She grabbed the phone records and walked out without asking if she could take them with her.

TWENTY-SIX

Louise was told that Mona Ibsen had been discharged when she returned to the psychiatric hospital.

"And it looks like the doctors are about to discharge your brother," the nurse said.

"But he's not even close to being ready for that!" Louise glanced down the hall toward the closed ward. "He seemed happy when I got here this morning, for the first time. His treatment is helping."

The nurse nodded. "It's wonderful to see the progress he's making. And it's clear in every way that he's much better. Just the fact that he asked for a shower and clean clothes is a very good sign."

"But surely that means he shouldn't be sent home now!" Louise was starting to feel desperate. "What if his depression returns?"

The nurse stood up from behind the glassed-in reception desk and walked around the counter to Louise.

"The policy here," she said, her voice gentle, "is that when he says he isn't having suicidal thoughts anymore, he'll be discharged. But, of course, that doesn't mean his treatment will be stopped. And you should take it as a positive sign."

She laid her hand on Louise's shoulder. "Your brother was in line for electroshock therapy. We were prepared for the possibility that he might become one of our long-term patients."

"Electroshock," Louise repeated quietly.

The nurse nodded. "It's a serious treatment, but it has a good effect on many of our patients with severe depression."

"When will he be discharged?" Louise glanced over at the closed ward again.

"Possibly later today or tomorrow." The nurse's pager beeped from her pocket.

Mona lived in a small apartment on St. Jørgensbjerg, not far from the harbor. Louise had driven by the row house years ago, when she'd first heard about Mona, but she'd never been inside. At that time, Mona had been visiting Gerd out in Svogerslev. There was something touching about those two and the close relationship they shared, Louise thought, but at the same time it was also sad that Mona's parents were so uninvolved, even though Mona was clearly struggling.

She finally found a parking space not far from Mona's apartment. She walked toward the building, which was a whitewashed two-story edifice with crooked blue windows. The neighborhood was cozy-looking, with older buildings, and Louise had the feeling that most of the people living around here knew one another. A village within a city, something that would feel claustrophobic to Louise.

Only seconds after Louise pushed the buzzer, the front door swung open, as if Mona had been standing by her door waiting for Louise.

"Come in," Mona said. Her voice sounded thin and childlike.

She wore a light pink wraparound blouse and loose, pale yellow pants. Her flowing white hair and pale-colored clothing made her look feeble, despite the fact that the antianxiety drugs had made her gain weight. Still, there was something insistent in her eyes as she asked Louise to follow her.

Her windowsills were filled with green plants that blocked people out on the street from peeking in. Louise looked around the low-ceilinged room, at the old-fashioned writing desk, the dark sofa, the oblong dining room table. Framed insects hung on the walls, carefully spaced in even rows. Big and small. Louise studied the largest of the framed collections, just inside the door. It was full of dried earwigs, pinned so densely that it was difficult to distinguish one from the next. The pattern the insects created gave it an artistic quality.

"Beautiful." Louise smiled at Mona, gesturing toward her artwork. There were also smaller frames that held single insects. When she'd first met Mona at Gerd's house, she'd been sitting at a table covered with dead insects that she was drying out, and Louise had been horribly repulsed. Mona had described how the living insects were put into a glass with a thin layer of gypsum on the bottom, then ether was dripped into the glass. And it was chilling to watch her pin the insects onto a sheet of Styrofoam. But now that Louise saw the finished products, it all made sense.

As Mona watched, Louise walked around the room and inspected each frame. There wasn't a single butterfly in the collection, and no beautiful moths, either. Not that Louise knew much about insect species, but most of them looked like plain old flies and beetles and wood lice. None of them seemed to be rare species, and although some of them might have been of interest to collectors, she wasn't knowledgeable enough to identify them.

Out of the blue, Mona asked, "Did you know that carnivorous beetles are also called predator beetles? If Susan's body was dessicated, like they reported in the newspapers, it's most likely she was eaten by larder beetles. They wait to attack a body until it's dried out, four or five months after death. But because Susan's body was lying there so long, there must have been earwigs and other beetles, too. They must have crawled around on her so much that they didn't even recognize it as a body."

She spoke matter-of-factly. Louise stared at her in equal parts fascination and horror.

"And if there were bluebottles in the cave when she died," she continued, "they would have laid their eggs inside her, and thousands of flies would have hatched underneath her skin."

"How did you get started with all this?" Louise asked, pointing around at the frames. "And how could you know that Susan's body had been taken over by insects?"

Louise walked over to Mona. She didn't like taking psychics seriously, but she couldn't help but be fascinated by Mona. "You said back then that you knew something bad was going to happen on the field trip."

Mona gave a short nod. "I knew someone was going to get hurt." Her face quivered slightly, as if her premonition had never let go of her. "I know you might find all this repulsive."

She gestured at the dead insects and bottles of chemicals around the room.

"But like Gerd always says, I've most likely never gotten over what happened, and now I'm trying to accept what it's done to me."

"Your nightmares?"

Mona nodded. "I can't get away from it. I try, but every time I hear about a missing person, it comes back, there's nothing I can do. It's part of me now. If people had listened to me back then, Susan would still be alive."

Her feathery voice sounded bitter now.

"I'm sorry I didn't make it outside in time when you came by my brother's house," Louise said. "Did you come because you wanted to talk to me?"

Mona nodded. She stared straight ahead, her face as blank as it had been in the school picture she'd left at Mikkel's house. After several moments, she said, "I wanted your help. I knew Susan was still on Bornholm. The others thought she ran away, even though I kept telling them she was there. No one believed me, no one listened. Until now. But I should never have said anything."

She kept wringing her hands, almost in desperation. "I could see the insects. And the darkness. I told them. I told the grown-ups to keep looking, I told the police she was there. That she was trapped, couldn't get out. But nobody listened."

Louise suggested they sit down at the table. When she pulled out a chair, she noticed a bucket on the floor, covered with plastic wrap. Inside was a dark brown, swarming clump of insects, all crawling around on top of one another. They looked like a single large organism. A few of them crawled up the sides of the bucket and out onto the underside of the clear plastic. Louise glanced at Mona; her face still showed no emotion. Then Louise noticed the lidded jelly jars pushed against the wall underneath the table, as if they'd been hidden in haste. All filled with living insects.

"Are you going to frame some of these, too?" Louise tried to sound normal, offhand.

Even though Mona nodded, Louise wasn't sure she'd heard.

The insects were creepy, but she shook off the urge to recoil. "I'd like to talk to you about the class picture you left in my brother's yard. Trine had a copy of the same photograph, too. Someone had drawn a circle around three of the girls on hers, but there were four girls circled on yours. You drew a circle around your own face. Why?"

For several long moments, Mona sat in silence. Then she quietly cleared her throat. "I'm afraid," she whispered.

"I know this is painful for you, to be confronted with everything that happened back then, and I'm sorry for bringing it up. But I wouldn't be here if it wasn't important to me. To me personally."

"It's okay. I'd like to talk about it."

"Good. Can we start with Trine?"

Mona looked away but nodded.

"How did you get along with her and her friends?"

"I didn't like them," she said with no hesitation. "They acted like they were the only people in the world who mattered. They made their own rules; they didn't care if anyone else got hurt. They didn't like me, either."

"What about the others in the class, how did you get along with them?"

Nymand had told her that his detectives had contacted all of the old 7C students except for a woman who had moved to Boston with her husband. They would all be questioned again. It annoyed Louise that she wouldn't get to talk to them herself. She wanted to ferret out how the rest of the class felt about Trine and her three friends. But she'd reminded herself to focus on finding Trine and leave Susan's death in the hands of Nymand and the Bornholm police.

"Our teachers let Susan, Trine, Pia, and Nina share a room. Everyone else slept in the dormitory. Except me. I stayed in a little room at the end of the hall. The other girls wanted it that way."

"But why?"

"They didn't like being around me. They thought I was creepy; they called me 'the Witch' because I kept warning them something terrible would happen."

Louise was surprised by how Mona's monotonous tone of voice affected her. It wasn't just that Mona had been excluded, or that their teachers apparently accepted this and hadn't done anything at all to try to help her integrate into the group of girls. It was Mona's face, so totally blank as she spoke. Not a hint of sorrow in her eyes, not a single quiver in her voice. She spoke of her exclusion as if it were only natural, expected.

"I was okay with being alone," Mona said. "I preferred sleeping in there with all the floor cleaners and soaps than listening to them whisper."

In a way, Louise could understand that.

"I just wanted to be left alone." Now Mona looked at Louise, as if seeking validation for feeling that way. "I've always liked silence, but that night when we were told to turn out the lights, it felt like the air started shaking and this weird feeling of heaviness seeped in through the walls and down from the ceiling. I couldn't stand being in there, I had to go outside. Sometimes I wonder about that; maybe I was sensing the other girls' nerves. Their room was right beside mine."

Louise didn't want to interrupt her, so she simply nodded.

"I snuck out and sat by the bicycle shed. I had a clear view; I saw the girls crawl out the window and run away. And come back. But everyone thought I was just trying to make trouble when I told the adults what I'd seen."

Louise leaned over the table and reached for Mona's hand. "I believe you, and I know you called Trine a short time before she disappeared. What did you want to talk to her about?"

Mona bit her lower lip. She looked like a little girl caught doing something wrong. But she straightened up, and Louise let go of her hand.

"I wanted to warn her," Mona said, resolute now. "It's all coming up to the surface now. I was afraid she might be in danger."

"Why would she be in danger?"

Mona gave her a long look, but then shook her head. "I don't know, I can just sense it. The past is catching up to us now that Susan's been found. You can't keep it hidden; it's going to come out."

"Did you call Pia and Nina, too?"

Mona nodded. She didn't seem to realize that if her old classmates had been hiding something, the calls could have been extremely frightening.

Neither of them spoke for a moment, and Louise took the opportunity to regroup.

"Did you hear that Pia drowned herself out in Dyndet three days ago?"

"Yes, Gerd told me." Her eyes turned blank. "Pia never answered my call, so I just left her a message."

"What did you tell her?"

"That they had to tell the truth."

"Mona, listen." Louise was pleading now. "Would you please, please tell me why you are so convinced they're hiding something? I know what you told the police back then, that Trine, Pia, and Nina got back to the hostel much later than they claimed. But there must have been something more. Did you hear them say anything when they got back, did you see something? What makes you so sure they aren't telling the truth?"

Mona looked almost paralyzed. She'd been struggling to pull her legs up underneath her, and now she began gently rocking back and forth in her chair. "They're disappearing, one by one. All of them who went out that night."

Louise studied Mona's face; there was something enormously irritating about the unwavering mildness of her expression. She wanted to shake her, wake her up. If this had been a regular case and they'd been in an interrogation room at police headquarters, she probably would have thought Mona Ibsen was crazy and would not have paid much heed to her statement. But there was a certainty, an assuredness in her manner that made it hard to dismiss her.

Mona turned back to Louise. "They left the hostel the night before Susan disappeared, too. And the other three came back without Susan."

"What do you mean?"

"They weren't close friends, not at all, not like everyone thought. They didn't like Susan, or else they'd had a fight or something. That night Susan came back alone a little while after the others, and she was crying; she even sat outside their window and cried quite a long time before crawling back in. And the next night she didn't come back at all. The other girls shut Susan out. It's their fault she disappeared. Nobody believes that, though."

TWENTY-SEVEN

Camilla was packed and ready to go home. She'd just put her porta-
ble coffee mug into her bag and told the editorial office she needed
two pages for the story about Susan Dahlgaard's school friends when
her cell phone rang.

All afternoon she'd been trying to get in touch with Nymand to
confirm that the police were now officially linking the suicide of Pia
Bagger to the search for Trine Madsen and the discovery of Susan's
corpse. When she'd spoken to him after meeting with Nina Juhler,
he seemed to agree that the three old friends might be covering for
one another and hiding something. She no longer believed they'd
split up with Susan at the harbor that night, and when Nymand told
her he was sending two officers out to interview Nina, Camilla took
it to mean he agreed with her on that, too.

But four or five hours had gone by, and she still couldn't reach him.

Camilla picked up the phone. "Nina's gone," said Louise. Louise
gave her a recap of her conversation with Mona, explaining how the
three friends had had some sort of disagreement with Susan and that
Susan had been upset the night before she disappeared.

"When did you see Nina?" Louise asked.

"I got there about eleven, and I left about a quarter till noon. What's going on?" Camilla slung her bag over her shoulder and ran down the hallway. She heard her friend take a deep breath.

"After I spoke with Mona, I got in touch with Nymand, told him he needed to bring Nina in for questioning, for her protection as much as anything. But when they got out to Birkerød, she was gone. The door was open, and her wallet, phone, and car keys were just lying there. She's vanished."

Camilla rushed over to her car. "Just like Trine."

"Just like Trine."

"Call her mother." Camilla told Louise that Nina's mother had been taking care of the house while her daughter was away. "It sounds like they're close. Maybe she knows where Nina is."

She backed her car out and headed toward Nina's whitewashed house at the edge of the woods.

"The police have already sent techs out there," Louise said.

"That was quick." Camilla made a note to herself to call the office secretary, tell her to definitely include in the article the fact that the police were now connecting the two cases. "They must have found something since they're already getting Forensics involved."

Louise didn't answer.

"She could just be over screwing the neighbor," Camilla said. "Or on a long run in the forest." Then she remembered all the cigarettes Nina had smoked; maybe she wasn't the running type after all, even though she was tall, thin, and long-legged.

"Are you out there now?" she asked.

"No, I'm with Mikkel. He's being discharged, we're driving him home to Osted. I can hear that you're on the way, though."

"I just *knew* those three girls were hiding something. I told Nymand, too, but I should have grilled her more when I was there."

"No, that's his job. The Bornholm police are questioning the men again, too. They're only missing one of them, Daniel Axelsen, the truck driver, because he's out on the road."

"Surely the trucking company knows where he is?"

"On the way to Poland, they say."

"If he's been anywhere near Nina, they can catch him on surveillance cameras at the ferry, at the bridge, phone towers, whatever the hell else. It can't be that hard."

"They're working on it."

Camilla heard voices in the background. "What about Mona?"

"When I heard Nina was missing, I called Mona and convinced her to go over to Gerd's place so she wouldn't be alone. I have to run, Mikkel's coming out now."

The freeway traffic was heavy. Camilla tried to call Nymand several times in vain. Frustrated, she gave up and called the Communications Department at Roskilde Police and asked what was going on out in Birkerød, and if there was anything new concerning Nina Juhler.

"No comment." They hung up.

Just as she was exiting the freeway, Camilla finally got a callback from Nymand. He got straight to the point.

"Rick says you spoke with Nina Juhler right before she disappeared. I'd like to talk to you. Now."

"Why the hell do you think I've been calling you all day! I've heard she's gone. What happened?"

"Were you out at her house when you spoke with her?"

"Yeah, she'd just gotten home, straight from the airport. Her suitcase was still in the hallway when I got there."

"Where are you now?"

"Just off the Roskilde exit."

"Drive out to the house. I want you to see if it looks the same as when you left. And Forensics will need your DNA."

Camilla said she'd be there in less than twenty minutes.

Nina Juhler's car was still parked in the driveway, but now police vehicles lined both sides of the narrow street. Camilla swung in behind the last one in line. A neighbor across the street was standing in his front yard, clearly curious about all the commotion.

A uniformed officer stopped her as she approached Nina's house. She explained that Nymand had asked her to come and then she waited patiently on the far side of the hedge. Finally, the captain came out of the house with a tech, who provided her with white coveralls, a hairnet, and a mask.

"Just for while we're inside," Nymand said.

Camilla had already zipped up the thin paper coveralls, and when they reached the front door, she pulled the blue plastic shoe covers on over her sandals and followed him inside.

The dark gray suitcase was gone, but the shoes she'd noticed earlier were still there, as were the coats hanging behind the door.

Camilla stopped in the doorway to the living room. The terrace door was closed, the pack of cigarettes was still lying on the shelf. It looked every bit as nice and tidy as it had earlier that day. She heard voices upstairs; the techs were going through the entire house, Nymand explained.

"I can't see anything that's changed," she said. "Except for the suitcase, it's not . . ."

Camilla stared at the table, where the vase with flowers from her mother stood. The letters had been opened, and possibly there were fewer of them now. Or else it was because the newspapers were gone. An opened envelope lay askew on top of the stack of papers, as if someone had tossed it there. Beside it were two dead insects, but even from a distance it was obvious the open envelope was full of them.

She pointed. "Where's that from?"

Nymand followed her eyes. "You're thinking about Mona." He shook his head. "We spoke with her, and she denies sending a letter to Nina. She doesn't even know her address. The techs are taking the letter in."

"It's easy enough to say that," Camilla said. She asked if they'd checked to see whether Mona and Nina had kept in touch over the years.

"According to Mona, they haven't had any contact. Or as she put it, they don't know each other anymore."

Camilla peered at the insect envelope and saw that the address had been printed on a label stuck to the front. She took a step toward it as if to pick it up, but Nymand put an arm out to stop her and so instead she leaned down to peek inside. The envelope was full of all kinds of dead bugs. Flies, big and small; long brown earwigs with scorpion-like claws behind; wood lice with their gray, round crab-like bodies. There were also many enormous, metallic green beetles with thick, black, curly legs. She shuddered.

"Let's go." Nymand laid a hand on her shoulder and nudged her toward the hallway. "We'll take your car."

"Go," she repeated. "Where? We can talk here just as well."

He shook his head and nudged her again, explaining that he'd take her into the station and interview her there. "Do you have a recording of your conversation with Nina?"

Camilla nodded, said it was on her phone.

"At the moment, you're our primary witness. You're probably the last person to have seen Nina Juhler and the last person she was in contact with."

Camilla stopped and shook off his hand. "I'm no idiot." She glared at him. "There's something you're not telling me, otherwise you wouldn't have called in the techs so soon. What happened?"

They stared each other down for a moment before he put his hand on the small of her back and led her to her car.

It took a few tries to turn her big SUV around on the narrow street. When they were on their way to Viby at last, he told her they had checked Nina's phone for incoming and outgoing calls.

"I understood from Louise Rick that you left Nina about a quarter to twelve."

She shook her head at him. "You could've just asked me. But yeah, right around there."

"Okay. At 11:50, the first unanswered call was made to Trine Madsen's phone from Nina Juhler's phone. Seven more unanswered calls were made in the next twenty minutes. At 12:13, Nina Juhler called 112 and asked the dispatcher for the police, but then the call was cut off. My people arrived at the house at 12:58. They found the door open and Nina Juhler was gone."

"But you didn't know she'd called 112 before you came here?"

"No. After you and I talked, I sent two officers out to speak to her about Susan. We're working with the Bornholm police on the case. It's not certain yet if there was a crime, or if Susan Dahlgaard's death was accidental, but right now our colleagues over there are focusing on how she ended up in Echo Valley. We hoped Nina Juhler could help with that, but now she's gone, too."

They kept Camilla for four long hours. Two young female officers were in charge of the questioning, and even though they were very friendly, when they pressed her to go through her meeting with Nina for the third or fourth time, Camilla was exasperated.

"It's all right here, for chrissake," she said, pointing at her phone.

She'd given them permission to make a copy of the recording, though she did consider refusing in order to protect her source. But she knew the police didn't have much to go on and the search for Nina took priority.

"You ended your conversation by telling Nina Juhler that it was time she told the police what really happened the night Susan disappeared. Is there anything you know about that night that you haven't told us?" They kept at it. Camilla repeated that she didn't know what had happened, but it was clear to her that the three girls had lied and must know more than they claimed. She also tried to convince the two officers of her theory that Susan hadn't split up with Trine, Pia, and Nina after all, and that the four of them had gone out to the abandoned house to wait for the Bornholm boys together, as had been planned.

"We'll probably never find out," one of the officers said. "The house was torn down long ago, and anyway, it's been twenty-five years; there wouldn't be any evidence left after that long even if it were still standing."

"Yes, but it could still explain why she was in the area."

It wasn't any harder than that, she thought in annoyance, but she willingly answered all their repeated questions. At one point, pizzas and colas were brought in.

It was past nine when she walked out of the police station. Before leaving she'd tried to get in touch with Nymand, to ask if there was any news, but she was told that he'd left. During the questioning she'd asked if she could call her newspaper and update the article she'd handed in, to prevent the competition from beating her to the latest developments. But the officers wouldn't allow it. And now that the printer deadline had passed, she could only feed the new information to their online site. She wanted to be able to tell her boss she'd tried her best to let *Morgenavisen* know about the connection between Nina Juhler and Trine Madsen as soon as she'd confirmed it. She hadn't mentioned Pia Bagger. Her paper still respected the families' privacy when suicide was involved.

Of course, Nina Juhler would be a big story if the police didn't manage to find her. There had been no official announcement of a search, and Camilla couldn't stop thinking that there might be a perfectly logical explanation for Nina leaving. Which meant she would be in for a shock when she discovered the police had treated her home as a potential crime scene.

Camilla had told the two officers that Nina might simply have followed Camilla's advice, she might have called the police to tell them the truth about that final night on Bornholm. And maybe she got cold feet and hung up. But it was odd, though, that she would call 112, the emergency number.

And then there was the envelope with the insects.

Her thoughts kept swirling, and by the time she got home, around ten, her mind was exhausted. She turned the hallway light on, then instantly froze when she heard a faint noise from the living room. Slowly, silently, she lowered her bag to the floor.

For a moment she stood listening; she heard breathing, something moving. With the door behind her still open, she cried out, "Hello?"

She waited. The timed light in the stairway behind her clicked and shut off. "Anyone here?" She yelled loudly in order to sound braver than she felt. But then she heard someone sniffling.

"Markus!" She ran into the living room. He was sitting in the armchair by the window, his legs pulled up underneath him, arms folded around his knees. "Oh, honey!"

In an instant she was by his side. His face was hidden in the dark; the light from the street was no more than a few scattered reflections on the ceiling.

"What happened?" she whispered. "Is it the baby, did something happen?"

She put her arms around him, and suddenly she was overcome by a feeling of wanting to protect him. Him and his little baby. He cried on her shoulder, and she rocked him gently until he was ready to lift his head and dry his eyes.

"Honey." Camilla stroked his bristly, boyish hair.

"The baby's gone," he whispered, still sobbing. "And we can't see each other anymore. She broke up with me. She says it's Grandpa's fault."

"Grandpa?" She shook her head in bewilderment. Her father had shown ten times more sympathy concerning Markus and Julia and the baby than she could ever have conjured up, though her initial shock had faded by now.

"Julia had a miscarriage?" To her surprise, a jolt of grief struck her from out of the blue.

"She had an abortion." Her son sounded so much older than his years.

"An abortion! Why in the world is it your grandfather's fault? What did he have to do with it?" She pictured her father in his old reliable slippers. "He told me you had a great evening together, he was happy for you two, he liked Julia very much."

"She says it was the way he took it; it made her realize how serious it was. Like she really understood then that she was expecting a baby and we were going to be parents."

"Hmmmm," Camilla mumbled as she kept stroking his hair.

"Grandpa wanted to celebrate. He congratulated us and said he was looking forward to the baby. I thought it made her happy, that after all that time someone else finally felt the way we did. But it didn't."

He was calmer now, and Camilla scooted over a little bit so that they could see each other in the dim light.

"She didn't want it after all. Maybe she just thought it was a game we were playing. But I wanted it."

Camilla spoke softly. "You wanted *her*."

He nodded. "But she broke up with me. She sent all my stuff over in a taxi. She doesn't want to see me anymore."

"But what about her parents?" Camilla felt helpless.

"She didn't even tell them. I thought she had; she said she did, anyway. That's why I came home and told you, so you'd know about it, too, right away."

Her arms felt like lead as she reached for him again. "I'm sorry you feel so terrible. Don't you think you'll get back together?"

He shook his head. "She says I only want to tie her down. That it'll be my fault if she doesn't get an education."

"What a load of crap!" Camilla stood up and turned on the sofa lamp, furious at how unfairly he was being treated. "Why does she have to say something like that? You did everything right when she told you she was pregnant; the way you acted is the definition of re-sponsibility. Don't listen to her. There aren't many people willing to sacrifice their teenage years the way you were. You've done nothing wrong."

Silence.

"She's got my ticket for the Roskilde Festival," he finally said.

"We'll get it back." Camilla had an overwhelming urge to give lovely young Julia the dressing-down of her life. At the same time, though, something inside her loosened up, fell back into place. She felt a physical sense of relief.

"Is this the weekend you're going to borrow the boat?" she asked.

He nodded. Camilla couldn't help thinking how strange life was.

One moment it was plotting a course for one destination, the next it sent you off toward another. And though it hurt to see his broken heart, it was also an enormous comfort to feel the wind blowing in a new direction.

Camilla tucked Markus into bed in his room, which had mostly stood empty since they'd moved into the new apartment. She could hardly remember the last time he'd let her care for him that way. Seventeen years old and so tall now. And about the same age as the Bornholm boys had been when they'd met the girls from Osted.

She sat at the foot of his bed, rubbing his feet while they talked about TV series and movies. He was indeed grown up now, but still so touchingly young at the same time. It struck her how difficult it was at that age to foresee the consequences of your actions. And how quickly things could turn. She thought back to when she'd been seventeen, how she used to stay up so late at night even on weeknights with school the next day. Suddenly a memory popped into her head of herself sitting on the floor in Ole's room, together with several friends, listening to the Ramones and passing a bottle around. The electricity in the air between the girls and boys . . . They played spin the bottle and came up with challenges for one another:

"If it points at you, you have to go out on Hovedvejen and strip, then run across the road twice before you come back."

"If it points at you, you have to go in and kiss Ole's dad while his mom watches you."

"If it points at you, you have to kiss someone in the room."

"If it points at you, you have to walk over to the neighbor's and piss on their doormat."

But every time there was a way out: you could chug the rest of your beer instead of doing the challenge.

.   .   .

Markus was asleep. Camilla leaned over carefully and turned off the lamp beside his bed.

Back in the living room, she texted Louise. "What if the girls did some kind of dare to show off to the boys? Maybe they saw or did something they never told anyone about?"

Moments after sending the message, Louise called. She sounded tired.

"Nina still hasn't shown up. I just talked to Nymand. Tomorrow they're going public and making it an official search. They've already notified all the other police districts on Sealand. What did Nina say when you talked to her?"

Camilla was too exhausted to go through it all again. "She said they split up with Susan at the harbor, and that she, Pia, and Trine sat on a bench and looked out at the water or something."

"How far is that abandoned house from the place where Susan was found? You've been there, can you walk between them?"

"Definitely! The house was on the corner where you turn to get to Echo Valley. I don't know the exact distance, I was driving, but it didn't seem all that far. You could walk it, anyway. What are you getting at?"

"I'm thinking about something Mona said, that the night before she disappeared, Susan came back to the hostel crying. After the other girls were already back. Mona thinks something happened between the four girls, they had an argument or something, and Trine, Pia, and Nina left Susan behind. But it could have been Susan not wanting to go back with them. And maybe something bad happened when she was alone with the boys."

"Like, they might have hurt her?"

"I'm not thinking anything specific; I'm just lying here trying to fall asleep. I just can't make sense of it, that's all. If the girls did something to make Susan cry, then why did they all go out together the next night? And if it was the boys who'd made her cry, why didn't she tell the other girls about it?"

Silence. Camilla had been brushing her teeth while Louise talked, and now she spit out. "Sorry."

"They were at that house," Louise said. "Why the hell else would she end up all the way out in Echo Valley?"

"But someone else must know what happened. Someone must have kept the secret besides them."

They both spoke at once. "Mona."

TWENTY-EIGHT

BORNHOLM, 1995

Susan kept to herself at breakfast. She didn't even glance at her three friends when they all walked over to the long table to make their lunches and get ready for the day's outing.

Lena and Steffen yelled at them to hurry up. Trine had a hangover; she'd made several trips to the bathroom the night before to throw up. She'd told Lena that she was sick, that she wanted to stay at the hostel, but Lena wasn't buying it.

On the way to the castle ruins at Hammershus, Carsten wrecked his bicycle by riding it up a slope that was steeper than he'd thought. They all had to wait for his bicycle to get repaired, and as they sat in the ditch beside the road waiting, Susan came over to the other three girls.

"Skipper asked yesterday if we all wanted to meet at the harbor tonight." She acted as if nothing had happened between them. "They invited us to the old abandoned house where they hang out. They want to party with us. Do we want to party with them?"

Without thinking, Trine said, "Sure we do."

Pia nodded, but Nina said nothing.

After a few moments of awkward silence, Pia told Susan that she was sorry they'd left her alone at the beach.

"It's okay," Susan said, looking away. "We just hung around and drank some more. It was a good party; it's too bad you guys missed it."

She still hadn't even glanced at Trine, but when they got up and walked over to get their bikes, Susan jogged up beside Trine and quickly said, "I shouldn't have asked you that last night, it was an awful thing to do. I see that now."

"Anybody want to go swimming?" Nina asked after dinner. She'd been standoffish all day, Trine thought, and she hadn't said anything about what had happened the night before, either. But now she was thawing out, and it looked like maybe she'd decided to forgive Susan.

The four girls and several others in the class decided to go out to Hullehavn after they'd cleared the tables. Trine's hangover had finally eased up during dinner, and she thought that a swim might help her feel more normal.

Several of the boys jumped straight into the water from the bridge. Lena and Steffen had decided to tag along, and they started building a bonfire with a few of the others, right on the same spot as the one from the night before.

Susan sat out on the wharf, talking to Mads. Trine had had a secret crush on him since fourth grade, but nothing had ever really come of it. Maybe he didn't even know, she thought. She remembered the feel of Daniel's arm around her again. It had been nice, but he hadn't kissed her. She hoped he would that night. Then she wouldn't be the last one of the four friends to try something with a boy. She looked over at Nina and Pia; they hadn't kissed anyone yet, either. But she'd noticed Pia hanging around close to the lanky boy,

Tonny. He was a little gawky maybe, but in a nice way, totally different from Aksel in their class, who acted so snooty.

"Time to head back," Steffen called, but of course a few of the boys had to jump off one more time, and Trine remained seated on the sand until Pia walked over and pulled her up.

"Come on. We don't want Lena to think we're planning something. Have you seen those two?" Pia nodded over at the wharf, where Susan was still sitting close to Mads.

Trine nodded. Pia knew how she felt about Mads.

"Don't pay any attention to her, she's just trying to make you jealous." She linked arms with Trine, and they walked back to the hostel together.

Before the four girls went to their room, they had walked two of the hostel's bikes around to the back of the building and hid them there so they could get away quicker that night. Trine and Nina pedaled, Susan and Pia rode in back. They wobbled down the hill to the harbor, laughing all the way, and for a few moments Trine forgot all about how nasty Susan had been to her. It wasn't all that dark, but black clouds were starting to blow in from the sea.

"How long does it take to bike out to that house?" Pia shouted against the wind.

"It depends on if you're riding in back or not," Trine said, bearing down on the pedals.

"About half an hour," Nina said. She always knew about things like that. She'd been a Girl Scout once.

Trine spied the boys from a distance, standing beside the convenience store, gesturing wildly. There was no one else in sight. Trine noticed Tonny was missing from the group, but then he appeared on the path that ran up to the hotel. He handed something to the others.

"Hi," Susan shouted, but the boys were too absorbed in whatever they were talking about. At last, Skipper looked up and noticed Susan, waving as he caught sight of her.

Pia jumped off the bike, and Trine leaned it up against a low wall across the street.

Skipper broke away to greet Susan, but the other boys continued talking quietly among themselves. He kissed her. Stretch shouted that it was time to go.

"Can we ride out to the house with you?" Susan asked as she followed Skipper back to the group of boys. Stretch shook his head; he was acting more standoffish tonight, and he seemed annoyed at the girls for coming.

Trine was about to join Daniel when Stretch started pulling him away. Skipper let go of Susan and said they should bike out to the house.

"We'll meet you out there," he said, walking away. "We'll pick up some beer on the way."

Susan grabbed his arm. "But where is it?"

"Ride out to Echo Valley." He explained that the house was just before the turnoff to the valley, right on the corner. "You can't miss it, the roof's caved in on one side. Go on in and wait for us."

Trine felt sweat running down her back by the time they reached the sign pointing to Echo Valley. The good thing about Bornholm, Nina had said, was that there weren't all that many roads, so it wasn't hard to find your way around. All they had to do was bike up the road that led away from Svaneke, straight ahead all the way. Through Østermarie and down Almindingevej. Nina had, of course, brought along the map they'd been given the day they arrived. Typical Nina, Trine thought. She laughed when Pia started singing: "Our driver is blind, and out of her mind."

The moon had disappeared, and scattered but heavy drops of rain had begun to fall when their shaky bicycle lights finally illuminated the house, half hidden behind tall trees and wild thorny bushes. Red brick, dark blue wood trim. The glassless windows were like big gaping black holes in the dark, an unnerving sight. Trine kept close to Pia as they stood out on the lawn, staring up at the house, until finally Pia walked up to the rotting door and pushed it open.

There was an old rickety table just inside the door with a big lantern on it, which they turned on as soon as they stepped in. They found tea candles and matches in what had once been the living room.

"What a great place!" Pia walked over to a plush, mustard-colored sofa and plopped down. Paintings hung crookedly on the flowery wallpaper, their gilded frames like the ones in Trine's grandma's house. Two cups with rings of dried coffee inside stood on the coffee table.

The boys were right. It looked like whoever had lived there had suddenly gotten up off the sofa and left the house and never come back. Books still stood on the bookshelf, and on the top shelf lay an open book that someone had been reading. There were ceramic vases on the windowsills that still had the shriveled remains of flowers drooping from them.

But what made the greatest impression on Trine was the abandoned kitchen. She found old-fashioned pots and iron kettles in the cupboards. A blue jar of Nivea cream stood on the windowsill behind the tattered orange curtains. Greasy plastic containers filled with flour and sugar. A faded box of oatmeal. Cans of tomatoes, their labels torn. At the bottom of a drawer lay a pack of spare blades for a cheese cutter.

They'd been through the entire house and had been waiting for an hour when Pia finally said she was tired of waiting. "They're not coming!"

"They'll be here," Susan said, confident as usual. "They know we're out here."

"I don't want to wait anymore," Pia repeated.

"I'm staying," Susan said.

"It's stopped raining, let's go outside," Trine suggested, to keep herself from falling asleep. Nina had already curled up on the couch. It was past one a.m., and the moon was peeking out now and then from behind the dark clouds.

They woke Nina up and walked down the road to the parking area where the class had stopped earlier on the way to Echo Valley.

"Maybe we can get into the candy store," Susan said. She broke into a run, and the others followed, panting by the time they reached the store. It had a row of benches in front, and several big trees loomed above.

"How do we get this grate off the window?" Pia looked at Susan, who had just walked around the building to try the back door. Without a word, Susan lifted the big rock she'd found behind the store and started hammering at the hook holding the grate in place. They could see the rows of candy just behind the window.

"There might even be some money!" Pia said.

Trine felt a rush of adrenaline. She didn't see how Susan had done it, but suddenly the grate was loose. "What if there's an alarm?" Trine was fidgety; all the courage and excitement she'd felt as they ran through the darkness had vanished.

Nina hung back, and she stepped even farther away when the window glass shattered. They stood still and listened, but at first nothing happened. Then Susan reached through the broken window and started gathering up candy.

"We have to get inside, get the good stuff behind the counter," Susan said feverishly. Then the alarm went off, a sudden explosion of sound, a howling so loud that the four girls instinctively fled across the parking lot to the forest and up onto the trail, heading toward the shelter where they'd eaten their lunches earlier that week.

Pia was the first to stop. "Who's going to come?" she said, panting for breath. "There's nobody around here, and it'll shut off eventually."

Other than the howling alarm, everything was quiet. There was a big white house at the edge of the valley, but it looked dark and silent. Just then a light came on in the house, and a door opened. A deep voice yelled something, and instantly the girls took off deeper into the forest. Away from the parking lot, the candy store, and the white house, the entire ground floor of which was now lit up.

They ran so fast that the air whistled in Trine's ears.

Now they were far enough in the forest that they couldn't see the lights from the house, and they crawled behind some heavy bushes to hide themselves even more thoroughly in case someone was coming.

"What were you thinking?" Trine reached out for Susan. "You shouldn't have broken that window. What if we get caught?"

"You were all in on it." Susan shoved Trine back so hard that she almost lost her balance. "You're all so childish. You don't think the boys could see that you've never had a first time? Everybody knows you're still a virgin. And you even think you have a chance with Mads."

She laughed scornfully, her white teeth gleaming in the dark. "He just laughs at you. None of them want anything to do with you. Especially Daniel. He said so the other night, after all of you left."

"Stop it," Nina said.

Pia had been in the middle of opening a bag of candy, but now she tossed it aside and stepped toward Susan. "What's the matter with you? Don't talk that way about any of us, we've never done anything to you. And what about your parents? They didn't even want you when you were born."

Trine quickly backed away.

"You don't know the first thing about my life!" Susan snapped.

The alarm had stopped, but Trine caught glimpses of the flickering beam of a flashlight, searching up between the trees.

Her eyes stung at the thought of Susan and Daniel talking about her behind her back.

"Stop it!" Nina said.

Susan whirled and stuck her finger in Nina's chest. "You don't think I noticed how you were watching us yesterday? You don't think I've seen how you can't take your eyes off me? You stay out of it, you little dyke!"

After a moment of total silence, Pia lunged at Susan. Trine staggered toward them, weaving around the trees.

"I know why your mother didn't want you!" Pia hissed into Susan's face. "Your mother couldn't even take care of herself."

"You don't know what you're talking about." Susan was back on her feet now.

"As a matter of fact, I do. My mom's a social worker, and she told me about your mother and the two foster families who threw you out because they couldn't stand you!"

Susan's face contorted into a sneer of anger, and she swung wildly and rammed her fist into Pia's arm. Pia hunched over, surprised and shaken by the physical attack. "Stop it, you hit me really hard."

But Susan didn't stop. She kept swinging blindly, until suddenly she sank to the ground, sobbing, her face in her hands. "Leave me alone, I never want to see any of you again. Never ever."

The forest was quiet again. Dark clouds scudded across the sky as the wind picked up. Nina and Trine put their arms around Pia, who was gasping in spurts. The three of them stood and watched as Susan got to her feet and began walking away from them, farther into the dense forest.

Suddenly Pia shook Nina and Trine away and charged at Susan, shoving her hard. Susan fell and rolled down the trail toward the small bridge below.

"And we never want to see you again!" Pia screamed.

The moon disappeared behind a cloud, but not before Trine saw Susan's golden hair spread like a fan around her head. She lay completely still.

Trine called Susan's name as she took a few tentative steps toward her. Her feet slipped on the wet stones where Susan had fallen.

"Just leave her there," Pia said.

"We can't do that!" Trine looked pleadingly at Nina, who had turned away, frightened. But she joined Trine, and they clambered down the slippery rocks together.

"Susan," Trine said when they reached the bridge. She squatted and tried to pull her up into a sitting position. The clouds were heavy now, but only a few drops of rain fell here and there.

"I think she hit her head," she told Nina, who still looked frightened. "She's not moving or anything, maybe she passed out."

Pia stood behind them, farther up the slope. "Oh, come on! She's just pretending."

"She's bleeding."

Susan began moaning, a garbled sound. Her hand shook when she tried to raise it to her head, as if she couldn't judge the distance correctly. Slowly she sat up.

Trine reached out to help her stand, but Susan slapped it away. "Get away from me! I want to go home, to my brother in Copenhagen; you all can rot in Osted hell."

She wobbled as she got to her feet, then she glared at them a moment before staggering off into the forest.

"Come on, let's bike back to the hostel," Pia yelled, impatient now.

"We can't just leave her here! She's hurt." Trine set out after Susan, fumbling along in the darkness until she felt the slippery wet wooden bridge planks under her feet.

"If she wants to go to Copenhagen, let her. Let's go!" Nina had walked back up the slope, and now Pia put her arm around her. "It's her own fault, she's the one who attacked me, and you heard all the stuff she said."

Trine called out Susan's name again and took a few cautious steps in the general direction Susan had gone in, but the hushed dark forest had closed up behind her.

Few words were spoken on the way back, and none at all when they finally reached the hostel. They were soaked, exhausted, cold, and shivering.

As they crept toward the window, Trine whispered, "Do you think she'll come back?"

"I hope not," Pia said through chattering teeth.

Trine could hear that she didn't mean it, that she was just as nervous and scared as Trine. Nina said nothing. None of them noticed Mona sitting in the bike shed, out of the rain.

Inside their room, they threw their wet clothes in a pile on the floor and crawled in under their quilts.

"It was really lousy, the boys telling us they'd meet us and then not showing up," Nina whispered.

"Really lousy," Pia agreed.

Trine was despondent. "If Susan doesn't get back before breakfast, Lena and Steffen will know we've been out again."

"But Susan was the one who talked to the guys and made the plans to meet them," Nina said. "We just tagged along."

"She'll have to take the blame when she gets back," Pia said.

They lay for a while in silence before making a vow. They swore they would never tell anyone, no matter what, that they'd been out to the abandoned house.

TWENTY-NINE

Louise sat watching Mikkel as he slept. He breathed deeply, peacefully. All night long, she and her parents had taken turns sitting with him. First her father, then her mother, who had woken Louise at five to take over so that she could catch a few hours of sleep before getting the kids up and off to school and day care.

For a few hours Louise had stared at her phone, scrolling through photos of Jonas. And of Eik. She'd lingered on one of the earliest photos she had of him, in which he was leaning up against an unmarked police car, with his shark-tooth necklace, his shaggy hair. Looking at it hurt. Then she scrolled through the photos from their last night together. He'd tried to explain how he felt, and she'd tried her best to make sense of it. Maybe Camilla was right. That, in fact, she was the one who had ended it, not Eik. She couldn't handle the way he had set her feelings aside. Maybe she had ended it without truly understanding what he was trying to say.

She heard her mother get up, the murmur of her parents' voices behind the bedroom door. Mikkel turned over in his sleep.

"I miss you all," she wrote to Eik. "I hope you're okay." She'd written back and forth with Jonas, but this was her first message to Eik since they'd split up. She wondered if she should add an emoji, a heart or red lips.

But before she could hit send, her phone rang. She went out into the hall so as not to disturb Mikkel. At first, all she heard was incoherent sobbing, and she couldn't even tell if it was a man or a woman.

"Hello, I'm sorry, but who is this?"

"It's Mona." Louise couldn't believe it, it couldn't be Mona; all this loud blubbering sounded nothing like her usual light, childish voice.

"Gerd?"

Now it was quiet on the other end of the line, as if the person were fighting to get their emotions under control. "Gerd!"

"Yes." She sounded vague, furtive, but then she began crying again.

Her mother came out into the hallway and froze at the sight of Mikkel's closed bedroom door.

Louise whispered that he was sleeping, that she had just stepped out to answer her phone. Her mother opened Mikkel's door a crack and Louise glimpsed her brother inside.

"You have to come over," Gerd said, "something's happened!"

"Gerd, listen to me." The professional Louise, the police officer, took over. "Take it nice and slow, just tell me what happened."

"Please come." She began sobbing uncontrollably again.

Louise raised her voice. "Has something happened to Mona?"

"I don't know," she wailed. "Come to Mona's, you can see for yourself."

"I thought Mona was with you! I thought you were both in Svogerslev!"

Louise was already pulling on her coat. "I'll be back soon," she told her mother, who stood holding a sleepy Malte. "I have to drive over to Roskilde."

. . .

On the way there she thought about calling Nymand but decided to wait until Gerd could explain what had happened. She was more annoyed than worried that Mona wasn't with Gerd, though the woman's emotional outburst disturbed her. Louise noticed that her breathing was quickening with apprehension, and she forced herself to exhale slowly and deeply.

She recognized Gerd's bottle-green Berlingo in front of Mona's small building. The St. Jørgensbjerg neighborhood was still quiet as she tossed her bag over her shoulder and rushed up to the door. Gerd was sitting at the dining table, her face puffy from crying and her hands in her lap, palms up. She almost looked as if she were asleep.

Louise approached her gingerly.

"What happened?" She squatted down in front of her and tried to make eye contact. "Where's Mona?"

Gerd looked up at her and shook her head slowly. "I don't know."

"But she was with you!" The night before, when there was still no news about Nina, she'd even called Gerd to make sure Mona was there.

After her late-night conversation with Camilla, she'd realized she would have to speak with Mona again. Maybe she should have called Nymand last night, she thought. If Mona was more unstable than Louise had believed, either he or a police psychiatrist should talk to her.

"She *was* with me," Gerd said, "but when I woke up this morning at six, she was gone. I don't know when she left last night, but her bicycle and all her insects are gone, too."

Louise glanced around. No framed insects hung on the walls, and the bucket under the table and the small glass jars full of insects had also vanished.

Louise stood up and pulled out a chair. "Have you checked to see if anything else is missing?"

Gerd shook her head lethargically. "I'm afraid something happened to her, that she did something bad."

"Bad?"

"To herself." Gerd added that she'd already called the acute psychiatric hospital, but they hadn't heard from Mona.

"Has she been suicidal in the past?" Louise asked.

Gerd's eyes were glazed, but she was making an effort to pull herself together. "She's been in the psychiatric system as long as I've known her. It's a latent fear in all of us, that someday she won't have the strength to go on living."

It took several moments for her to pull herself together to stand, then she asked Louise to follow her. They walked through the tiny kitchen behind the living room and into a room that overlooked the small backyard. A desk stood in the middle of the room, a bookshelf along one wall. A stack of the frames Mona used for her insects lay on the table, along with several glass and plastic shadowboxes from IKEA. But there wasn't a single insect in sight.

Louise glanced around the room.

"Everything's gone, she's taken them all," Gerd said. "Those insects have been a big part of her life ever since she was a teenager. They were her hobby, they steadied her, helped her fight off her anxiety."

She began crying again, and Louise led her back to the living room.

"Gerd. I'll have to contact the police, but I'm begging you, *please*, tell me if you know anything about Mona and Susan that hasn't come out already. I have the feeling that Mona knows more than she's told us, and I'm afraid it's put her in danger."

"I don't know anything," Gerd said, still sobbing. "Nothing at all."

. . .

It was only a few minutes past eight, but Louise could hear from Nymand's voice that he'd been working for quite a while that morning already.

"What do you think?" he asked, after she gave him Mona's address. She heard him walking away from his desk.

"I think we don't know what we're looking for." She took note of the fact that he didn't object to her use of the word "we," including herself as part of his team. "The only people who know what's happening and why are all gone now. And we have no idea where they've gone or what kind of threat we're up against."

"Exactly," he muttered. Louise heard a door closing in the background. "Should we send the techs out?"

"I don't think anything here indicates that Mona has been a victim of a crime. I'm thinking more along the lines that she was planning to leave."

"She fled?"

She looked around. "She spent time packing up all the insects," she said, well aware that he wouldn't understand what that entailed until he arrived. "She didn't just run off on the spur of the moment."

Louise told him about her late-night conversation with Camilla. "It seemed logical that Mona might have been the one who sent the letter with the insects to frighten Nina, but now I'm not so sure. If we're working from the theory that Mona knows something about Susan's disappearance, but she's desperate because no one believes her, and then she tries to scare Trine, Pia, and Nina into spitting out the truth about Susan's death—why does she disappear, too? It doesn't add up."

She'd often brainstormed this way with her colleagues in Homicide when they were trying to figure out a possible motive in a killing. They would just toss out ideas about how a person might react to a given situation. They didn't always make sense, but sometimes they turned into leads that no one had noticed previously. It was a way of trying to explore the human psyche, looking at as many different possible intentions and emotions as you could. Often the more you looked at various angles, the more it would begin to become clearer which avenues were worth investigating further and where police resources should be allocated.

"I'll ask Wiinberg from Bornholm to send over the transcript from when the police first questioned Mona Ibsen," Nymand said. "Then we can check to see if there's anything she said back then that was overlooked."

Louise asked for permission to read the transcript, too. She gave him her private email address.

"By the way, when does your leave of absence end?"

She heard his car moving faster now; he would arrive soon. "I've got almost two months left," she said.

"And then you'll be heading up Homicide. Are you okay with the reorganization of the investigative units there?"

Louise had nothing to say, really. She'd put everything having to do with Homicide out of her mind during her leave. Hadn't even answered the last emails Toft had sent. No doubt he just wanted to be courteous, to keep her up-to-date while he filled in as temporary head, but she'd been unable to concentrate on anything he'd sent while she was away.

"I guess you know the reception for Rønholt is Friday. Are you coming?"

"No," she said without hesitation. She'd received an invitation. Her old boss at Missing Persons had included a note that Louise also hadn't answered. She felt sick at the thought of regular working hours, mail sitting in pigeonholes. She simply didn't want any of it anymore. And that went double for the new job waiting for her, where she would now be heading up the entire division. It would be hours and hours and hours behind a desk. She had been flattered when they offered her the job, had seen the promotion as a huge vote of confidence.

"I'm not returning to the Copenhagen Police," she heard herself say. "I've told them I'm not accepting the position."

Which wasn't true. But the moment she said it, she felt a tremendous sense of relief. Suddenly she felt like she'd been trying to climb a mountain carrying a large, heavy bag on her back. Step by step. Up, up, up, with bowed head and curved back. And now she'd just dropped the bag to the ground.

"How did they take it?" Nymand sounded startled.

"Fine," she lied. "They have Toft, you know, he's doing a good job filling in."

She would get in touch with the police commissioner, Human Resources, and Toft the moment she got back from Roskilde.

A few minutes after they'd hung up, Nymand knocked on the front door and walked in. He glanced around the low-ceilinged hallway for a moment before entering the living room. Gerd was sitting on a chair in the dining room, with her spine very straight and her hands folded in her lap.

"Maybe she wanted to get away from me," she whispered to Louise as Nymand walked toward them.

Louise rubbed Gerd's shoulder and sat down beside her.

Nymand took a seat across from them. "What do we know?"

"Mona went over to Gerd's house after I spoke with her yesterday," Louise said. "I'd suggested it because I thought she shouldn't be alone, not until we knew more about Nina and whether or not she'd left home of her own free will."

Gerd listened intently to Louise, but said nothing.

"Mona slept over at Gerd's in Svogerslev, but sometime in the night or early morning hours she left the house and came home. And before she left here again, she packed all her insects and took them with her. And she had a *lot* of insects."

He looked confused.

"She had five or six shoeboxes full of them at my place," Gerd stated. "Plus, all the jars in my living room."

Nymand frowned. "Shoeboxes filled with dead insects?"

Gerd nodded.

"She's a collector," Louise explained. "Beetles and flies and all sorts of other flying creatures. She's been collecting them for years."

"So she catches and kills them, keeps them in shoeboxes?"

"Or cardboard boxes." Gerd pointed out at the yard.

"In other words, we're talking about quite a few dead insects," he said. Louise and Gerd nodded. "And both of you believe she took them with her?"

"There's a lot of evidence that points to that," Louise said. Gerd didn't answer.

Louise walked through the kitchen and over to the back door, then opened it. It gave onto a small tiled terrace, and just to the left of the door lay a stack of empty boxes, including the shoeboxes Gerd had mentioned. It looked like someone had just moved in and then stuck all the used boxes behind the building. She walked farther out into the yard to see if the insects had been thrown away in the garden, but she didn't see anything.

"Could she have stuffed them into bags and taken them on her bicycle?" Louise asked Gerd, who was now standing in the doorway. "Where did Mona usually go to collect insects? Maybe she's taking them back to where she found them?"

"Usually she goes to the forest behind the psychiatric hospital, St. Hans. But you can find these types of insects in plenty of other places. It's not like she has only one particular spot. Being in the forest makes her feel peaceful, and she likes to collect insects anytime she walks around in the woods."

Nymand didn't beat around the bush. "We're afraid this is a suicide, right?"

Louise nodded. Gerd collapsed onto the floor of the tiny kitchen and Louise reached out just in time to cushion her head. Nymand took a step forward, as if to catch her, but he was too late and didn't manage to get to her before she slid to the floor.

"Gerd!" Louise grabbed her shoulders. "Gerd, wake up!"

They carried her out to the living room sofa. Nymand grabbed an embroidered pillow from the easy chair and slid it under her head, while Louise kept calling her name.

Gerd opened her eyes suddenly and looked at Louise in despair.

"I've always tried to be there for her," she whispered, "but she has a darkness inside her that she never let me see."

Louise leaned down and hugged the older woman; it was distressing to see the misery in her eyes as she processed the fact that she might have lost Mona forever.

"We'll do everything we can to find her," Louise said.

"It could already be too late," Gerd whispered. Tears streamed down her cheeks.

Yes, Louise thought. *It could be too late.*

THIRTY

When Louise stepped through the glass doors and into the psychiatric hospital's reception area, the nurse quickly stood up from the desk behind the glass wall and walked over to her.

"Is it Mikkel?" She looked worried.

Louise shook her head and said she was there to ask about something else. "It will only take a minute; do you have the time?"

The nurse's smile wilted a little bit, but she nodded and told Louise to follow her to a small meeting room.

"Mona," Louise said, after the nurse closed the door.

"I can't talk about our patients," the nurse said.

"I know, I know, of course. But you are aware that she's disappeared, and right now I'm afraid something has happened to her."

Louise realized the nurse had no idea she had a connection to Nymand and the case. She apologized and said she came from the Copenhagen Police and was helping Nymand with the search they'd just initiated. She pulled her police identification card out of her wallet and showed it to the nurse. She didn't mention anything about her leave of absence or the fact that she was between jobs. Or, rather, out of a job.

"Canine patrols are on their way to search the forest. I'm sure Nymand's people have already asked if there's anyplace you can think of that she might have gone. We're assuming she left her home in the early morning hours, on bicycle."

"We've talked about that ourselves, too," the nurse said. She seemed to have taken it in stride that Louise was also a police officer. "My shift began at eight, and, well, we're all worried. We hope there's an innocent explanation for her disappearance. She asked to be discharged the other day, she wanted to go home. We determined that she was doing well. You saw her yourself, and she wasn't displaying any of the signals we look for that would indicate suicidal thoughts. There have been a few times in the past, though, where we've suspected she might be having those thoughts and we've had to keep a closer eye on her, like we did with your brother."

Louise realized the nurse might be blaming herself for not being observant enough with Mona. "I spoke with her yesterday; I definitely didn't get the impression that she might be thinking of suicide. But everything with Susan has stirred something up in her, that seems clear. Actually, I was more worried that she was feeling scared. It seemed like she was afraid of something."

The nurse studied her. "Anxiety," she said. "You're thinking maybe she's retreated into herself because of an anxiety psychosis. And maybe that anxiety has now driven her to suicide."

Louise shook her head. "I don't have any real understanding of how these things work. I just very much want to find her. That's why I'm interested in whether there might be places she likes to go to that she might have told you about. We know that she likes to walk in the forest, that she spends a lot of time there catching insects, but can you think of any other places she's mentioned? Places where she feels safe?"

She wanted to ask the nurse whether she'd ever heard Mona talk about Bornholm or Susan, but that would have to wait until they'd found her. There was the issue of patient confidentiality, and it would be up to Nymand to question the personnel and see if he could somehow get around the patient confidentiality roadblock.

"The forest, yes. And the cliff out by the fjord. She liked to sit there and look out over the water. But I haven't heard her talk about any other places."

"What about her childhood, did she ever talk about that? Could there be a place she might want to go back to, maybe a place she enjoyed visiting as a young girl before the field trip to Bornholm, before her problems started?"

The nurse shook her head again as she tried to remember. "Maybe her parents would know. To be honest, I don't know much about them, we've seen so little of them. Maybe they were more involved when Mona first became ill. But in all the years I've been here, Gerd is the only one who comes when Mona needs to be admitted. Once in a while her mother visits, but not often. It's my impression that Mona doesn't have a close relationship with her parents."

Louise thanked her and stood up to leave. She promised to keep the hospital informed. "And of course you'll notify the police immediately if Mona shows up. We need to keep in mind that there might also be a simple explanation for why she's gotten rid of all her insects. Maybe Susan's body being found after all these years has offered some sort of closure for her. And now she'll be able to put the case behind her."

Out in the parking lot, Louise stopped to watch the canine search unit drive by, heading toward Boserup Forest. She called Nymand.

"No sign of her yet" were his first words. "We're starting with the area closest to St. Hans and down to the fjord, then we'll walk a human chain through the forest. And we haven't found her bike yet, either."

"What about Nina Juhler?"

"Nothing on her, either. It's like she's disappeared into thin air, as the cliché goes." He said that her neighbor across the street had come home shortly before the police arrived. He knew that Nina had been gone for quite a while, and he had been worried that the police might have been there because of a break-in. "He hasn't seen her or anyone else at the house."

"Do you mind if I speak with Mona's parents?" Louise said.

"We already talked to them. They haven't seen or heard from her since her birthday, several days ago, when they invited her to dinner. But she'd only just been admitted, and Gerd suggested they hold off on dinner until she was doing better. So they only spoke on the phone."

Louise asked if they were searching for her anywhere else.

"We've just gone out with a press release; they'll announce the search on the local news and P4 Sealand radio. And it's on social media. Twitter and Facebook."

Louise had expected him to take a more cautious approach, to feel it was too early to fear the worst, wait a bit longer before committing so many resources. But no. He'd even brought in officers from a local special unit that assisted police districts with particularly complicated investigations.

In the background she heard someone giving orders: the search teams had been briefed, and the human chain through the forest was starting. She felt the familiar rush of adrenaline, the electric anticipation that always accompanied a search, as she listened to the sounds in the background of the call.

"Would you be okay with me dropping by to see her parents? I know you've been there already, but . . ."

"Go ahead," he said. He gave her an address in Rorup. "When you were talking to Mona about going to stay with Gerd, did she have any reaction to hearing about the search for Nina Juhler?"

"Not specifically, but when I was with her, she told me she was scared."

"Scared of what?"

"At the time I assumed it was just everything: Susan, Trine, Nina. She seemed shaken up, but she also said she wanted to talk. And that's when she told me that she thought there had been some kind of disagreement between Susan and the three other girls back then, like I told you. She didn't say anything more, but I think the thing that still bothered her was the fact that Trine, Pia, and Nina never told anyone about their argument with Susan, or whatever it was that happened to make Susan cry. They pretended everything was fine. Mona didn't believe them. But she felt like nobody listened to her back then."

"Call me when you've spoken to her parents."

"I will."

It would take her about fifteen minutes to reach Mona's parents' farm in Rorup, which was only a few kilometers from Mikkel's house. She called her mother and told her she was heading back. Her mother said that Mikkel was still asleep, and Louise offered to drop by a bakery and bring home pastries for breakfast.

"If you two need some time at home by yourselves, I can hurry back, and Mikkel can come to the bakery with me."

She thought of their summer vacations in Lerbjerg when she and Mikkel were young, and they would talk their dad into driving to the bakery on Hovedgaden for pastries: thick cinnamon rolls, Danish horns. Though it wasn't exactly the healthiest of breakfasts, it was still her favorite.

"Let's all have a cup of coffee together when you get here," her mother said. "It's been so long since the four of us have spent time together."

Louise agreed. She couldn't even remember how long it had

been. She'd moved out first, then Mikkel, and then Trine had come along.

She felt a jolt of happiness at the thought of being together, just the four of them, but then she realized something was missing. Right now, more than anything, she wished Trine could join them. And there was only one thing to do about that. She had to keep looking and find her. Find all three missing women.

Nymand called again as Louise was parking behind a church that was near where Mona's parents lived.

"We've searched Pia Bagger's house. And we also spoke to her parents."

"And?"

"And we found a letter with dead insects. It was on the same table where her brother found the class picture."

Camilla had told him about the picture, on the back of which Pia Bagger had written "Sorry" before drowning herself.

"Did her parents know about the envelope? Did Pia say anything about it?"

"No, but we're contacting everyone she knew. We've already talked to her brother; he doesn't seem to know much about her private life. They mostly bonded over his children. He remembered the other girls from Pia's class, but like he told Camilla, the girls went their own separate ways after what happened on Bornholm."

"Did you find anything on the letter?" she asked.

"It hadn't been postmarked, so someone dropped it directly into her mailbox. We sent it to the techs, priority."

"What about the letter to Nina?"

"No stamp or postmark on that one, either."

"Did the neighbors see who delivered the letters?"

"We're checking that."

"I'll look through Trine's things as soon as I get back from seeing

Mona's parents. I've already searched Trine's closet and didn't find anything. But I'll check it all one more time."

The gravel crunched under Louise's feet as she walked up the Ibsen family's driveway. A horseshoe knocker hung from the front door, and she knocked three times before the door swung open. An elderly man leaning on a cane was in the doorway, and Louise had the impression that she'd interrupted his morning nap.

"Hello," Louise said. She introduced herself and said that she knew their daughter, Mona.

"Yeah, we hear she's caused problems again." He sounded tired.

"That's not true, not at all," Louise shot back. "On the contrary, we're very worried, we're afraid something might have happened to her."

"Who is it, Jørgen?" asked a voice from inside the house. A few moments later, a gray-haired woman appeared behind him in the hall.

"They want to talk about Mona," he said.

Suddenly Louise had become a "they," but she gave Mrs. Ibsen a friendly nod and asked if she could come in.

"It's the police," he said.

"Well, come on in then, come inside." Mona's mother tugged at her husband to make him step back and give Louise room. "We don't understand what could have happened. They say she's gone."

She led Louise into the living room. The low windows revealed a backyard filled with berry bushes and trees. "She doesn't usually just disappear like this."

Her husband dragged himself over to the recliner. It took him some time to lever himself down into the chair and then he looked away and slowly shook his head at his efforts.

"Please have a seat," Mrs. Ibsen said, pointing at the sofa. Before

Louise could say she only had a few quick questions, Mona's mother was already on her way to the kitchen.

She carried in coffee cups and an assortment of cookies, and only after carefully arranging the entire spread on the coffee table did she ask what Louise wanted to talk to them about.

"I'm wondering about what Mona was like as a young girl, before the class field trip," Louise began. The old man muttered in irritation. "Before she began having problems. Can you tell me about her?"

"She was a happy girl, very active," the mother said. "She loved sports, especially handball. Sometimes she had handball tournaments almost every weekend, and they practiced two or three times a week. So she got out a lot, but she might have been a bit shy and quiet around people she didn't know. Just the opposite of her big sister, Ida. She had a whole different personality."

Mona's father growled again, but this time his wife didn't let it pass.

"That's enough, Jørgen! Ida was eleven years older than Mona; it was a pity they were too far apart to play together and such. It might have been different if they'd been closer in age; Ida might have been able to understand Mona better."

Something in the way she talked about her older daughter made Louise uneasy, but she didn't interrupt.

"Ida joined Youth for Peace right out of school, and the year after that she was part of that Next Stop Nevada—have you heard of that?"

Louise faintly remembered the peace movement, the group of young people who flew over to the United States to join the protest against testing nuclear weapons in the Nevada desert. Mostly she remembered the newspaper photos showing a busload of Danish kids driving across the country—and there had been that song Søs Fenger had written for the occasion, "Ticket to Peace."

"They were both crazy, each in their own way," their father muttered from his chair.

"Stop it, Jørgen!"

Mona's mother glanced apologetically at Louise. "It's always been hard for us to understand what went wrong. Why they had such problems."

"Why they just couldn't be normal," he nearly shouted.

Louise observed the way Mona's mother stopped herself from snapping back at him and instead leaned over the table. "What do you think could have happened to her?"

Her worry seemed genuine despite how they seemed to feel about their daughters.

"Hopefully nothing has happened," Louise said. She wanted to ease their minds, though she sensed a tension between them that she didn't fully understand. "Is it possible she's been in contact with her sister?"

"She'd have one hell of a hard time doing that," Jørgen said.

His wife looked down. "Ida chose to leave this life in 1992."

"Threw herself in front of a convoy of semis, up on Holbæk motorway, if you must know," he said.

Louise turned to him. "I'm sorry."

"It was all that hippie business."

Louise realized that his gruff manner was just his way of handling his emotions. She felt bad for him.

"It ruined her," he continued. "But then when Mona started up, too, with all these feelings she had about things, it was too damn much to take."

"The night Ida killed herself," the mother said, "Mona came into our bedroom and woke us up, saying she'd dreamed that something had happened to her sister. She wanted us to get ahold of Ida. I finally got her settled down and back to sleep. But then we got woken up again when the police called and told us what had happened. They wanted us to drive over to the hospital and see her. We wouldn't let Mona go; I stayed home with her and Jørgen went alone."

"Is there anyplace you can think of that Mona might go to?" Louise asked. "She's not with Gerd in Svogerslev."

Jørgen growled again, and out of the corner of her eye, Louise saw him put down the paper he'd been pretending to read.

"We're so happy Gerd is able to reach our daughter," her mother said. "The two of them get along so well. She's always been able to handle Mona in a way that Jørgen and I never could, and that's been good for her."

That was too much for him to take. He strained to get to his feet, grabbed his cane, and pounded it on the floor in anger, then slowly stomped out of the room. He slammed the kitchen door behind him.

His wife ignored his outburst and pointed at the yard. "Mona always liked the outdoors. She loved to hide under the bushes. She made little caves in there and we were supposed to find her. The swing is still out there, but it's been a long time now since she's been home."

She apologized and swiped away a tear under her glasses. "She also liked the graveyard. She used to sit over there whenever she felt sad. When the other kids teased her, or if something happened in school. At first we tried to get her to find somewhere else to sit. But Gerd said back then that it was good she had her own little places to be by herself, to be happy. So we let her, even though people thought it was strange, a child liking to be in a graveyard."

Louise was just trying to wind up the conversation and had her bag over her shoulder when suddenly the kitchen door burst open, and Jørgen wobbled in so fast that he nearly lost his cane. The two women were startled.

"Oh God, it's . . . God no!"

He made a retching sound as he leaned over the table, as if he were about to throw up.

"Jørgen, what is it!"

Louise jumped to her feet and in two steps she was by his side. He turned his back to her and lowered his forehead to the table. His shirt was dark with sweat. Without raising his head or saying a word, he managed to point toward the yard.

"What's wrong, Jørgen?" his wife asked.

Louise ran outside, and immediately the tree with the swing caught her eye. A wheelbarrow was leaning up against the trunk, and nearby was a rake, a bucket, and a trowel. When she walked over to the berry bushes, she saw the mound in the grass, like a newly dug grave—the dead insects. Mona's body lay beneath them. As Louise threw herself onto the ground to pull Mona free, she glimpsed crumpled-up trash bags under the nearby bushes, a half-full bottle of water, empty medicine bottles.

Louise heard herself scream as she rolled Mona onto her side, into the recovery position. "Call an ambulance!" she yelled toward the house as she stuck two fingers into Mona's mouth, down her throat, and she heard the crackling, crunching sound of dead insects being crushed as she swept her fingers back and forth. Mona's body was still warm, but Louise couldn't find a pulse. Again she tried to provoke the gag reflex, but nothing happened. Either Mona was deeply unconscious or she was dead.

There was no reaction from inside the house, so she tore her phone from her pocket and called Nymand. He answered on the second ring.

"We need an ambulance and an emergency vehicle here in Rorup, right now!" she yelled. She swore at herself for sitting inside and drinking coffee and chatting while Mona lay only a few meters away, slipping into death.

Mona must have sat on the grass and dumped bag after bag of dead insects over her legs and body before lying down. Like a summer day on the beach, being buried in the sand, Louise thought.

In the doorway, Mona's mother leaned against the door frame, crying. Louise waved her over as she began speaking calmly to Mona. Told her she wasn't alone, that there was help on the way. That everything would be all right.

"My little Mona." Her mother sank to the grass beside her, still crying as she covered her mouth with one hand and reached out with the other to Mona's cheek. Her hand shook as she caressed her daughter's thin, pale skin. When Louise finally heard the sirens, she stood up and ran out to the street.

"She's out back in the yard," she shouted. She noticed Mona's bike, leaning against the side of the house.

The four men pulled out a stretcher from the back along with the equipment to give Mona oxygen.

"I don't know if she's alive," Louise said as they ran around the house. She helped Mona's mother to her feet and put her arm around her. The men quickly surrounded Mona, lifted her onto the stretcher, and put the oxygen mask to her face. It all happened so fast that it was over before Louise and Mona's mother had even reached the door to the house. One of the men came over and asked the poor woman if she wanted to ride along to the hospital. But she shook her head slowly and said it would be better if Gerd was there, if their daughter woke up.

Louise winced in pain at hearing that. She was about to say that it might be good if her parents were there, too, but then she reminded herself that she couldn't just barge in and erase this family's entire history. She didn't know what would be best for Mona, even though it was obvious to her how much Mona's parents missed her.

"You can ride with me," she offered. Then she remembered about her own parents and Mikkel, who were waiting for her with the coffee already brewed.

She texted her mother: "I hope you don't mind waiting a little bit. It'll be a while before I can get there."

It had been a long time since she'd sent a message like that, since she'd left a loved one hanging because of her work as a police officer. She also realized how long it had been since she'd felt this adrenaline rush, and it was immediately clear to her now that turning down the new job as the head of the Homicide Department was the right decision. She wasn't ever going to be happy sitting behind a desk and thinking strategically, that just wasn't her—she belonged on the ground helping people.

Mona's mother hurried to pull on a thin summer coat over her dress. "But how do you think she'll feel about it?"

"She's not going to send you away, I'm sure she'll be happy to see you." The truth was that she doubted Mona would wake up again. But at least her mother would be there when the doctor declared Mona to be dead.

When they opened the front door, Louise saw that Mona's father was standing next to her car wearing a windbreaker. Louise acted as if she had been expecting him to come along, too, and she helped him into the front seat and then called Nymand.

"I'm on the way to the hospital with Mona's parents." She made it clear that they were in the car with her so that he would know she was limited in what she could say. "There's not much else here." Suddenly she realized that she actually hadn't looked around.

"I'll send a few officers out there," he said.

"You should probably also get in touch with Gerd," Louise said.

He promised he would, and Louise promised in return that she would report back from the hospital. The emergency physician had said that Mona was in extremely critical condition, and Louise was well aware that in many cases that simply meant the patient had yet to be officially declared dead.

She stopped in front of Roskilde Hospital's emergency room entrance. Nymand called again and told her that they hadn't been able to reach Gerd.

"She's not answering her phone."

"I'll drive over and pick her up," Louise said.

She helped Mona's parents out of the car and led them into the reception area. Surely someone at the information desk could help them, she thought.

The two elderly people looked bewildered as they stood clutching each other, but after a few moments Mona's father cautiously started leading his wife toward the desk.

Louise pulled up outside of Mona's building and was puzzled to see that the front door was open. Then a police officer appeared in the doorway.

"I'm sorry, but you can't go in."

Louise told him who she was and said that she'd spoken with Nymand.

The officer nodded. "But there's no reason for you to see this. There's blood, a lot of it. She used a kitchen knife."

Her knees began to give way. "Gerd."

He looked at her blankly.

"Elderly woman, gray hair, pageboy cut?"

He nodded.

Louise leaned up against the door frame. "Is she dead?"

He nodded again.

"Did she leave a letter behind, any kind of a message?" Louise asked.

"No. We haven't found anything."

"I'd like to see her." She pushed her way past him, and he did nothing to stop her.

Gerd lay with her hands folded over her chest. He hadn't been exaggerating; in Danish police jargon, it was a splatter death. There was blood all over the floor and on the small table beside the sofa. Gerd's face and hair were covered with splotches of blood, too. She'd cut deep, and she'd known what she was doing. She'd also pulled a blanket over herself, and her bloodied hands held an old photo of Mona.

Louise peered at Gerd. She went over their last conversation again, recalled Gerd whispering that she might be the one Mona wanted to get away from. She also remembered how Mona had confided in her that she was afraid.

Without hesitation she reached into Gerd's bag and pulled out a small set of keys.

She called Nymand. "We need to get to Svogerslev. I think Gerd was the one Mona was afraid of."

THIRTY-ONE

The light over the dining room table inside Gerd's small house was on, even though the whole room was hot and stuffy from the sun shining mercilessly in through the glass door to the terrace. Her bedroom lamp was on, too, and the blinds were still down. Clearly she'd left the house in a rush.

Nymand stepped into the room. "Are you thinking that Gerd scared Susan Dahlgaard's friends enough to make them run away, and even threatened one of them so much that it drove her to commit suicide?"

"I'm not sure what I think," Louise said. "But I'm afraid that might be the case. I think she felt that those women ruined Mona's life. That they were the reason her Mona fell apart."

She opened the door to Mona's bedroom. The bed was rumpled, a suitcase lay open on the floor with some of Mona's pastel-colored clothes inside, and a toothbrush and some tubes of cream had spilled out of a tipped-over toiletry bag. It looked as if this bedroom had also been abandoned in a hurry. Louise stood in the doorway and carefully studied the entire room.

It had all happened so fast after Louise had told Mona that she should go over to Gerd's. Louise, afraid that Mona was in danger, had sent her straight into Gerd's arms—even though Mona had just sat across from her and told her she was scared.

"Here are the envelopes and labels, the same kind as those delivered to Pia Bagger and Nina Juhler," Nymand said when she came back into the room. He showed her what he'd found on Gerd's heavy oak desk, which was nested between floor-to-ceiling bookshelves. A printer stood on the lowest shelf, and he unplugged the cord.

Louise told him that Mona had denied sending the letters.

"And if we believe it wasn't Mona, that means somebody else here knew about the dead insects," he said.

Louise nodded as she reached for the mouse on the desk. Gerd's computer screen lit up. She thought she might have to type in a password, but instead a lasagna recipe from the Danish Broadcasting Corporation's website popped up.

"Does the house have a basement?"

"I don't think so . . ." She was checking Gerd's Google searches; the school psychologist had been searching "gravhøje"—barrows, the very old burial mounds that were common around the countryside.

"We need to have some IT people look at this," Louise said, excited now. "She was checking out caves located in cliffs, only she was looking for ones that might be nearby."

She opened a new window and typed "gravhøje" into the search box. She scanned the results and recognized Gravhøj Roskilde and Gravhøj Lejre among the list of various other ancient graves and megalithic tombs.

Nymand walked out into the hall, and she listened with one ear while she kept going through Gerd's computer. She could hear him on the phone briefing his team back at the station.

"We'll need a detailed map of the area," he said, "and grab Thyssen from the radio, he's the one who knows this district best."

He ducked back into the room and pointed at the computer. "The techs are on their way, and they'll take it back with them. Let's head over to the station."

Louise glanced around Gerd's living room one last time, then followed him out.

"As of today it's been more than two weeks since Trine disappeared," she said when they reached the cars. "It doesn't seem likely that Gerd could keep her hidden for so long."

"You don't think she's alive?"

Louise shook her head. "I fear the worst."

Nymand had put together a team of fourteen officers. He boomed out orders and directed the team to start checking any kind of ancient burial site in the area, of which there were many: barrows, tombs, long dolmens, stone circles. "We need to look at any mounds with some sort of depression or a chamber underneath." He pointed at a map on the wall.

The department was understaffed due to the Roskilde Festival, the huge rock festival currently underway nearby. Louise had seen Nymand raging at a well-groomed man with several stripes on his shoulder, exasperated by the lack of personnel available now that he had a breakthrough in his case.

"Øm Jættestue is the most famous and well-preserved site in the area," Thyssen explained in his steady baritone voice. "But I'm thinking it wouldn't be easy to hide someone in there because there's so much traffic, with all the tourists and school classes."

On the map he circled the area around Roskilde. "But Hvedshøj Gravhøj is right out here in Himmelev."

"Let's go." Nymand pointed at two officers. "And you two take the tomb in Øm."

He pointed at two more sites while Thyssen marked out the various coordinates for the two teams.

Louise listened to them going through the list of the nearby ancient sites, getting into a technical discussion of round barrows, dolmen chambers, multiple chambers, vertical megaliths, capstones. They had just put another photo up on the wall when Nymand's phone rang. Louise listened in: it was the tech who had arrived at Gerd's house just after they'd left.

"They found diethyl ether in her car," Nymand exclaimed after he hung up.

"Mona used ether on her insects," Louise said.

"There was a sponge, too. They're bringing the car in now. It sounds like she had a small pharmacy in the back."

Louise tried to picture Trine alone at her house. Maybe she'd also received a letter with dead insects, just like Pia and Nina. Had she understood the message? And that day, maybe Gerd had come by just after she'd arrived home with the kids. Wouldn't she have been scared? Had she realized what was coming? But how would Trine even have any idea who Gerd was?

Louise's thoughts swirled. She picked up her bag from the floor and glanced around at the others, then she stood and headed for the door. Three new teams had been sent off and the room was still buzzing with activity, but suddenly all that mattered to Louise was being at home with Mikkel when they called to tell him they'd found Trine.

THIRTY-TWO

Camilla was sitting at her kitchen table when Louise called. Markus had just woken up; she'd let him sleep late. And her father had just walked in the door.

The evening before she'd called and told him about Julia's abortion and how terrible Markus was feeling. And in a moment of self-awareness, she'd asked him to come and talk to Markus. She was completely livid at how Julia had treated Markus; she could hardly say a single good word about her. At one point she'd almost called Julia's parents to blame them for their daughter's lack of responsibility, honesty, and basic human decency. But then she remembered that Julia hadn't even told her parents she was pregnant. And midway through her third beer, it hit her: The girl probably hadn't even been pregnant. She'd been testing Markus, seeing how far he was willing to go for her, and when it became clear he was indeed ready to commit, to go all the way, she'd gotten bored and dropped him.

"The coffee pods are in there," she told her father. She pointed at the Nespresso machine as she made an apologetic face for having to leave to talk to Louise. Markus was just out of the shower, and he came in with a towel wrapped around his waist to say hi to his grand-father. She closed the door to her office.

At once Camilla could hear that something was wrong. She recognized the quiet, clipped tone of voice from times when she'd interrupted Louise when she was working on an important case. But now Louise was the one calling her. Camilla waited patiently.

"Mona hasn't regained consciousness yet." Louise told her about the woman's suicide attempt.

"But she's alive?"

"She's alive, yes, and her parents are with her. I drove by the hospital on the way to the station to tell them Gerd is dead."

Camilla had already reached for a notepad. Habit.

"It turns out that Gerd essentially isolated Mona from her family. She took so much responsibility for Mona and her emotional health that Mona's parents felt inadequate. They were afraid they weren't good enough at picking up on how Mona was doing, her signals, that they wouldn't be able to help her when she had problems. So they let Gerd take over. I don't think they ever really understood what happened on Bornholm, whatever it was that set off their daughter's emotional illness. A few years before Mona was forced to go on the field trip, her older sister had killed herself. Maybe that's why they were so afraid of getting things wrong with Mona."

"But didn't her dad reject Mona, her interest in spiritual things?" Camilla asked.

"It doesn't sound that way to me when her parents talk about it. I think it's more that he tried to talk her out of believing in premonitions and such. It worried him; he felt it was the sort of stuff that had driven her older sister to kill herself. All he wanted was to protect her, but that wasn't how Gerd saw it."

"How's Mikkel doing?"

"He seems a lot more like himself to me. Now we're just hanging out here in the house, waiting to hear from the police. Nymand is keeping me informed. He's an old grump, but he's okay, actually."

"You do fine with old grumpy bosses," Camilla reminded her.

"Yeah, you're probably right."

Camilla was anxious to go out to the kitchen and hear what her father and Markus were talking about, but she sensed that her friend had more on her mind.

"Trine's mom just got here. Anyway, they found cooler bags and water bottles in the back of Gerd's car. Which would suggest that she was keeping them locked up somewhere. Together or in two separate places. Maybe she wanted to re-create what Susan went through in the cave on Bornholm."

"But she doesn't know what happened to Susan," Camilla said. "No one knows how she died."

"Maybe not. Or maybe it's just that no one's told us about it yet."

"You think Trine, Pia, and Nina knew what happened?"

"I think they said or did something that made Mona believe they did, anyway."

Camilla heard Markus and her father laughing in the kitchen and something unclenched inside her. An email from Frederik popped up on her screen. "Arriving 10:30" was all it said.

The night before she'd told him about Markus and Julia, and she'd started crying because she missed him so much. But she didn't remember asking him to come home, so she was surprised to see his email.

"Frederik's on his way home," she said.

Silence. Suddenly Louise shouted in her ear: "They think they've found her!"

Camilla sat with her phone in her hands. She was aching to get out there and cover the story. But after a few moments' thought, she joined her family in the kitchen instead and asked her father if he'd like to stay a few days now that Frederik was coming home.

THIRTY-THREE

"Where?!" Louise whispered as she closed the door. Nymand had called while Mikkel and her parents were out in the yard with Kirstine, Malte, and Liselotte. They had inflated a plastic swimming pool and filled it with water, and now screams were whizzing through the house.

"The dolmen out at Bregnetved; we have a canine unit out there. The dog is certain, but no one's going in before we get there. A team of doctors is on their way, too."

"Bregnetved, the place out here behind Osted?"

"That's the one. We're just now passing Glim, so we're almost there."

"I'm coming," Louise said.

"And it's about halfway between Osted and Birkerød, where Nina Juhler lives."

Louise stood for a moment at the kitchen counter, wondering if she should tell the others what was happening, but instead she decided to just slip out and leave a note on the counter telling them she'd be back soon.

She didn't feel good about leaving Mikkel, but she thought that she should know any news about Trine as soon as the police did, before he was told.

As she approached, she spotted the canine-unit vehicle and saw the dog lying beside it. Probably a happy dog, she thought, with all the praise it would have been given, along with water and treats. She pulled up next to the vehicle and parked in the ditch. Several other cars drove up as she was unfastening her seat belt. Nymand jumped out of the first one and strode right past her and on across the field. Louise recognized the same doctor from the ambulance that had picked up Mona earlier. Surely her shift was almost over, Louise thought.

The dolmen didn't look like much from where Louise stood. Just a mound of earth covered by tall, yellow, withered grass and a nearby tree with broad branches that cast a shadow over it. She followed the others toward what looked like a low stone wall constructed of large stones, hidden behind the wild grass. The dog handler and two other officers were around the far side with Nymand, pointing out the doorway. When Louise got there, she saw that there was a deep crevice between two imposing stones, and that it led to what looked like a low, narrow passageway beneath the mound. Nymand wouldn't be able to fit in there, she thought as one of the officers brought out a headlamp and squatted down in front of the opening. Seconds ticked by, and he still didn't move; narrow passageways apparently weren't his strong suit, Louise thought. And his partner was too tall and muscular to help.

"I'll do it," she shouted. They all turned toward her.

Louise walked over and put on the headlamp, then turned to the two officers. "Has there been any sign of life?"

"We think we heard something when we yelled inside. Possibly someone moving or breathing."

"But you had the feeling someone heard you?"

"We think there was some kind of a reaction from inside."

"Trine!" Louise yelled as she kneeled down and cautiously began crawling forward. The stone roof sloped higher just inside the musty, narrow passage, and she was able to sit up.

The stones were cool and the passageway felt clammy. Again she called Trine's name, and Nina's, too. She spoke calmly, said she was coming in and that help was waiting right outside. Her voice echoed in the cold darkness. Suddenly something big darted over her hand, and Louise jerked it back.

Gerd would probably have been able to almost stand, crouching, in here, Louise thought. She could have dragged someone inside. Louise struggled to sense any sound or movement in the dark space. There—something moved. And she thought she heard a low moan or a sigh.

The cone of light from her headlamp revealed a red water bottle. She spotted some kind of opening in the tiny, cave-like space; it looked like there might be a circle of boulders with a small opening in the middle. And now she could see a basket and a bucket blocking the narrow entrance between the boulders.

Then, a half-meter farther in, there was Trine, lying on her side, her arms over her head. She didn't move or react when Louise called her name.

Nina lay staring at her. Her head was resting on a rock at an awkward angle, as if she'd been sitting up but then lost all her strength and slid down the dirt wall.

"Nina." Louise took off the headlamp so it wouldn't blind her. "It's over now. You're getting out."

Tears began running down Nina's dirty cheeks.

Louise spoke slowly and clearly. "I'm going to yell back to the people outside that I found you and then I'm going out so they can get in. The next person you see will be a doctor or rescue personnel, and they'll help you out. Is Trine alive?"

Nina didn't react for a few moments, but then, though it clearly took an effort, she nodded. Louise couldn't stop the tears from coming to her eyes. She looked at her sister-in-law for a moment before crawling back to the entrance.

When she was within earshot of the others, she yelled, "Found them!" Outside in the fresh air again, she let Nymand put his arm around her shoulders as she told them that both women were alive. "But Trine is unconscious."

Mikkel paced the gray linoleum floor while they waited for permission to go in. They'd been at the hospital for two hours now, and she and Mikkel still hadn't been able to see Trine. The doctors were working to stabilize her; she was dehydrated and starving. It did look as if she'd had something to eat in the past two weeks, but she was exhausted, and she'd been heavily sedated. Earlier the doctor had said that she didn't seem to have been harmed otherwise. No beatings, no injuries. She'd been covered with urine and feces, and was extremely weak from lying down for two weeks, but she had no physical wounds. They believed Trine had been held in a coma-like state through injections of benzodiazepine or some other sort of sleeping medication. An anesthesiologist had looked in and written down a schedule for gradually reducing the dosage to prevent withdrawal symptoms.

But, most important, she was alive and would slowly return to them, Louise thought. It was hard for her to see how her brother would be able to handle getting both Trine and himself back on track, though. Trine had a lengthy period of physical rehab ahead of her before she'd be able to function normally.

Finally, the door opened, and the doctor and two nurses stepped out and said that she and Mikkel were welcome to come in. Louise peeked inside. Trine lay staring straight up at the ceiling. She let Mikkel go in first. Tears streamed down his cheeks, and he stumbled a bit as he approached Trine.

Louise watched as he sank down on a chair beside Trine's bed, reached out for her hand, and then leaned down and hid his face in it.

The doctor came over to Louise. "You need to be prepared. She's going to be traumatized for a long time. She's going to have problems with small rooms and being in the dark."

"But will she recover?"

At first he simply stood with his hands in his white coat pockets and stared into Trine's room, but then he nodded. "It's too early to say too much about her liver and kidneys, but right now it looks like it's possible she might get away without any permanent damage from the medications she'd been given."

Trine's eyes were closed now. Mikkel pressed his forehead against hers and stroked her hair, whispered to her. Louise wiped a few tears away. A sweeping wave of sorrow for her own loss nearly bowled her over, and she wobbled a bit as she found a chair, sat down, and lowered her head between her knees.

She didn't know how long she'd been sitting that way when she felt a hand resting lightly on her shoulder. Somehow she knew it was Mikkel. He put his arm around her and pulled her close, held her tightly.

"Thanks," he whispered.

"How is she?" Louise spoke into his shoulder.

He cleared his throat and pulled back a bit. "Trine didn't take our cigarette money to use herself," he said, his voice thick with emotion. "She emptied the jar because she wanted to put the money in the bank, so she could pay for the vacation house we'd rented. The money is still in her pocket."

"Go on back in there to her," Louise whispered. She let go of him. She needed a moment alone as she struggled to get ahold of herself. She bent her head again, stared down at the floor. And she stayed that way until a firm hand grabbed her arm and she heard Nymand's voice saying it was time to go.

As he helped her up, she knocked over her glass of water and it splashed out across the linoleum as he led her away.

It wasn't until they were sitting down in the cafeteria and he'd set a cup of black coffee and a cheese sandwich in front of her that she started to feel a little bit like herself again.

"Eat," he said.

For a second Louise wondered how he had time to sit there. He should be at the police station, celebrating their success.

"It's not true." Nymand leaned over the table. "What you told me, it's not true!"

She frowned in puzzlement and took a big bite of the cheese sandwich, as if it were a shield to protect her.

"You didn't quit. Personal Crimes expects you back on August 15."

"It's not going to happen," she said after she finished chewing. "I just haven't told them yet."

He studied her for a moment. "I suggest you talk to Søren Velin. I'd like to recommend you to head up our region's new mobile unit."

"I'm not going to head up anything!" she said, though she was surprised to hear him mention her very first partner from the Homicide Department. They had worked together for a year before Velin transferred to the previous mobile unit, where he'd stayed until it was shut down. Now he was a captain at the National Police Research Center, but she'd lost contact with him.

"It's going to be a special unit of experts who will be assisting various police districts with their most difficult cases."

Louise knew very well what the new special unit would be doing. The national police leadership had been forced to admit that disbanding the old mobile unit and spreading the country's best homicide investigators to the four winds had been a mistake.

"And it's not only homicide," Nymand continued. "The unit will also be involved in complicated disappearances, which you're familiar with from your time in Missing Persons. If, for example, we hadn't found Trine and Nina ourselves, we would have asked for assistance."

She was aware of that.

"You have to be a part of this. You'll be supporting the entire country."

"I'm not working right now," she said, hoping that would make him stop.

"Sitting behind a desk, that's not you. You need to be out in the field."

That much they agreed on.

"You'll need three recommendations. I'll see to it that you get them."

"Recommendations?"

He nodded. "From people in leadership. From Flemming Larsen in Forensics, Lieutenant Detective Mik Rasmussen, and me."

Louise wanted to stand up and walk away, but she was too tired.

"Let's think about it," she said when he started fidgeting because she'd been silent for too long. And she nodded, to convince him that she would consider it.

"What did Nina Juhler say?" she asked.

His shoulders sank, and he seemed to deflate slightly. Louise had the sneaky feeling that he'd promised other people that he would convince her about taking on the mobile unit. And that was annoying. Very annoying. She took a deep breath, but she said nothing more about it.

He stirred sugar into his coffee. "It doesn't look like Gerd intended to kill them. Nina didn't have that impression, anyway. It was more that she wanted Trine and Nina to tell her what really happened the night Susan died. But they claim they don't know, because when they left, she was alive. And Gerd didn't believe they were telling the whole truth."

"So she tried to get the truth out of them by putting them through what Susan went through?"

He nodded. "Nina woke up while Gerd was driving her to the dolmen. She'd given Nina ether, then tied her up and carried her over on a wheelbarrow."

Louise thought about the old-fashioned anesthesia while Nymand explained that Gerd had ordered the ether on the internet and printed out the receipt.

She remembered the wheelbarrow in front of Gerd's house. And the Berlingo, which had a low trunk. That must have made it possible for her to pull Nina and Trine out of the car and into the wheelbarrow.

"Bizarre," she mumbled.

"Yes. And both women are thin and not very tall; that made it easier."

"But do you really think Gerd planned all this out in advance?" Louise asked.

He shook his head. "I think it evolved over time. I'm sure she was very worried when Mona's condition worsened after Susan's body was found. Nina says that Gerd wanted them to step forward and say what really happened in Echo Valley so people would know that Mona had been telling the truth. But when she realized that Nina and

Trine didn't know anything, she must have snapped somehow, otherwise she wouldn't have held the two of them captive for so long."

"I think she was probably also deeply unhappy," Louise said. "Mona has gotten worse over the past several years; she's spent more time in the psychiatric ward, taken more medications. Gerd probably started wondering how long Mona could last at that rate. She saw how Mona reacted when Susan's body showed up; it must have driven her crazy with sorrow, to the point where she felt that she needed to try to make the three women confess."

"Maybe. And it terrified Pia Bagger so much that she killed herself. Gerd would be facing charges for that if she were still alive."

"But she's not."

"No. She's not. And she was right that the three women were keeping a secret. A secret they should have admitted long ago."

"Nina talked about it?" Louise asked.

He nodded. "She admitted that they lied back then. They made a vow to one another to never tell a soul about being out in Echo Valley that night. She justified it by saying that they were just kids, they didn't realize what the consequences would be, but they did leave Susan alone out there. Nina says they were just fooling around, waiting for their new Bornholm friends to show up. They went to the Echo Valley parking lot, to try to break into the candy store. The alarm went off, and they ran into the forest to hide. She says they might have been a little hard on Susan; they teased her. At some point Susan fell and hit her head. They tried to help her, but she wouldn't let them; she pushed them away and ran off."

"So they agreed to lie?"

"They didn't dare say they'd been out all night; they didn't want to get sent home from the field trip. That's why they made up the bit about leaving Susan at the harbor and then coming back earlier. They didn't know Mona had seen them, and when she said they were lying, they doubled down on the lie, you might say. They promised one another that they'd all stick to the story they'd already made up. They felt they couldn't change it. The search for Susan was on, and they'd lied to the police. But Nina says they convinced one another that they couldn't have done anything to help Susan because she ran away into the forest."

"But they could have done something," Louise said. "If they'd told the truth, the police could have sent a canine unit into Echo Valley and saved Susan."

Nymand nodded. "That's what Nina blames herself for, too. But again, she says they didn't know the seriousness of their lie. They thought Susan went back to Copenhagen, like she said she was going to. Or at least they hoped she had. Nina pressured the others to keep the secret; she was afraid of her father. Apparently all three of them were."

Louise hadn't heard about a father from Nina, only about the mother who looked after Nina's house while she was gone.

"He died several years ago." Nymand paused for a moment. "Nina started crying when she talked about it, about how serious it would have been for her if he'd found out that she'd sneaked out and broken into the candy store, she and the others. It seems he was a strict man; he'd already threatened to send her off to boarding school. Something of a tyrant. The girls broke off contact when they finished grade school. Nina says that what happened back then has stuck with her, that many times over the years she'd thought about what a relief it would be if the truth came out. But that was before Susan was found. And because she'd pressured the others to keep quiet, she wasn't going to be the one to break their vow. All three of them had ended up with good lives, and she wasn't going to ruin that."

"They were thirteen years old, not little kids! They were old enough to kiss boys, and certainly old enough to take responsibility."

He nodded slowly. "But they didn't. They lied their way out of it."

"Gerd wanted to pressure them to do just that, to take responsibility. She wanted a just ending to what she felt had ruined Mona's life."

He nodded. "And in a way, she got it."

Louise thought about how paradoxical it was that Gerd, in her eagerness to get justice for Mona, had instead exposed her to the thing that scared her the most. She'd been the one to make more of Mona's old classmates disappear. "Yes. In a way," Louise agreed.

She thanked him for the coffee, then stood, intending to return to Mikkel and Trine.

THIRTY-FOUR

Immediately the darkness surrounded her, closed in on her. She couldn't see the opening to the cave anymore, and at first she didn't understand what had happened. Her entire world was an impenetrable darkness and sudden absolute silence. The pain in her head made it hard to think clearly, and her drowsiness pulled at her. It took a while for her to realize she was penned in.

She panicked and tried to sit up, but another wave of nausea overcame her. She vomited again, and it ran over her hand. Though she was dizzy, she desperately ran her hands over the tree bark in front of her, which cut her fingers. She screamed when she realized a large tree had fallen during the raging storm and now completely blocked the narrow opening. She put her shoulder to the trunk, pushing and shoving with bloody fingers. Tears flooded her cheeks as she again screamed desperately for help. For several moments she put every last ounce of strength she had into trying to budge the tree, but it might as well have been a brick wall. She was trapped.

Panic dulled her senses, and her screams became hoarse. Nothing was visible in the darkness. Her tears were burning her cheeks now, and she lay down in her vomit. The cuts on her arms and hands stung. Her strength was gone, leaving only a feeling she'd never experienced before: the fear of dying. She thought about her friends, hoped they would look for her despite what had happened. Hoped they had stayed in the forest or had gone for help. Hoped that someone was trying to find her.

Her nausea refused to go away, and she succumbed to the dizziness, floated in and out of consciousness. She no longer remembered what she was running from as the darkness once and for all swept over her.

THIRTY-FIVE

As Louise was headed back to Trine's room, she was suddenly over-come by an overwhelming sense of longing. In her mind she saw Eik, felt his arms around her, the sense of security that leaning against his chest gave her. She longed for him, for the sensation of being loved and being missed by someone. She was drained from all the intense emotions that flared up in the wake of being so close to people who had recently lost someone. She thought about Mona and how she would feel when she woke up and learned about Gerd. About Pia's parents, who now had an explanation for why their adult daughter had chosen to drown herself. All that despair left Louise so alone.

Louise veered toward the exit, then walked across the lawn to-ward a bench nestled under a huge linden tree. She pulled out her phone and opened the message she'd been about to send to Eik when Gerd had called. Now she deleted the last sentence and added a new line: "I miss you, and I'm so looking forward to all of you coming home." She added three hearts and clicked send.

ACKNOWLEDGMENTS

So many memories from my own class field trip to Bornholm emerged while I was writing *A Harmless Lie*, but the book is entirely a work of fiction, and all the characters are a product of my imagination.

I've lived in Osted and Viby on Sealand, and I know the area particularly well. I did take the liberty of moving the Bregnetved dolmen over to the other side of the road, to fit my story better.

I spent much of my childhood in Osted, and I'm sending many warm thoughts to my old friends. I haven't included any of the specific things we did together, but those childhood years had such great importance in my life, and I still carry them with me. I'm also sending a very special and loving thought to Henrik (Red), who died all too young but has never been forgotten.

Many people have helped me research this book, and my heartfelt thanks go out to them for their openness and all the time spent answering my questions. Their help has been invaluable.

Thank you, Captain Bjørke Kierkegaard of the Mid and West Sealand Police, for allowing Louise Rick and me to bother you.

Thanks to head nurse Ulla Falkner, who time and again patiently answered my questions, and to nurse Anne Dorte Stagested for

showing me around the acute psychiatric hospital in Roskilde.
Thanks for going along with pretending that Mona Ibsen was one of
your patients.

Many thanks also to chief physician Steen Holger Hansen from
the Department of Forensic Medicine, who has aided me in all of my
books. Thank you for your willingness to play along with my stories
every single time I show up. And thank you, chief anesthesiologist
Marie Louise Rovsing, for your enormous help concerning ether.

Brian Ellebæk, dog trainer: You saved me when I reached a point
where my story simply wasn't plausible. I rewrote it to make it work.
Thank you.

And thank you so much, dear Facebook friends, who not only
support and back me up and cheer me on, but are lots of fun. You're
also an encyclopedia of class field trip memories. It has been *so* much
fun weaving your anecdotes into this book. I can imagine several of
you reading something that sounds familiar to you.

Also, my good friend Michelle Kristensen loaned me her diary
from her Bornholm class field trip, from which, among other things,
I borrowed a bicycle crash. It's fantastic that you saved this diary.
Thanks!

Thank you, Lars and Andreas. You're the same ages as the girls
on Bornholm in the book, and you helped me with names and other
such things. But thank you even more because you help keep my life
from falling apart.

My thanks to Lotte Thorsen for reading and for your never-
failing sharp and useful input; it's an enormous help.

It's been a tremendous pleasure for me to work with my new editor, Stinne Lender. You have totally embraced Louise Rick, me, and
the entire story. Thank you for accompanying me during my research on Bornholm and for your serious involvement in the story.

And I owe a debt of gratitude to my team at Politiken Publishing. You are all a great gift. It's also been wonderful working with the Nordin Agency; you have always wanted the very best for me, and that gives me a sense of security and happiness.

My most loving thanks go out to my son, Adam. You're the best part of my life. And even though you've given me a great deal of inspiration through the years for the characters of Jonas and Markus, you are not at all the model for Markus's story in this book.

Finally, thank you so much, dear readers. You give me so much encouragement. Thank you for spending your time on the stories that keep popping up in my head.

ALSO BY SARA BLAEDEL

THE LOUISE RICK SERIES

The Midnight Witness

The Silent Women

The Drowned Girl

The Night Women

The Running Girl

The Stolen Angel

The Forgotten Girls

The Killing Forest

The Lost Woman

THE FAMILY SECRETS SERIES

The Daughter

Her Father's Secret

The Third Sister

ABOUT THE AUTHOR

Sara Blaedel is the author of the number one internationally bestselling series featuring Detective Louise Rick. Her books are published in thirty-eight countries. In 2014, Sara was voted Denmark's most popular novelist for the fourth time. She is also a recipient of the Golden Laurel, Denmark's most prestigious literary award.